RED WEATHER

RED WEATHER

Janet McAdams

THE UNIVERSITY OF
ARIZONA PRESS

TUCSON

THE UNIVERSITY OF ARIZONA PRESS

www.uapress.arizona.edu

Library of Congress Cataloging-in-Publication Data
McAdams, Janet, 1957–
  Red weather : a novel / Janet McAdams.
    p. cm. — (Sun tracks: an American Indian literary series ; v. 71)
  ISBN 978-0-8165-2035-0 (pbk. : alk. paper)
  I. Title.
  PS3563.C263R43 2012
  813'.54—dc23
                    2011043552

Publication of this book is made possible in part by the proceeds of a
permanent endowment created with the assistance of a Challenge Grant
from the National Endowment for the Humanities, a federal agency.

Manufactured in the United States of America on acid-free, archival-
quality paper containing a minimum of 30% post-consumer waste and
processed chlorine free.

17   16   15   14   13   12   6   5   4   3   2   1

Contents

RED WEATHER

Autobus Esmarelda

After all these years, it was hard to imagine they were still alive. In the cold still hour before dawn, when other people woke to think of unpaid bills, of all their unkindnesses, their keenest embarrassments, Neva lay awake watching different versions of her parents' lives flicker by like home movies. She imagined amnesia or imprisonment. A new city where they were unknown and their days full—new house, new jobs, new children. Sometimes what flickered by were possibilities too terrible to think of. But she always pushed those away. Better not even to imagine. When her brother lay awake, what did he see? It was something she and Harker no longer talked about. But they were always there, a shifting space at the edge of her vision, at the acute corner of consciousness.

She'd left Atlanta in a rush. The train to New Orleans, the flight to Mexico City, another train, and now the last bus—the trip to get here was a blur. After so many years of waiting, she had simply moved. She had followed the only trail that had been offered in years, the only trail rising from the tangled threads of their history. She had not panicked, not thought much about where she was, what she would do when she got there, not until she saw the families on the bus with her, hovering in their own orbits, more apart from her than she'd been from the landscape outside the train window. Panic—even more than she felt looking out the side of the swaying bus at the hundred-foot drop. How had she come here, and where was here? It might take her days to get back to Atlanta. It might take weeks.

With wet palms and a mouth dry as the landscape she'd passed through the day before, she shut her eyes, breathing slowly and counting, counting each inhalation, each exhalation. She couldn't think about it, couldn't think, because she might start screaming, might cry, throw up. She closed her eyes, trying not to be sick, imagining the scene on the bus, the Indian families huddling together protectively, the sneery tie-dye guy who made a point of speaking Spanish with the driver, his girlfriend who never spoke. What if the bus driver put her off? She counted each breath, and when she got to eighty-nine, she heard one of the little girls behind her say "Abuelita" and turned to see the grandmother fishing a banana out of a bag and giving it to her granddaughter.

They stopped in four small towns, villages really, where there weren't real bus stops, pulling up in front of a small market, then a fruit stand, until finally they just stopped along the highway at a place the driver and the family of nine seemed to recognize. At the first stop, a father and son got on with huge bundles and got off again at the next stop. After that, people left the bus steadily until there were only Neva, the American couple, and a man in a maroon sports coat.

Over the tape player Neva listened to the same mix repeat itself: Sonny and Cher's "I Got You Babe," the Monkees' "Last Train to Clarksville," Jefferson Airplane's "Volunteers of America." She slept, waking when the bus stopped, so stiff that stretching her legs was painful, to see the bus driver beckoning her to the front of the bus. Everyone else was standing in the dirt road by the side of the bus. "Señorita," the driver said, and she took her backpack off the rack and stumbled outside where the bright light and heat felt like a wall against her swollen face. She tipped her head down. The driver opened the compartment in the side of the bus and handed out their luggage: a large cloth rucksack for the tie-dye couple, a black valise for the sports coat man, and Neva's duffel and brown suitcase.

The others walked away. "Where are we?" she asked the driver, who answered "La frontera" as he was climbing back on the bus. *The border.* He looked back to her. "Coatepeque," he said, pointing.

Finally, she thought. *Esmarelda* was written in dirty white script across the bus's sea-green exterior. The driver turned the bus around in a quick U in the narrow dirt road, and Neva dragged her bags out of the way just in time. The others were headed directly into the bright sun. She hoisted her backpack onto her shoulders, picked up the duffel in her left hand, and reached for the hard-shell brown suitcase with her right. Her father's suitcase. There was a long white scratch in the side that hadn't been there before, and one of the corners was pushed in. Her back ached. Her right arm felt as if it might pull clear out of the socket.

The tie-dye couple turned back to look at her. "It's a long walk to the border," the man told her, nodding at her load—the backpack, the duffel, the hard-shell suitcase. She couldn't tell if he was friendly. He carried only the rucksack, patched together out of bright purple and orange fabric. His girlfriend had a string bag over one shoulder, a bottle of water, a mango and banana jostling inside it.

It's my whole life, Neva wanted to say. All that's left. But she remained quiet, trudging behind the couple, slower and slower, until she could hardly see them ahead of her. The landscape had changed so much since she got on the train in Mexico City. She could tell she was entering a different country. The trees were lusher, the light a thicker yellow. And the houses were wooden instead of stone or stucco. Coatepeque. Such a tiny country. Why here? she wondered. Why would they have come here? It had been in the news recently, but she couldn't remember why. Some children were playing with a cart, taking turns pushing each other in it. As she went by, they turned toward her, calling out "Dame cinco!" and held their hands out. Cinco what? she wondered, too tired to root around in her pockets for change. She set the suitcase down and opened it. It was crammed with the heavy objects of her former lives: a blue wool suit, boots, the marble track from her grandmother's farm in Alabama, oak and sanded by hand—she couldn't leave that. She'd never known her grandfather. Her mother had a photo of him in his shop sanding something, maybe the marble track. In the photo he looked thin, cheeks hollow, the straight black hair falling into his eyes as he squinted over his work. But you wouldn't have known he wasn't white. She remembered the shop where he must've labored over this toy she and Harker had played with. So much dust and grit covered the shop's windows you could barely see out. She and Harker had been told not to go there because the roof was sagging; the grown-ups were sure it would fall on them. They went once or twice anyway, but there wasn't much there. It wasn't at all like an attic. Only Mason jars of nails, a stack of boards in one corner, spider webs everywhere and then in her hair and across her face.

But she could remember dropping one marble after another on the zigzagging wooden gutters, watching them make their way back and forth, from top to bottom, until they spilled out onto the flowered rug in her grandmother's sitting room.

She made two piles, repacking the suitcase with what she could not bear to abandon. But even half empty, the suitcase tugged at her burning right shoulder. She stopped again, rooting through for extra socks, underwear, a pale blue bikini, stuffing them into the duffel until she could hardly zip it. Into her pocket she put a tobacco tie wound with red thread and a little prayer wheel made from quills. No, not from my ancestors, she could hear herself explaining. She remembered her brother

Harker saying, "We're Creek. We didn't grow up in a tipi. Our family's in Alabama." Two little objects she had saved from those heady days in Atlanta, when their house had filled with people from Oklahoma and South Dakota and North Carolina. Her Uncle Gus laughing when he gave the ties to her and her brother. Laughing, but meaning the gift seriously. Not knowing then about all the trouble that was to come.

The rest of it she left in the suitcase and did not look back at it, at any of it, the objects that had followed her for years, from Atlanta to Alabama and back again. From Atlanta to here, where she would leave them. She felt them tug on her bones, on something deep in her belly, but she left them. Their stories would change, and they would enter the lives of strangers, newborn, adoptees who learned to speak a different language.

She motioned to the group of children who waited by the side of the road, setting the marble track up gingerly in the yellow dust. "Juguete," she said, making a rolling motion with her index finger along the wooden track. The children looked puzzled. She searched in the dust for a small round rock and tried to roll it down the track. There was silence as they eyed her, up and down, whispering to each other, until a little boy shouted, "Canica!" He ran across the road and disappeared into a row of ragged bushes, his bare feet kicking up small clouds of dust that lingered as Neva and the other children sat motionless and silent. He reappeared a moment later, squatting near Neva and setting a handful of marbles down in the dust between them. He selected a cat's eye and set it on the track. As it rolled faster and faster down the zigzagging course, the children said "Oh!" in unison, and the little boy put another marble, a blue agate, on top and caught it at the bottom in his hand.

The children were laughing as she walked toward what she hoped was the border. She looked back once to see that one of the little girls had put on her high-heel sandals and towered over another little girl waving Neva's blue silk scarf in the still air.

Ciudad Coatepeque

Neva's gold wedding ring had stretched the many miles between Atlanta and New Orleans. Her diamond solitaire had taken her high into the thin air over the Gulf of Mexico and down on the other shore. Her camera far into southern Mexico. The gold bangle she'd inherited from one of her mother's friends had brought her here, across the border to Coatepeque, and bought her meals for a week. Coatepeque—a country that barely made the news, eclipsed behind Nicaragua's revolution and El Salvador's death squads.

She pawned everything when she left Atlanta, and if she didn't find work soon, she didn't know how she would manage. She'd thought of calling her brother, but the last time they talked on the phone he had made her so angry she slammed the receiver down. Even if she swallowed her pride, called him to say, You were right about Will, how would he get any money to her here?

The man in the Atlanta pawnshop had spoken to her from behind a cage. Almost exactly an arm's length behind the cage, jewelry shone from glass cases—heavy class rings with dark red or blue stones, brooches in the shapes of animals or flowering branches, a man's thick gold ring crusted with diamond chips—a "gent's ring" her father called them. On the walls were electric guitars, a shiny black vacuum cleaner, too many eight-track tape players to count. The long, pointed nail of the man's left pinky stood out against his short, meaty fingers.

"I don't get much for shortwaves," he said. "Nobody wants 'em—" He broke off.

"Let go of her purse, Philip," he said, and Neva turned in surprise to see a young man with a runny nose holding her purse in the air behind her, the strap still wrapped around her shoulder. "Let it go." When Philip released her purse, it swung against the counter with a thump. He was a blur out the front door of the shop.

The man sighed. "He really ain't so bad. Just a pothead."

She was careful after that. In the restroom of the Amtrak station, she hid money in small caches all over her body. Two twenties flattened under the insole of her left shoe. Two more safety-pinned between her breasts. The rest tucked into a little cloth purse hung from a belt loop inside the front of her pants. She worried that she would forget where she'd put the money, so she drew a picture of herself in her journal, with a star over each and every cache. She kept one day's spending money in the pocket of her jacket, the one with the zipper. But no one ever looked twice at her money, not even after she crossed the border, and every bus stop was a chaos of men shouting, "Lady, lady, over here, lady," of children selling sweets and cheap souvenirs, of policemen walking the length of the bus, thumbs tucked into the waistbands of their uniform-green pants, automatic rifles slung across their bodies.

Ralph, the man who was supposed to rent her an apartment, was late. On the other side of the zócalo stood the white, pyramid-shaped Heroes Monument, its base plastered with posters from the last legislative election. Politics seemed to be everywhere in Coatepeque City—graffiti spray-painted on walls and wooden fences, posters layering every vertical surface. A boy and a girl sat on the first step. He bounced a small red ball; the girl watched, reaching for the ball once, then pulling her hand away as the boy caught it with a deft motion.

A mariachi band hovered in front of her, music bursting from them, sure that she would relent and drop a few coins into the sombrero the little boy—the bandleader's son perhaps—held out to her. The bandleader played a guitar the size of a cello. A powerful, clear tenor voice emerged from a frail-looking singer who leaned on a cane and closed his eyes while he sang.

As her money dwindled, Neva had started ignoring the bands. She was too broke. She took a paperback out of her bag and started reading. It always worked. In a few minutes, the mariachi band drifted away, still playing, toward the verandah of the Grand Hotel. They knew every American had money. They knew that even the poorest American tourist had ridiculous amounts of money. That if they persisted, he or she would reach down into a deep pocket and produce a few coins or even an American dollar if the tourist had forgotten to change money. She was still not used to being around people who looked like her mother, who looked like Gus, her mother's cousin, to being around them all the time.

When the band moved away, she saw two women on the park bench across from her. They had watched the encounter. One of them smiled and shook her head at Neva. The two women glanced at Neva once or twice and talked in near whispers to each other. One was tall with blond hair pulled back in a braid. She wore tight black pants and a Mexican blouse. The other dressed a little like a missionary, a plain denim skirt and brown sandals, her dark hair cropped short. Neva strained to overhear their conversation, catching a word or two of English. She felt starved for English, disoriented to have been in Spanish for so long. She was beginning to dream in Spanish. Last night, for instance, she was trying to tell Will why they shouldn't operate on the cardinal they found after it dove into its reflection in the glass door leading to their patio. "But we aren't doctors"—"Este . . . we are here, pero no somos médicos" she kept saying, over and over, as the cardinal began to look more and more like a baby with a beaky mouth and flushed red cheeks, as she followed Will through the hospital while he picked up blue surgical gowns for the two of them, rubber gloves, a mask, a scalpel. But the r in "pero" began to roll into "perro," the Spanish word for dog, and before she knew it, Will had become the black dog her brother Harker brought home in the fifth grade.

She and Harker kept the dog secret from their parents. They made it a place under the mulberry bushes in the side yard. They left it a blanket to sleep on, a bowl of water, and a plate of leftover chicken and dumplings. The next morning, the water, the food, and the dog were gone, the blanket scrunched up into a nest. They spent hours looking for it, calling it, but they had no name for the dog and had to settle for "Here! Here!" clapping their hands as they called. Perro. They could've just called "Perro."

Will, she thought. I don't want him here. Not even in my dreams.

She knew the women weren't talking about her, felt invisible here, the way she'd hoped to disappear when she married Will. That evening in the kitchen with Will's friend, Brian. "The mysterious Neva," he'd said, tugging on a piece of her hair. When had she gotten so quiet? His breath smelled of wine. He leaned against her, warm and a little sweaty. "Will's little secret." She had no idea what he meant. Miriam had come in then, to nurse Emma, the new baby, and Neva had never found out. Yes, she wanted to disappear. She was tired of being Neva Greene, the girl whose parents got *involved with something*, then vanished. The woman who looked a little foreign. Or something. But she didn't want to be Will's little anything. And now she wasn't.

The women seemed to be American, though the shorter, dark-haired one could've been French or Italian, if she weren't dressed so badly. They were eating lunch, pupusas, a Salvadoran dish of fried corncakes stuffed with cheese and piled with cortido, a relish halfway between kimchi and cole slaw. The tall one had covered herself entirely with a large cloth napkin to catch the hot sauce that dripped into her lap. She ate with relish. Neva's mouth watered a little. Food here was wonderful. She ate like a starving woman—mangoes, cucumber slices dusted with chile, anything with salsa verde. She expected to get fat. Will had always insisted they eat cautiously, ordering that there be no ice cream in the house, complaining when she made the yogurt from whole milk. But she didn't get fat. The knobs that had been her wrists and elbows softened. She felt her body straightening, pulled upward into the bright tropical sun. Her legs toughened up from all the walking and carrying luggage. Solid as trees, she thought, as she felt the warm granite of the zócalo through the soles of her sandals.

She thought about how weak she'd been when she got here. That first night, back aching from carrying luggage, sand in her eyes from lack of sleep. Just add it up, she'd thought as the boy at the hotel desk had chattered on in Spanish and English. Please, she thought, if you don't hurry, the restaurant will close. Tomorrow is Sunday and nothing will be open. I will die of hunger.

"Okay," he said, grinning. He punched a sequence of numbers into the adding machine and listened with satisfaction as it rasped out a long piece of white paper. "You owe forty-five."

Neva fished through her backpack for her billfold and began counting out the notes.

"No, no, no," he said, shaking his head at her. He sighed grandly, as if she were a cute but misbehaving child. He began adding the numbers on a piece of paper.

Dishes clinked in the restaurant downstairs. "Thirty-eight!" he shouted with triumph in his voice. "I will take you to your room."

"It's okay," Neva said. "I'll take the key and come back later." She gestured to the restaurant downstairs, but was too embarrassed to say, I'm hungry. I have to eat. How had she been living, if hunger was unseemly? How lucky to escape.

"No, no, no," he said, shaking his head. There was a sweetness about him that made her ashamed of the irritation she felt. He pointed toward the restaurant, "Restaurante." Then up the stairs. "Cuartos." He held up a brass key wired to a block of wood. "I have the key!"

He reached behind him for a pair of crutches Neva hadn't noticed, swung his whole right leg out past the ends of the crutches, weighing himself on it carefully before he lunged forward with the crutches, his movements slow and methodical. His left leg was amputated above the knee. Neva had forgotten there was a war here.

3

The Central Plaza

Like every American male Neva met in Coatepeque, Ralph wore a hat. It wasn't as large as some of the hats she would meet, or as bright. Grime ringed the brim, and old sweat stains clouded the crown.

He nodded at the two white women on the bench opposite. "You Neva?" he said, as he sat down next to her. His nose was a map of broken blood vessels. So many of the gringos here drank until you could read it in the skin of their faces. "Whew!" he said, running a soiled red handkerchief around the backside of his neck. "I bet you never bargained for weather like this!"

It hadn't seemed so hot to Neva, but she was a southerner, so acclimated to hot temperatures that when the thermometer dipped into the seventies she put on a sweater. It was probably hotter in Atlanta, where people raced through the heat from their cars to their offices. It would be even hotter in Alabama, hot and steamy. The light here in the mountains of Central America was a different color of yellow, clearer at this altitude. Sometimes she missed Alabama's thick air, the way looking through it was like looking through a pane of old glass—everything softer on the other side.

The women were watching them. One of them caught Neva's eye and smiled at her. Neva smiled at her feet. When she and Ralph rose, the women rose, too. "Hey, Ralph," the dark-haired woman said.

"Deborah." He nodded at both of them. "I talked to the guy about your cistern. He says he'll be out next week. But you know how they are here . . ." He grinned at her.

"Well, no, I don't know," she said. "But if you've talked to him, that's fine."

"We could run out of water, Ralph," the tall woman said. There was a sharpness about her, cheekbones angular, posture athletic. Even without her rush of pale blond hair she would have stood out, not just pretty, but sexy, at home in her body.

Ralph started to say something, but the dark-haired woman cut him off. "Are you looking for an apartment?" she asked Neva.

Neva nodded.

"Not the Santa Clara place—" She turned to look at Ralph.

"It's all I have," Ralph said. He took his hat off and fanned his face.

"Ralph, I don't really think Santa Clara is a good place for Neva. Your name is Neva, right?" The dark-haired woman took a breath as Neva nodded. "I'm Deb, this is Kira." She gestured at the blond woman. "Santa Clara is two bus trips into the city."

She looked at the other woman, raising her eyebrows slightly, and turned back to Neva. Ralph jingled his car keys impatiently behind her. "We have an extra room to let. Why don't you come look at it?"

Ralph shrugged. He seemed a half-hearted landlord, one who would just as soon let her leave with the women so he could go back to whatever bar had rouged his cheeks with morning Gallos. But Neva was imagining the Santa Clara apartment—a studio he had said. She didn't care if it was small or in a distant, quiet part of the city. In her mind she could see the French windows, the light streaming in through them in the morning. She imagined sitting in front of the window each morning, drinking coffee from a white mug with a blue ring around it. She imagined intense quiet. No one watching her, no one asking her anything about herself. She didn't want friends here, didn't want to be cracked open by anybody. And she needed to be able to keep her secrets. Their secret. Why she was here. What they had done. Where they had gone.

She looked at the women. Kira glanced at Neva as she scrubbed her fingers with a wadded paper napkin, but the other waited expectantly. She saw their interest in her and shook her head. I cannot let you near me, she thought. I cannot let anyone come too close. I have waited too long for this and you might get in the way.

Ralph played the radio loud in his Land Rover as they bumped along the cobblestone roads, and music blared in sudden blasts from every store they passed. Each turn they made, Neva thought: This is *it*. Hoping for the blue house with the balconies, the yellow one with the pots of red geraniums in the doorway. The roads turned to dirt, then dust, clouding behind the Land Rover, obscuring the view behind them. They were miles from the city. Neva had lost track of time. She began to get queasy from the winding road. On and on they went. I will never find my way back, she thought. "Stop," she said, but Ralph either didn't hear her or ignored her. They started up a long hill, Ralph's car groaning up the incline. "Please stop," Neva said louder.

"What'd you say?" Ralph asked. He downshifted and the car jerked forward.

"Stop," Neva said. "Go back. It's too far."

"Not a problem," Ralph said. "Not to worry about my car. She can make it."

"No, it's too far for me."

"It's nice out here. Isn't it nice?" Ralph asked.

It was nice. Beautiful. Green fields, clear air. Orange flowers climbed the bluff facing them.

"There's a bus," Ralph said. "Comes every morning and every evening. Change in Santa Tecla."

They stopped in the curve of a road reaching up into the mountains that flanked the capital. Beyond them were the high, glass-encrusted brick walls that surrounded Coatepequen houses. A black chicken pecked a white one; they scattered when Ralph honked his horn at them.

"It's too far." She was weak. She was spoiled. She had become a city girl. City Indian—*What are you? Some kind of city Indian?* Uncle Gus used to tease her mother. Every day a walk down a dirt road, then two buses. Every day: morning, then evening. She couldn't do it.

"There ain't nothin' else," Ralph said.

"It doesn't matter," Neva said. "I can always stay at my hotel." But she didn't know if she could. A tour was coming, and they were bustling around getting ready.

Ralph hesitated for a moment. "You want to get a beer?" he asked.

She ate a taco from a stand on the corner near her hotel and drank an orange soda standing at the counter. She had begged off from Ralph's offer of a morning beer and set about trying to find a place to live. She smiled at the teenage girl sitting in a lawn chair behind the counter and left three pesetas. The girl smiled sleepily at her. It was hot, the midafternoon air still and humid, and the girl was beginning to drift into sleep. Neva longed for a nap, but she went down the street to the library where English speakers could root through used copies of the few American books in the capital: *Love Story, Future Shock,* or *Valley of the Dolls*. The bulletin board was layered with announcements—furniture for sale, Spanish classes, travelers offering to take letters to the States. There were two advertising apartments to rent, though they were layered over with flyers for massage and Hopi ear candling. She scribbled the addresses in her notebook anyway and started toward the central plaza.

But it was siesta, and no one answered her knocking. She thought she might just go back to the hotel and take a nap, come back this evening or in the morning and try again. Across the plaza, Kira, the tall blond woman she'd seen that morning, was stuffing long-stemmed pink roses into a nylon shopping bag. "Shit," she said, pulling her hand out of the bag and putting her finger into her mouth. She noticed Neva watching her and looked first annoyed, then laughed, shaking her hand in the air. Neva was close enough to see the spot of blood where a thorn must have pierced it. Neva laughed, too. She was surprised to feel a little disappointed when the woman slung her bag across one shoulder, a leg over her motorcycle, cranked it, and took off.

But then she pulled up next to Neva and shouted over the noise of the motor: "You didn't like Ralph's place?"

Neva shook her head. "No," she said, "it was too—"

"Wait a minute," Kira said, turning the key and jiggling a wire under the handlebars until the motor cut off. "Sorry. Yeah, we didn't think you'd like it. Way out in the middle of nowhere.

"Look," she continued, "you wanna just come look at the room? It's 180 a month, cheaper if you pay dollars—everybody wants dollars. You don't have to stay there forever. Rent it for a week or two while you look."

"All right," Neva said. "Where do you live?"

"Just get on," she said, motioning behind her. "It's not far."

Something about her tone made Neva obey. The rent was so low. A week at the hotel would be a month in their house. Who knows what she might hear or find out in a houseful of Americans. This trip wasn't about her, her need to escape. It was about them. She had been too young when it happened. Too young to understand what could be worth risking everything for. Even now they seemed naive, foolish in their belief that anything could change. They had tried to save a genera-tion. If she couldn't save them, she might find a way to finish their story.

As Kira's Yamaha left the plaza, it occurred to Neva that if it had been Deb, who seemed the kinder of the two, she might not have gone. She didn't want to soften up around anyone. Will had trained her. The small town of Butler City, Alabama, had trained her. Waiting had trained her.

4

Atlanta

The day she left Atlanta, a Tuesday, she came home to find Will
sitting at the kitchen table. He was rarely home these days. When he
was, he argued with her, yelling and throwing things. When he wasn't
yelling, he sat in sullen silence, while Neva tried to find out what was
wrong, what she had done. She would begin: "Are you okay?" and when
he didn't answer her, she would ask, "Is something wrong?"

The apartment was so hot, though, so stuffed with stale air that
Neva said nothing when she got home. She opened the windows,
opened the kitchen door, propping it to let the late afternoon air in. It
wasn't much better. This was the hottest summer ever. "Hottest summer
ever," she heard on the car radio, on the sound system piped into the
grocery store. "Yep, the hottest summer Atlanta has seen this century!"
The weatherman would announce it as if he were at the county fair selling tickets to see mutated fetuses or women humping coke bottles.

Her head was killing her. She'd been running errands for hours in
the heat and the glare. She was blind in the dark apartment, red dots
swirling before her eyes. She set down her shopping bags. Will looked at
her but did not speak.

She stripped in the bathroom and stepped into the shower, wanting
to lock the door. Started with cool water, turning it gradually to warm
when she finally got chilled.

"If you would just, you know, pull a face or joke around like you
used to, I wouldn't get so mad," Will had said to her a few days before,
with genuine pleading on his face. "You never do it; you never do it
anymore: joke me out of my bad mood—"

It was true. She never did that anymore. She tried out various faces
as the water bounced off the back of her neck. She blew her cheeks out,
pulled her lips down like Red Skelton. Nothing was funny. She was
tired. It was the heat. Working all day, tutoring at night. She'd even quit

the one class she thought she could manage this summer. The idea of humoring Will exhausted her like another job, the night shift, second shift—no time off ever. We are all wounded by something, she wanted to tell him. Her face didn't want to move into a smile. When she forced her face into a grin, she felt the corners of her dry lips cracking.

She couldn't. She was all out of distractions. She let the hot water pound her back, her head. Her feet were lobster red when she stepped out of the shower. Will stood in the doorway, thin as a rail, head tilted to the left, hair tufting up from the cowlick on the back of his head. All that boyishness she'd fallen in love with. His cheeks looked pinched and pale, and a faint sour smell rose from the rope sandals he wore.

She missed her friend Miriam. They had drifted apart after Will and Brian's quarrel. After Will had quarreled with Brian. Neva had tried, but she'd had to sneak, and she'd had to sneak without Miriam knowing it. Miriam could never understand what it was like to live with someone like Will. Miriam probably thought all men were like her husband Brian. And Neva knew that Will would get better. That someone would publish his thesis. He would find something permanent when his lectureship ran out. When things were better, he wouldn't need her so much or worry about her being disloyal.

Once, when Will had gone for a run, Neva had called Miriam. The phone had just begun to ring when Will came back for his cap and caught Neva on the phone. He pushed the hang-up button with his index finger and took the headset from her. "Who was it?" he said, so quietly, she forgot the danger.

"Nobody," she said.

Will looked down at the phone in his hand. His sharp intake of breath was sudden. "Goddamit, goddamit, goddamit," he screamed, banging the headset down with each goddamit, first against the base of the phone, and then, when the phone had slipped off onto the floor, against the top of the sideboard. "Goddamit, motherfucker," he said. The sideboard was soft wood, hundred-year-old English white pine, the kind of antique Will's mother passed along without a backward glance, but Neva thought it was beautiful. The phone made thick dents in the wood each time Will slammed it down.

Stop it, she thought, and backed away.

But on that Tuesday, Neva tried everything. It was so hot in the apartment. First, she was quiet. Then she pleaded. Then she did try to joke.

"You think it's funny?" he asked, looming over her.

"No, no," Neva said, backing away until she was up against the kitchen counter.

"You think you're so damn smart," Will said.

The phone rang. Will glanced at her as if to pin her into place. She heard him laughing in the other room after he picked up the phone. She knew, then. Hadn't she always known?

"I'm going out for a bit," he said, keys jingling in his left hand. It was a new expression of his—"for a bit" or "just a bit of that." Neva wondered who else talked like that.

She had been dazzled when Will first noticed her. But as the months went on, it was an intense sadness in him that had drawn her in, that had kept her there. She had begun to wonder if she'd mistaken disappointment for sadness. Will had grown up believing the world was there for the asking. (The *taking*—Neva could hear Harker's voice in her head.) And when it wasn't, his disappointment began to turn into something else—anger, even rage.

"You just go," she said after he left, leaving the front door slightly ajar as he always did. She slammed it shut, then opened it and slammed it over and over, until the picture on the wall behind her crashed to the floor. "Goddamit," she said. She slid to a sitting position with her back against the wall and turned over the picture, the sunflower print she'd rescued first from the farm, then from the thrift shop. The glass was cracked.

She flipped it over and began peeling off the paper backing, twisting the metal clamps under it and easing the cardboard off. The garish postcards beneath startled her. Four of them, each lined up with one corner of the frame, the picture sides facing out. She pried them out and lined them up on the beige carpet before her.

Tropical scenes. A bright hibiscus with a hummingbird floating over it. A mountain overwritten with white letters: *Volcan Ixtapel!* A beach with dark sand, bright sun rainbowing off it. And the last: Ciudad Coatepeque, a blocky cathedral behind a row of palm trees. All sent to the Atlanta address, but months after the house had been closed up. Long after the white station wagon had disappeared into the red dust of a north Alabama road.

The messages were brief, generic, written in thick black letters. *Great weather so far. Having a wonderful time! Love, Herman and Lily.* Each one signed the same: *Love, Herman and Lily.*

Herman and Lily: the old family joke. She and Harker loved *The Munsters*, and their mother would watch it with them if their father was working late. Once he had surprised them midshow. Just as Herman Munster had called to his wife, "Honey, I'm home!" her father had appeared in the doorway and echoed Herman, "Honey, I'm home!" "That you, Herman?" she had responded, and the nicknames lingered, her Lily to his Herman, disappearing only when everything had begun to disappear.

And now reappearing, on the postcards before her.

If only they would reappear, right now, she thought. She had thought it a thousand times before. Why bother? But if only they would reappear. Pack her suitcases and drive her away from Will and this hot apartment. Can't they? she thought. I could open the window and call out.

I will pick up the phone and a voice will say, Here we are, we'll come get you. Everything was a mistake, a dream, the leaving. You didn't have to live like this. It was all a mistake.

I will take this piece of brown paper, Will's favorite silver pen, and write. *Mother, Father,* I will write. *Herman, Lily.*

Strike a match and watch the words flare up, the ashes float out the window, catching in my mother's hair, my father's salt-and-pepper beard. Maybe it's gone completely white by now.

No, they can't come get me, she thought. No, they can't. And even if they could, I don't know their number, don't know if they have a number, if they're living or dead. I wouldn't know what kind of car to look for. An old Volvo? A Ford station wagon?

Would they both come? Or only her father while her mother stayed at home to prepare a room for Neva, fresh sheets on the single bed, a casserole in the oven, in case she was hungry. Maybe they would call Harker, and he would come home for the weekend to see her, just to see that she was all right.

"Okay, okay," Neva said to herself. No one will come, so I will go. She emptied her underwear drawer into the suitcase. Then she put half of it back, so that Will wouldn't notice right away. Two dresses from the closet, jeans, boots.

She opened the top drawer of the bureau where Will kept important papers. She found her passport, but put it aside, wondering if he would look for it and know she was gone for good. Her last paycheck was there, clipped together with checks Will was going to deposit in the checking account. She unclipped it, rearranging the rest of the checks, hoping he wouldn't notice.

She knew there was a roll of money somewhere, and she rooted around until she found a single sock with a lump in the toe. She shook it out. It wasn't money but a box of foil-wrapped condoms. The box was open and about half full. She felt a flutter in the flesh between the base of her spine and her belly. If that flutter had a voice, it would have said, *Oh.*

Oh. She stared at the drawer, the handful of dark socks, nail clippers, some change, and a gauge to measure the air pressure in tires. She heard a horn honk and pulled the shade up to see the cab she'd called waiting at the curb.

She found the money, a roll fat as a cucumber, took half, then two-thirds, fluffing the remainder out so the roll looked nearly as big. She took Will's wedding ring and the nail clippers. She put the ring back and fished her passport out of the manila envelope marked *Important Papers.*

She thought of the early-morning queasiness, the late-afternoon headaches from the Pill. I hate using rubbers, Will had said; it doesn't feel intimate. And Neva, he said, we're not ready for children, smiling at her as if she had been begging for one. She hesitated in the doorway, then zipped everything into the side pocket of her purse. It weighed a ton. The cab driver honked his horn three times, each honk lasting a little longer.

She stumbled when she got out of the cab, breaking the strap on her sandal, though she didn't know it until she stumbled again and fell down in the lane in front of the entrance to the Amtrak station. She hadn't cried at all, but this time she cried, resting for a minute on all fours until she crawled back onto the sidewalk and stood up. A woman in a green dress stood in front of her, so close their noses were almost touching. Her eyes were black as a deer's, and a gray rope of a braid hung over one shoulder, nearly to her waist. She put her arms around Neva, the bracelets on her arms jingling as they went past Neva's ears. "You," she said, then paused, "will be all right."

Neva found herself relaxing into the woman's hold. The woman's voice was low: "I've seen this sort of thing before. You will be all right." A train whistled as it approached the station.

Neva closed her eyes, felt the woman's grip relax, then let go entirely. She opened her eyes, but there was no one on the street. She thought she saw a swirl of green rounding the corner. David and Frances Greene, where are you? she thought. Herman and Lily. She went into the station.

5

The Indian Wars

The moped crept, then sped up. Each time she turned or wove between two cars, Kira shouted, "Hold on!" When Neva leaned hard against her, she felt Kira's thin body, bony beneath a restless layer of muscle. They took turns where they leaned so sharply Neva could've touched the street with her fingertips. The hotels and stores turned to houses, white stone behind walls and metal doors. Neva felt dizzy, not with the ride but with a sense of shock that she had climbed on, that she had done exactly the opposite of what she'd planned—to disappear, to hide while she searched. She knew it was more than cheap rent that had made her come with Kira.

They pulled up in front of the only house on the street that had no broken glass lining the roofline. Stucco painted a glaring yellow, with red Spanish tile on the roof. A few broken ones lay on the sidewalk leading to the door. Kira kicked them into the patchy grass. "Bright, isn't it?" she said. "Everybody calls it the 'Yellow House.'"

Deborah, the woman with dark hair and missionary clothes, was in the kitchen. "Oh hi," she said, motioning her in. Neva followed her into a large, square kitchen. "You found her!" she said to Kira.

"You were looking for me?"

"We thought you might like to come to dinner. I'm Deb," she said, wiping her hands on a blue and white dish towel and leaning across the table to shake Neva's hand.

"We thought we ought to tell you about Ralph," Kira said.

"Did you rent the room?" Deb asked her, glancing at Kira, who shook her head. "Well, that's probably for the best. We were going to leave a note at your hotel."

"How would you know which one?" Neva asked.

Deb shrugged. "It's a small town."

But Coatepeque City was huge, not as big as Atlanta, more like

Birmingham. Highways and rushing traffic, and parts you could get to only by taking the bus and changing twice. Deb noticed Neva's raised eyebrows and said, "I don't mean Ciudad Coatepeque. I mean the expat community. You're looking for somebody, you ask around. They always turn up. A lot of foreigners stay at the Presidente. We didn't think you were American at first—we figured you were there or at the Mirador. Do you like it—the Mirador?"

Neva nodded. The hotel was nearly empty. Her tiny room had a miniature fireplace in the corner. A chilly red tile floor that stung her feet when she got up in the middle of the night to pee, stumbling out of an impossibly deep sleep, so thick with dreams it took her most of the morning to shake them off. She hadn't slept like this since childhood, since before her parents left. Each morning she sat in the Mirador Room for which the hotel was named, with its view looking down over the city. The husband from the young couple who ran the hotel would bring her a cup of dark, muddy coffee and a tall glass of steaming milk to mix into it. The first morning she had gulped it down, feeling it rush into the tips of her cold fingers, the empty space beneath her ribs.

"So do you want to see the room? I've got to do a couple of things here," Deb said, chopping as she spoke. "I have to throw these peppers in in exactly two minutes, but then I'll take you up. Can you stay for dinner? We've invited a few people . . ." Something popped in the large skillet on the stove, and Deb jumped back.

It was a huge kitchen with a large, blocky wooden table in the center, on which were piled paper and plastic bags, a toaster oven, a blender, a basket of fruit, a mound of vegetables. Brown sauce had slopped from the skillet and was baking into a crust on the stove top. Peppers, tomatoes, and pear squash were piled on the counter. "Our last housemate left a bunch of stuff; so there's sheets—things like that. She left some clothes—her husband's kind of conservative." Deb turned to look Neva up and down. "I don't know if any of it would fit you—Kira's too tall and nothing really suited me. But we can take any stuff you don't want to the Madres."

"The Madres?" Neva asked.

"The Mothers of the Disappeared office. I do some volunteer work there. I'm a nurse. You could come sometime, if you like."

"Did she—your housemate—go back to the States?" Neva asked.

"No, she got married and went to live in Colonia García."

Kira rolled her eyes. "Hush, Kira." Deb turned back to Neva. "You might meet her tonight."

"Christina won't come. She always says she's going to—she never does." Kira ran a hand through her fuzzy blond hair and shifted her weight from one hip to another. "Anyway, I got to go. Get these scores copied before class tomorrow. Should I pick up anything?"

Deb looked around the kitchen. "Avocados if you see a stand. Beer. Oh, are you on your Yamaha? Never mind, we probably have plenty."

"Got it," Kira said. She moved so quickly her braid swung into the air.

"What does she mean, about copying scores?" Neva asked. She realized Kira was one of those people who never stood still.

"Kira's a musician. It's how she makes her living here—piano bar in the lounge at the Continental. And she has a little ensemble—they play around town and sometimes in Guatemala City."

Grease popped in the skillet. Deb pulled it off the burner. "You could just go up," she said, sighing as she checked her watch and set the cutting board down, dislodging a few chilies onto the tile floor. "Would you mind?"

"No, it's fine," she said, relieved that no one would hover. She needed to know how it would feel to be alone in the room, because she would need to stay there, to keep to herself if she moved in here.

Neva hadn't even noticed the door in the corner of the kitchen. Deb opened it and pointed up a curving set of stairs. "Just go up," she said.

Neva folded back the shutters and looked around the room, the gray stone floor, the white stucco walls. It was a peaceful room. A beautiful room. Still, she felt panicked, her throat tightening up, her palms damp as she clutched the bedspread. Ready to run home and I haven't even gotten started, she thought. I haven't even begun to look for them. At the Mirador, she'd had to fight the urge to stay in every day, to lie in her bed as if she were floating, floating, never to land but never to sink into dark gray water either. Only when she closed her eyes, the images clicked by like a speeded-up slide show, featuring a man with graying hair and a worried face, a woman who looked like her but surely had to be someone else. I am taller than she was, Neva thought, then corrected herself. Than she was then.

She sat down on the bed, trying to imagine sleeping in this room, reading a book in this room, changing into a nightgown, writing a letter. "It's a small community," Deb had said. Maybe that was the key to finding them, to finding out about her parents, or at least finding out if they had ever been here. Get to know every gringo in Coatepeque. I have spent too much time waiting, she thought. But I have come here, and now, maybe in this room, this house, I will find a way to unlock the past.

She untangled a strand of hair caught in one of her earrings, remembering the Indian woman who'd sold them to her, when the bus between the border and the capital had stopped for lunch. In front of the restaurant, three women sold rugs and jewelry made from black jade and silver. A German couple from the bus had hovered, Peter, the husband, standing to one side reading from his guidebook, glancing up every once in a while to scrutinize the women, their clothes, and the bright red, purple, and yellow rugs they were selling. "Hmmm," he said. Then after a while, he said it again and shut the book. The wife stood next to Neva. "Beautiful," she murmured over nearly every piece of jewelry, but she bought nothing.

Neva picked up a pair of earrings and held the silver hooks against her earlobes, feeling the weight of the jade rectangles suspended from them. She held some money out to the woman selling them, who picked a few coins out of her open palm.

"Nada más?" Neva asked. The woman waved her hand, her palm facing Neva, in a gesture that seemed the equivalent of shaking her head, *No*.

"They're so poor," Neva said to the wife, Marthe, as they walked away.

"Well, better poor than what happened to them in your country," said Peter, walking up beside them. "The diseases and everything. You're not from out west, are you?" he asked.

Neva shook her head.

"You could play one," he said. "I mean a Red Indian, in a film. With your coloring."

Neva looked away, to where the purples and dark greens of the high plateau gave way to the dense forest below. Red Indian. She hadn't heard that since she was a child. Maybe she could play a Red Indian in a movie, the way she played a white person in real life, at least most of the time.

"I've always wanted to go out there, see it—your west. I've heard there are still some buffalo living. Is that true?"

"I don't know," Neva said. There were no buffalo in Atlanta. She'd heard of a park in southwest Oklahoma that had a few, but she'd never seen them. Europeans thought America was one big Wild West Show. Six-shooters. Storybook Indians. They thought all the real Indians were dead.

"Who was that Mexican guy you were talking to?" Will had asked her one Atlanta evening just before they left a meeting downtown. He had his arm around her shoulder, his hand tugging a little on a lock of hair that had crept out of her braid.

They stood in a circle with Miriam and Brian. Neva saw Miriam watching Will's hand on her hair.

"His name is Bobby. He's not Mexican. He's Choctaw Indian."

Will whistled between his teeth. "Wow, no kidding. Imagine." He looked around the room for Bobby, but he had already left. "I'm sorry I didn't get to talk to him. Native American, huh?" he said, correcting her.

There was silence among the four of them.

"Why didn't you introduce me? You talked to him long enough." He tugged harder on the lock of hair, tilting her head to the side a little.

"Well," Neva said, "I didn't know we talked all that long." She put her hand to the side of her head, trying to pull her hair loose from Will's fingers.

Miriam leaned forward. "You know, Will, we were hoping you guys might come to dinner tomorrow night. I could invite Lori and Kevin to come, too. The vidalias are in. We're going to buy a whole crate and make some goulash."

Will let go of Neva's hair and dropped his hand until it rested on her hipbone. A long brown hair was caught in the ragged nail of his index finger.

"Kevin's kind of a jerk," he said. "Did you already invite him?" he asked Miriam.

She shook her head. "No, you're right. It would be more fun if it was just the four of us."

Bobby was in the doorway, turned back to look at Neva. He hadn't left after all. He raised his hand to catch her attention. "Don't forget," he said. "You've got folks in Oklahoma."

She waved back quickly, then looked down at the ground. She didn't look at Will. Please, she thought, Miriam, don't say anything. Why had she told her, when she hadn't told Will, hadn't told anyone? But she knew the answer. Miriam was the only person she had trusted completely since her parents left.

"What was that about?" Will said. "Neva, what was that about?"

"Neva's grandfather, Will," Miriam said. Perhaps she sensed some danger. "Was your grandfather Cherokee or Choctaw?" she asked. "Wait—are you and Bobby related?"

It went on and on in the car riding home. Alcatraz, Wounded Knee, small pox, blankets. How terrible it was, what they did to those people. How much? He wanted to know: how much was she? Sundancing, he said, that was a noble thing. A people who could do something like that. He had always wanted to. How could it happen to people like that? People brave enough to torture themselves, to be strung up. He'd seen that movie. Neva kept her hands on the steering wheel and didn't respond. He was drunker than she'd realized.

"How much?" he asked, stumbling through the back door into the kitchen. "I mean," he said, "I knew your skin was a little darker than . . . how much? Really, how much are you?"

"I don't know, Will." She turned on him and shouted: "I don't know *how much*. There are no records. There are only stories. I don't know and I don't care."

"It's awful that you're ashamed," Will said, stroking her hair. Examining her face for cheekbones, she imagined. White people were obsessed with Indian cheekbones. Or folds in her eyelids. If he kissed her, would the tip of his tongue search for the scooped-out valleys of shovel teeth?

Shame, she thought. What did he know about it? About passing? What had it been like for her mother, so alone in her skin, so alone her whole adult life until she met Gus, an Oklahoma cousin so distant, you'd need a piece of paper the size of Georgia to chart their family tree? When she began to meet other Indians in Atlanta? When she heard about Wounded Knee, about AIM? About what was happening to Native women—to Native *girls*—in reservation hospitals?

"I'm not ashamed," she said. She opened the refrigerator and took out a package of chicken. Blood pooled against the cellophane.

"Then why did you act like that at the reception?"

"Let it go, Will," she said, leaving the chicken, the dinner she was supposed to make. She walked through the sliding glass doors onto the tiny balcony.

He followed her. "You should reclaim your heritage. There might be records. Miriam's sister works at a library, doesn't she? We could get her to look it up."

Records, she thought. Records could kill you. Names written down somewhere. They write down your name and one day they come to get you.

"Fuck the records," she said.

"What did you say?" he asked.

Shut up. Just shut up. She felt the words but could not speak them. Not on this, she thought; on this I won't be bullied for once. "I'm not ashamed," she said.

"You're at least part Indian," he said, taking her face between his hands.

She thought of the old man on that highway in Florida, the missing photos of her grandfather. The children in Cherokee, North Carolina, a town her family drove through on their way to the Smokies each year. Billy Jack becoming a brother to the snake. The stoic Indian with the single tear in the antipollution commercial. Choctaw, Miriam had said, or Cherokee. Not Creek. In Alabama, school children memorized the names of the five disappeared tribes with a mnemonic: Four *Cees* and an *Ess*. Cherokee, Choctaw, Chickasaw, Creek, Seminole. No one taught them the differences. The teacher had ticked off the tribal names, first on her fingers, then her thumb, folding each into the fist of her hand.

Neva twisted out of Will's reach. "There's no such thing. You're either Indian or you're not." She tore into the cellophane and laid the chicken pieces out on the wooden butcher block.

"Neva, your people would never have attacked Vietnam." His voice was slurred. "They would never do what our government is doing in Guatemala."

Oh my god, she thought. Does he not know there are Indians in Guatemala?

He tugged on the braid that ran down her back. "Hey," he said, backing away a little when she pulled the cleaver out of the drawer, "don't scalp me!" He smiled at his own joke, and for just a moment she fingered the edge of the cleaver, imagined its sharp edge tracing his hairline, from forehead to neck and around the other side, wondering what it would be like to jerk his stylish hairdo clean off.

She opened another drawer and began rooting through it for bobby pins. She twisted her braid into a knot and secured it.

"Come on," Will said. "It was a joke."

The *English* invented scalping, she wanted to say. Because Irish heads were too bulky for the hunters who brought them back for a bounty. But she kept quiet, knowing he'd use it as evidence, a story to tell their friends about his Native American wife. Something she'd read in a book. When one of her anthropology teachers had said something so amazingly stupid about Indians, she'd gone to the library and spent a day and an evening pulling books off the shelves, trying to find out something real. A pale student with dark hair had told the professor he was Creek. "Cree," the professor, some Yankee from Harvard, had insisted. "I'm sure you mean Cree."

"Neva—" Will put his hand on the back of her neck. "Aren't you going to skin it? You know I don't like it with skin on it."

"Maybe we should become vegetarians," Neva said. She raised the cleaver and brought it down hard on the piece of chicken stretched before her. The breast and wing separated cleanly into two parts.

6

Dauphin Island

"Yes?" Deb asked, when Neva came back downstairs.

"Yes," Neva nodded. "I'll bring my stuff over in the morning, if that's okay."

"Or you could just stay," Deb said. "You could meet some people tonight." She turned to face Neva. A little tomato sauce clung to a lock of her short, light brown hair. "And then you can go up whenever you want to. That room is really quiet."

The pot on the stove popped, spattering red sauce. "Don't be put off by the mess. I know this looks terrible, but I'm really a good cook."

Neva tried to smile, to say something back, something teasing, friendly, but her face felt stiff and out of practice.

"I'll put this ragout on the back burner. We'll borrow Jamie's car and go get your stuff. Watch this and I'll run up and ask him."

Neva poked the contents of the skillet with a wooden spoon. She smelled oregano, a slight sweetness, a little vinegar. A month, nearly two, since she'd cooked anything, since she'd stood over a stove.

Deb came down the stairs with a slight, dark-haired man behind her. "Jamie says he'll drive you, Neva."

"Oh no," she said. Already it was beginning, taking from people and owing them later. "I don't want to put you out."

"My dear." Jamie took her elbow and guided her toward the door. "I would like nothing better than to sit in the Mirador Café and drink coffee. You may take your time packing up."

"He means it, Neva," Deb called from the kitchen.

"I'll hurry," she said, as she left Jamie sitting at a table in the breeze-way outside the Mirador. He waved a cigarette at her. "Take your time," he said, his eyes intent on the plaza, where children carried bundles of belts and purses, handstitched in the lavish Coatepequen style of red and blue satin thread. A few university students stood in a cluster, arguing and gesturing. A man in a tractor pulled a small train around and around the square. The five carts behind it were filled with children. Parents waved at their children as the train chugged by.

"Okay," she said. She didn't have much—what was left from the bags she'd packed before heading out of town: clothes, a few books, a picture of her and her brother taken once when Harker came to Alabama, on vacation from college in Wisconsin. A blouse she'd bought at the first stop across the border. The four postcards. Those were wrapped in plastic, tucked carefully in a stiff cardboard envelope. No, not much. Packing wouldn't take long, and she could sit on the bed for a few minutes, take a last look at the Mirador Room with its startling view of the city. She would miss it, the view, the dark, silty coffee. Her room, the most. It was the only space she'd ever felt was entirely hers. If it didn't work out—at the new house—she could always come back here. She wouldn't always be broke, not if she started teaching next week. What she'd heard about teaching had been right—everybody wanted to learn English. But cheap as the hotel was, she couldn't stay here much longer.

"Wow, you weren't kidding," Jamie said when she reappeared. He eyed her one bag. "You've redefined traveling light."

"Well, I started with more," Neva said. She hovered, ready to go, but Jamie motioned her into the chair opposite.

"We have plenty of time before dinner," he said. "And you look like a woman with a story."

Neva laughed. "Do you know women without stories?"

He toasted her silently with his coffee cup. "Your secret is safe with me."

She pushed a smile onto her face. "There really is no secret."

"Everybody in Coatepeque has a secret," he said.

"What about that little girl?" Neva asked, pointing to one of the children in the toy train.

"Her secret is that she just picked her nose and wiped it on her little sister's dress," he said.

"Not really," Neva said.

"Really, I swear." He doubled over laughing, and Neva joined him, laughing until she was teary-eyed. The first time in a month.

When they stopped, she said, "I've been trying to learn Spanish. I heard you could get work teaching English here, so I thought I'd give it a try."

"No one at home to miss you?" Jamie asked.

"No, my boyfriend and I broke up a couple of months ago. I've just been living with friends. Seemed a good time to do something like this."

"Something like this?" He raised his eyebrows. "So you're just an elderly runaway?"

"Is twenty-six elderly?" Neva asked.

"I think so," Jamie said. "How old were those boxcar children? They ran away, didn't they?"

"Yes," Neva nodded. "You've got it. I loved that book. That's my secret. When I was a kid, I always wanted to run away. I finally worked up the courage." In the plaza, the train sat still, its driver waiting for more children to appear or for the day to be over.

"What?" Jamie said. "You were far away."

"Oh, I was just thinking about runaways. Real ones, I mean. I'm sorry I don't have a more interesting story," she said.

"We could invent one for you." Jamie squinted at her. "You're that Russian princess that's always turning up."

"Anastasia?" she said. "That would make me about eighty."

"International jewel thief? Bank robber on the lam?"

Neva shook her head. She held out her empty hands. "Too broke," she said. "What's your story?"

"Bor-ing." He drew the syllables out. "Business degree. Got tired of sitting in a cubicle in New York—unlike all the do-gooders here. The house will be full of them tonight—Nurse Deb and all her helpers. I came to pack some money away before going back to New York. It's just taking a little longer than I expected."

"There's got to be more," Neva said. It was impossible to tell his age. Graying at the temples, but he groomed himself like a younger man—perfect hair, the fingernails immaculate. A lemony aftershave wafting toward her.

"Of course." He reached for her duffel and slung it over his shoulder. "There's always more."

He opened the car door for her. "I'll keep my secrets, Neva, and you keep yours."

After the indictment, her mother dreamed the same dream night after night. Neva sometimes woke to hear her stumbling into the kitchen, usually when there was the faintest morning light showing through the blinds. Her mother dreamed about the dogs from her childhood, Choo Choo and Devil, who had lived long, happy lives, then died peacefully, in their sleep. Choo Choo first. For a week, Devil searched the house for his friend, moving in a circle through Choo Choo's three favorite haunts—the rag rug next to her mother's bed, under the dining table, the foyer, where he could lie on his side and still look out one of the long windows next to the front door. Both dogs had been old and arthritic, could no longer climb the stairs, and didn't like to go outside if it were cold or raining. After a week of circling, Devil had slipped away, too. After falling asleep one evening, his breaths became slow and shallow until they just stopped. He had not even twitched.

But when her mother dreamed about the dogs, their deaths were long, violent, agonizing narratives in which she was trying to save them from hunters or soldiers, where they fell down wells and she searched for a rope long enough. Once a herd of cattle trampled them to death.

The next morning, Neva found herself alone in the sunny kitchen, which seemed especially quiet after the noisy party the night before. She stirred her coffee and remembered the few times she got out of bed in the middle of the night and joined her mother at the kitchen table. The first time she found her there she'd felt a sudden fear, a ghost walking over her grave. "Where's daddy?" she asked, thinking of him leaving, being taken while she slept, unaware. Her mother laid her cold hand on Neva's arm. "He's asleep. He hardly sleeps at all these days, so I didn't wake him." Her mother told her the dream in detail that night, but later she only told the endings. "Trapped in a burning barn," she would say, or "Eating poisoned meat."

One night she whispered: "Drowning, at the beach where we took you and your brother that summer."

That summer they went to the beach. The Gulf coast that started in Mississippi, stretched across Alabama and into the Florida panhandle, as the water grew bluer and the sand whiter. The rental houses wooden on pilings, stocked with scratched Teflon and a huge battered aluminum pot for boiling shrimp. Harker was eleven and Neva had just turned nine. Their parents rented a small house on Dauphin Island, so close to the ocean the bed sheets felt damp and the windows were sticky with salt. Neva and Harker met some children on the beach, the Willises—two redheaded brothers named Jimbo and Teddy and their sister, Alice Ann, a skinny ten-year-old with thin blond hair and a scar running the length of her left calf.

"Alice Ann had cancer," Teddy, the younger boy, confided to Neva when Alice Ann had gone back to their cabin for her flippers. When she returned, she dove into the gray waves and swam, a shiny arc moving away from them fast. From a distance, she did not look quite human.

They had played on the beach with the Willis children all that day and the morning of the next. They buried Alice Ann in sand, making her a parody of a woman with giant hips and breasts, her slight yellow head sticking out at one end. When an afternoon storm set in, Teddy said, "Come on over to our house. We got Yahtzee and Monopoly."

The Willises were different from her family. They had brought a television with them, which Teddy and Jimbo had hauled up the rickety wooden stairs.

"Do you remember the Willises?" Neva asked Harker years later. "Those kids on the beach?"

"How the parents almost didn't let us go to their house?" Harker's words echoed over the line.

"No, I don't remember that."

Harker sighed. "Neva, you act like they were saints. They had their prejudices. They weren't perfect." But she didn't remember. You always blamed them, Neva thought. But it wasn't true. She was the one who blamed them. Throughout their childhoods, Neva had accepted everything her parents said, did, arranged, and Harker had been the one to balk, to argue, to rebel. When the trouble came, they switched sides. She was just enough younger than Harker to believe that everything had been taken from *her*. Harker was angry at them, sometimes about some things. But he didn't blame them. At college, he joined every activist group; he started an American Indian student group. He organized demonstrations. He kept his last name. He didn't hide from anyone, from who he was.

"Are they gone?" Jamie stuck his head through the kitchen door.

"I guess," Neva said. "I just woke up."

"Did you have a good time at the party? Is there coffee?" Jamie wore a striped bathrobe that reached nearly to his ankles. He poured himself a cup and peered out the window over the sink. "Deb's car is gone. Why didn't you go? You look like a beachy sort."

Neva shrugged. "Tired, I guess. I wanted to get settled. Where did they go, exactly?"

"My dear, you've never been to Tesoro?" Neva shook her head. "It's very beautiful—black sand, very tropical, that sort of thing."

"I've never been to the beach here. It sounds nice."

"A little hungover?" Jamie asked.

"Not really. Just tired."

"Did you have a good time? At the party, I mean."

Yes, she thought, it was a good time. More or less. The helicopter pilot who drooled on her. Actually drooled. Spit dripping onto the sleeve of her dress. The marine from Atlanta with his questions. Was anywhere safe from questions? Everyone here wanted to know *why*? Why was she here?

But there was her long conversation with Penny, the possibility of some tutoring, at the German School or the Lycée. "Yeah, it was fun. I'm not much good at parties."

"You should drink more. Oh God, I love Saturdays." Jamie stretched, the sleeves of his bathrobe falling away from his pale arms. He looked around the kitchen. "What I would give for the *Times* and a bagel."

"Oh right, you're from New York," Neva said. Yes, she could see it. If she squinted, turned her face away from the bright landscape, the bougainvillea pressed to the window, the volcano, arcing over the courtyard wall, she knew Jamie. She saw him in Manhattan black or a Brooklyn sports coat, brown with the elbows out. Reading a newspaper on the subway. She nodded.

"Do you know New York!?" He sat up.

But Neva shook her head. "Not really. Do you miss the city, living here?"

Jamie shrugged. "I miss things, people. But I was sick of living in a tiny room. Sick of schlepping things—you know, the way people in cities carry bags of stuff with them everywhere?"

"But people do that here, don't they?" Neva said, thinking of the plastic net bags Coatepequen women carried—between them, if they were too heavy, on their heads if they weren't.

Jamie laughed. "Well, you're right of course, but *we* don't. They do. We don't." He paused. "I told you I wasn't one of the resident do-gooders. Speaking of which, how do you like your new housemates? Present company excluded, of course."

"I thought you lived next door," Neva said.

"Yes and no. It's the old servants' quarters for this house. Mostly separate. Two rooms, kitchen, bathroom, a little verandah. But I poach here. It drives Kira crazy."

They heard the sound of a moped, quick steps in the gravel outside, the slam of the front door.

"Really speaking of which," Jamie said.

"Hey," Kira said from the doorway. "Is Deb back?"

"We haven't seen her." Jamie said. He stretched in an exaggerated fashion, his robe gaping open over a white T-shirt. "I should probably do something. Get dressed or something before the sun goes down." He winked at Neva, picked up his coffee cup and put it in the sink.

"Thanks for helping," Kira said. She sighed, washed his cup and put it in the rack. She leaned against the counter, so that Neva had to crane her neck when she spoke.

"Do you remember Helen, who we thought was gonna come last night?"

"Right, but she didn't," Neva said.

"I saw her at the El Presidente today, and she said they need a tutor at the Escuela Internationale. Go Monday at four. If they like you, they'll do some sort of orientation; then you'll start right away."

"This Monday? As in day-after-tomorrow Monday?"

"Yeah, she's kind of expecting you, so you should call if you're not going—"

"Oh, I'm going. Thank you so much. I really appreciate it. Wow, that's just fantastic. Thank—"

"Jeez, don't make such a big deal about it." Kira was rooting around in the refrigerator. "There's Deb," she said, without looking up.

Deb set her keys on the table, her satchel in the empty chair. Its green canvas mouth gaped open to toothy rows of file folders and white paper. "What's up?" she said.

"Kira got me an interview at the International School," Neva said.

Kira stood up and snorted. "It's no big deal. Besides, nobody ever calls it that. In English it's just 'The International.'"

"They ought to just call it the Escuela Estados Unidos. The US version of international. Those families have a thing for the United States," Deb said. "But that's great, Neva. When do you start?"

"Day after tomorrow. It's downtown, right?"

"No, a couple of blocks off the Zócalo. You can walk there and take the 6 bus back—it runs 'til ten. In fact, I could drop you there tomorrow so you'll know where it is."

"You don't have to work at the hospital?"

"Oh, I don't work *at* the hospital," Deb said. "I am a nurse, but I work for an NGO."

"A what?" Neva asked.

"National Do-Gooders Organization," Kira said.

Deb's smile was tight. "Hush, Kira," she said. "I work for a non-profit, Neva. Across Borders—we focus on children and mothers."

Kira mimicked a woman rocking a baby in her arms. "Rock-a-bye, baby," she sang, "in the treetop . . ."

Neva ignored her. "You *focus* on them . . ." she said to Deb. "What does that mean? You focus on them?"

"Mostly nutritional stuff, prenatal," Deb said. If she heard the edge in Neva's voice, she ignored it. "Early childhood. Later if we can manage it."

"When the wind blows, the cradle will *splat*!" Kira opened her arms, letting the imaginary baby fall to the ground. "Good-bye, baby!" she waved to the floor.

"Kira thinks we should be dispensing birth control—"

"Does she?" Neva said, her voice so low neither of them seemed to hear her.

"Be quiet," Deb said to Kira, who had started humming "Rock-a-bye, Baby" under her breath. "But it's not what we do. It would be hard to do here. It's a Catholic country, for pete's sake."

"That's how you can tell Deb is really mad." Kira made a face at Neva, trying to draw her in. "She says things like 'for pete's sake.'"

Neva waited for Deb's tight smile to return, but instead she broke into laughter. "Shut *up*, Kira," she said, but she smiled in a way Neva had never seen, dimples in both cheeks. They had an odd relationship, Deb and Kira, a lifetime of history, though from what they had told her, they hadn't known each other for more than a year or two. Maybe everything ran in fast motion here, with the war only a valley away, flowers so brightly colored they didn't seem real, fruit bursting its seams from ripeness. Everything crueler or sweeter, saltier or noisier, even the way the day's intense heat gave way so quickly to the evening chill.

She remembered climbing the stairs behind Teddy Willis that summer day so long ago, the way the freckles on his back had merged into palm-sized orange splotches. The grape Kool-Aid that turned their mouths blue. She had been too embarrassed to ask to use the bathroom, too shy to tiptoe through the living room where the grown-up Willises watched TV, so all afternoon she'd held it, sitting with her legs squeezed together. They'd sat in a circle on the shallow porch overlooking the beach. Mr. and Mrs. Willis sat side by side on the divan facing the television and the plain, windowless kitchen. All afternoon Neva would look up to see the back of Mr. Willis's unmoving bald head, Mrs. Willis's hands patting her bouffant back into place.

Alice Ann sat with her legs folded to one side, the left one next to Neva's right hand. The scar ran like a long red dagger, and Neva's fingers brushed it once when she shifted her weight from one hip to the next. She shuddered both at the touch of it and the worry that she had hurt Alice Ann—the scar looked like a wound, vulnerable and tender. But Alice Ann didn't seem to notice.

Harker and Neva had never played Monopoly, but they learned the rules. Harker soon owned all the railroads and a monopoly of yellow deeds. Neva advanced her token—the iron—cautiously. She traded with Jimbo, then Harker, until she had her own monopoly and had started to put houses on them. The game ended when Teddy snuck off Kentucky Avenue, Harker's property. Harker was furious, even more outraged when Teddy read the rule aloud from a printed piece of paper he took out of the Monopoly box.

"You didn't tell us that rule," Harker said. "You can't do it if you didn't tell us."

They had taken sides quickly—Neva and Harker against the Willises. They had argued so loudly, Mrs. Willis had risen from the living room couch and told Neva and Harker to go home. "I'm not going to have people yelling in my house," she said. Her bouffant leaned slightly to one side, and her skirt was wrinkled.

Their only beach vacation because the trouble had started soon after. When she and Harker got back to their cabin, her parents were on the porch, drinking iced tea and watching storm clouds building on the horizon over the green water. It was windy; they watched as a few fronds of saw palmetto blew by, then an entire rosemary bush and a child's pink plastic bucket. Her parents were relaxed then; they bought copies of the same books and read them together. They cooked together from a French cookbook her father had ordered from Time-Life.

One of her father's patients had given him a recording of the soundtrack to *Zorba the Greek*—"He thought I would understand him better"—and they had put the record on one night after dinner and danced, first her parents, then all of them in a chain around and around the house, through the living room into the dining room, up the two stairs of the landing and down the other side, and around again and again until they were damp and exhausted.

What happened to that record, Neva wondered? Or the French cookbook? What happened, what happened? The old question rose like a slender black snake curling up her spine, but she pushed it away, as she always had.

7

The International

After Neva had been tutoring for a week, Mr. Kremer, the vice principal, called her into his office. Her palms were sweaty. There were stories that he compensated for stupidity with bullying, with strange deductions from paychecks for using too much chalk, that he didn't like it when teachers pinned things to the bulletin boards because it made them look messy. He asked her if she liked tutoring, but before she could answer, he said, "Do you speak Spanish? You look like you speak Spanish."

Neva shook her head. "No, not really," she said. They sat in silence for a few moments, Mr. Kremer's face wrinkled with concern. He asked again, "Are you sure you don't speak Spanish?"

"No," Neva said, "no, I don't. I wish I did. I've been studying—"

He leaned forward across his desk and interrupted her. "Carla Sobel is pregnant."

She wasn't sure she knew who Carla was exactly—the tenth-grade teacher with the ponytail, she thought. She waited, unsure why he was telling her this.

"Well?" he said.

"I'm sorry?" Neva asked.

"Do you or do you not want the job?" He sat back in his chair with the tips of his fingers arced together into a tiny church across his face. There was a black mole right in the center of his forehead, a thick hair sprouting in the middle of it. He asked the question through the church of his fingers, the words rushing out like a relieved congregation after a long sermon.

"Teaching the tenth-grade class?"

He moved his fingers in and out like an accordion. "You are a teacher, aren't you?" he said.

When Kira asked at dinner, "How's the tutoring?" Neva told them about the job offer.

"There was one weird thing in the interview," she said. "He kept insisting that I could speak Spanish. I hope it's not a big problem that I don't."

Jamie was squinting at her. "Well, señorita," he said. "You could *pass*."

At Neva's baffled look, Deb said, "For Coatepequen. Jamie means you could pass as a Coatepequen."

If she had thought about it, she would've responded that she was too tall. After dinner, she looked at herself in the mirror in her room, trying to see herself as a stranger, a woman climbing off the bus as she was climbing on, a cashier at Kismet, a teacher at a Coatepequen high school. Yes, she could see it—the Indian hair, the eyelids. A señorita to tourists and expats—but to a Coatepequen? She didn't think so. Belonging had so little to do with the looks you were born with. What mattered was how you moved, the story your shoulders told, that your hips carried. What mattered was what was written on your face, your history, the history of your grandmothers, of the land that claimed you.

That Saturday, she dressed up a little, the way Coatepequen women did, digging deep into the clothes the mythic Christina had left behind. Stockings, eye shadow. She rode the bus to the central market, watching the women, trying to mimic their body language. It was different. The men's looks were routine, not acute. A teenage girl shared her seat and began to talk to her in Spanish. But the women were not fooled. Their cool friendliness was business as usual.

So on Friday, she became Carla's teacher's aide, scrambling to find enough material to fill six classes a day before Carla left at the end of the term. The students worked in workbooks, learning to change sentences into clauses, to put adverbs before adjectives, learning that "Everyone" was singular and took the pronoun "His." When she taught literature, Carla outlined the story, interpreting it for the students as they worked through it. The students wrote down everything she said, except for a trio of boys in the back row. "Why don't they take notes?" Neva asked. "Oh," said Carla. "The girls take notes for them."

When they did poetry, Carla went through the poem line by line paraphrasing. "Whither art thou going, waterfowl?" became "Where are you going, duck?"

"Miss Sobel," one of the boys in the back asked, "why is he talking to a duck?"

"Because he loves nature," Carla told him. Neva saw pens moving. She leaned toward Regina Vides and saw her writing *Poet Loves Nature* in elegant script.

She didn't know if she could do it. She mostly sat in a desk off to the side and wrote down everything the girls wrote down. She had a month to learn, a month before she walked into the room without Carla, without, she thought, a real teacher.

At the end of her first week as Carla's teaching assistant, Carla's doctor ordered her home to bed for the rest of her pregnancy. "Kremer says you'll have to start Monday," Carla told her. "Sorry," she said, twisting her mouth, but Neva could see she wasn't sorry. That even before her feet had gotten swollen, she had grown tired of paraphrasing poems about ducks. She left Neva a box crammed with what she called teaching materials, some that she'd inherited from the tenth-grade teacher before her. Neva brought home everything—the textbook, the workbook, old exams—and spent the entire weekend in her room going over them. She felt sick. They would eat her, she thought. They will just eat me up.

She lived in fear of Mr. Kremer. He seemed to have a lot of time on his hands. He whistled as he walked down the hallway, keys jingling. When the whistling went on by, she felt her body relax. But if it stopped suddenly outside her door, she couldn't concentrate, would stop mid-sentence if she were explaining something on the board, would stand up if she were bent over a student's paper.

"We go to the same beauty salon," Susannah the tenth-grade teacher told her months later. Susannah had befriended her the first week, her irreverence a godsend. "He gets perms. How could you be afraid of a man who pays to make his hair look like *that*?"

But she felt like a guest in Carla's classroom, an imposter. She was sure Mr. K—as all the teachers called him—would find someone better, a real teacher.

At the end of the first week, she tumbled into an exhausted, fitful sleep, dreaming that angry children were pulling her hair. She knew them, recognized their pale gamine faces, but they weren't anyone she knew in real life. She was teaching at an orphanage where the children were wild. She tried to teach them the Spanish word for key, *llave*, but they only pulled her hair harder. They were feral children, barefoot, growling instead of speaking. Abandoned children, who had learned from the grass and the bushes, from crows and foxes. She was their teacher, the one expected to teach them to be human. And then she was one of them, running, running across fields of sharp rocks, hay mowed down to stubble, running before the humans could catch them.

She woke once, touching her sore scalp, remembering the mornings her grandmother had braided her hair in the minutes just before the school bus arrived. "Your hair is just like your mother's," she would say, reaching for the grosgrain ribbons to bind first one thick braid, then another. Neva's hair was jet black, reddish when the sun shone directly on it. All day, wisps would escape her grandmother's careful braids. She longed for the straight, shining blond or the brown curls of her classmates. But she was the new girl, the temporary girl. They did not talk to her at first. She remembered the loneliness: her parents gone, her brother away at college, visiting every holiday, but still, away.

She had hated them a little—not her classmates, but the girls, the women, whose might-have-been children were forever lost to them. The women written down and catalogued in BIA records. She had been old enough to sense it, the sickness and horror in her parents' voices when they talked about it. Sterilization. The body written out of history. But only now was she beginning to understand what it might mean to wake up in a body that had been tied and cut and changed. What loss means when loss is already the first fact of your history.

But who knew? Maybe it was harder to expect everything, like Will. Like all the Wills of the world.

She sat up in bed in the ink-black room—the noise from the street had finally stopped. The room was stuffy. Fighting panic, Neva felt her way to the wall where she knew the large shuttered windows were and ran her hands along the plaster, stumbling once on an armchair she'd forgotten, until she found the wooden edge of one of the windows and felt her way to the clasp in the center. When she opened the shutters, the room was light enough to see every object in it: the white iron bed in the corner, the heavy Spanish dresser and the elaborate mirror above it, a pale square framed in dark rickrack. Neva turned the armchair around so that it faced out the window. The city was as quiet as if no one lived there, and the slight breeze was cool against her damp face. Tomorrow, she would call Harker. After her wedding, everything changed. There were so many things she didn't want to tell him. Things that would make him dislike Will even more. She never thought the silence between them would stretch over so many months, across two continents. Tomorrow, she told herself. Tomorrow, I'll call.

Three days later, she got through. The only phone was in the hallway, on a carved brown table that rocked when you picked up the receiver. Dialing the States involved a long, complicated sequence of numbers. You had to shout a little, so she had waited for a chance to be alone in the house. Wednesday afternoons Deb volunteered at the Madres office and Kira rehearsed with her band. You could never pin Jamie down about his schedule, so she listened for him next door.

Harker's voice sounded sleepy through the static, though there was only an hour difference between the Midwest and Coatepeque.

"Harker?" she said, disconcerted to hear his name echo on the line.

"Neva? I can't hear you very well. Wait—"

"Okay," he said. "Where are you? This is a terrible line. Should I call you back?"

"No, I'm—I'm not in Atlanta," she said.

"I know. I tried to call you. Will—"

She cut him off. "I've left Will—"

"Well, about time," he said.

"Don't start, Harker. Just don't," Neva said. She could hear the note of irritation creeping into her voice.

"Sorry," he said. "Are you okay?"

"I'm okay. I mean I really left Atlanta. I'm in Central America, in Coatepeque."

"Wow," he said, and the word echoed. "Well," he said after a brief silence, "I'm glad. I always thought you should travel. You were always so afraid to venture out."

"I wasn't," she said. But he was right. Always so afraid.

"How long are you there for? Who are you traveling with? What was your friend's name—the one who made your wedding cake—" His words came out in a rush he was so excited—that she had left Will, that she had stopped waiting by the mailbox. She didn't know how to tell him why she was here, what she had come for.

"I'm not traveling," Neva said.

"What do you mean?"

"I just. I know it sounds crazy, but I sort of live here. I have a job—I teach English. I live in a house with some other Americans, two women, white women—"

"Is that okay?" he asked.

"Yeah, it's fine. They're nice. One of them is really nice—Deb. She does this work with pregnant women here, with nutritional counseling, stuff like that. Support after the baby is born, too."

Harker didn't say anything for a moment. Then he asked, "Well, that's good, isn't it?"

"Sure," Neva said. "It's great. It's just that the women are, you know, like Indians—"

"They are Indians," Harker laughed. "Neva, they *are* Indians—"

"No, I know. It's just that it brought back a lot of stuff. I keep thinking how if there'd been a group like hers, like Deb's, maybe those women in Oklahoma wouldn't have been sterilized. Maybe none of it would ever have happened."

They were both silent. "Neva." Harker spoke first. "I don't know what to say. There are so many maybes. So many what-ifs. You can't live like that. Be glad that somebody somewhere is helping Indian babies get born and helping them live. It's the least white people can do. It is what *they* were trying to do."

"Yes, I know. I know that," Neva said. "Trying," she said. "Everyone's always trying."

She stayed in her bedroom often those first few weeks in the house, out of the way, turning back up the stairs if she heard voices in the kitchen. She would hover, listening, half-longing to go down and half-determined to hide away, curled up and untouched. Most days, she woke early and walked the three blocks to the bus stop, or woke even earlier and walked the mile or so to the school. Afternoons, she almost always walked unless she had too much stuff to carry, passing the yard with three brown chickens, the drugstore, and Mami's Ice Cream, where so often some of her students were outside eating cones. "Miss!" they would call out to her. "Don't you want some ice cream?" But she would only wave and walk on.

She worried endlessly about doing something wrong at school. She worried about it at home—Deb and Kira's house. She didn't think of it as home. She couldn't relax at breakfast, jumping up to put the orange juice and the butter back in the refrigerator. Mopping up every spill and crumb before sitting down to eat. A couple of nights she skipped dinner because she knew how awkward it would be if she intruded on their meal.

They began to call up the staircase. "There's soup. Are you hungry?"

or "We're getting Chinese takeout—do you want some?" At first
she said, "No, that's okay," but the combination of smells—garlic or
oregano—and her own growing loneliness lured her down. After a
while, she stopped feeling like company, didn't carry her breakfast back
up the stairs to her room or make her excuses when one of them joined
her in the kitchen.

She started cooking enough for four. And though Kira had been
unable to resist asking, "What is it? Grits?" the first time she made
dinner, they ate everything. After every crumb was gone, Kira looked
at Deb. "We didn't even know she could cook." She learned to cook
Coatepequen food—fried plantains, rice with garlic and cumin, black
beans ground to a thick salty paste and sprinkled with the dry white
cheese Coatepequen women made in their kitchens. She bought
chicken at the market and roasted it in the small oven. She experiment-
ed with peppers and cilantro, learning to make marinades and relishes.

Around Kira, she always felt an edge of something, an edge she
could not lean against. Jamie and Kira fought a complicated war with
each other, teasing on good days, barbed on others, but the house
remained a friendly place with its share of small frictions. No one ever
wanted to clean up the day after a party, not even Deb, and there were
so many parties. Nothing, Neva had to remind herself, after living the
way I lived the last few years. Not if I'm the one who picks up every
plastic cup, who scrubs every wine stain from the rug. Nothing, when
the courtyard garden is lush with red and purple flowers, when a bowl
of mangoes and limes perfumes the whole kitchen, when I can turn
into bed each night and sleep. Sleep until the sun slants through a tall
window in a room that is mine. Sleep so deeply it is like dying and
coming back to life.

8

The Yellow House

Late one afternoon, as she chopped onions in the kitchen, she realized it had been a month, the time she'd promised to rent the room, and she had no thought of leaving. A month and what had she done with these thirty days? In the rush of sun and fruit drinks, of days at the volcano lake—of being included—what had happened to the search? I needed to get settled, she told herself. To figure out how to start searching. I couldn't just start asking questions. She didn't know who she was arguing with. Herself? Her brother? The absence that was her parents? Maybe they were just the excuse to leave Will, to leave behind the life— the existence—she'd made for herself. They were my excuse then, too, she thought. My reason for hiding away. Her brother would never have lost sight of them. He never hid from who he was.

In Coatepeque, Neva was still hiding. From who she wasn't. When new people at the bar began to ask her things, she smiled and stirred her drink. She changed the subject. She asked them: "Are you going to eat those peanuts?" or "Can you watch my purse while I go to the bathroom?"

She could've invented a past, but with teaching and tutoring, learning the bus routes, and always watching, asking, looking for a clue to follow, for a way to ask a question—with all of this, she would have had to keep a notebook ready to consult. If someone asked, "How old are you?" or "Where are you from?" she'd have had to pull the notebook out of her purse and flip it open the same way she opened her Spanish dictionary to look up a word she needed.

Cleveland, the Invented Neva Dictionary might say.

Twenty-seven.

No, not me, not ever. I've never been married.

Sally, a sister with golden hair.

A cat named Puff, border collie named Puck, who died when I was twelve.

Lawyer, nurse, Methodists. No, not interested in politics. Still married, still living in Ohio. Yes, they call every other week.

"I haven't given up," she said aloud, as if Harker were in the room with her. But she could see that she'd made a choice to put them away for a while, like a pair of dolls left over from childhood, tucked into a bottom drawer or a box under the bed. It was why she had married Will, to put them away, but his rage had made her miss them more. When he pushed her over the couch, she thought, for the first time in years, of the boy falling down the stairs. His bruised brain leaking slowly, so slowly, that he didn't die for days. She kept watch after Will pushed her, wondering when she would begin to talk, to tell stories the way the dying boy had. Half memory, half dream. Names and dates. Names that, in time, yielded more names. But she lived when he did not. She had a bruise on her left hip and the wind knocked out of her. He had an autopsy in an FBI office and a trial named after him.

She was thirteen when it happened, fourteen when they left. At first, it felt like a rising excitement, joyous and noisy. It began when her mother met Gus, one day at the Chattahoochee Arts Festival when he and Millie his girlfriend had just walked up to her, and Gus had said, "I don't know who you are, but I know you're Indian." ("He shouted it," her mother would say, laughing. "People turned and looked!") They discovered they were cousins of a sort—"white cousins," they called it, because they were related through their white kin, not their Creek blood. Gus was Oklahoma Creek through his father, but his mother's family was from North Carolina. "Third cousins once removed." Harker tried to explain it to her, but the math of it—like all math—eluded her. They called him Uncle Gus—it was traditional—and as it was also traditional for a woman's male relatives to take a special interest in her children, Gus did his best.

The house was filled with people that summer. "The Indian Summer," Harker and Neva called it when they were older, without a trace of irony in their voices. Gus and Millie came. She was Lakota from Rosebud and made tiny little bags stitched from rabbit skin with the fur turned inside. She gave Neva and Harker one each, with little polished stones inside. "Is this traditional?" Harker asked. "Traditional" had become his new favorite word. "What do the stones mean?"

"Oh nothing," Millie said. "I just saw the stones at Woolworth's and thought they were pretty."

Her mother changed so much after she met Gus. What had it been like for her, growing up in a small Alabama town, watching her Creek father, always a little unsure who would shake his hand and who would turn away? Neva couldn't imagine it. One hundred and fifty years and half a dozen generations after the Removal—no one outside of North Carolina even thought about Indians being in the south. How much easier it must've been for her mother in Atlanta, a city where you could find any color of skin, but still, it wasn't the same as being recognized for what you were. An Indian ancestor made for bragging rights in the south. Unless it showed, Neva thought. Then it was a source of shame.

Sometimes other kids were there, but mostly Neva and Harker hung around the edges. The adults talked about Wounded Knee constantly—it had only been a year since the truce was reached and AIM left. "They're still shooting people up there," Millie's brother Marvin, who was visiting from South Dakota, said.

Years later Harker told Neva that they were wild to do something—their parents, Gus. "Anything would have done, any issue," he said. But Neva didn't agree. There was something special about its horribleness, about sterilization, to her father, a doctor and the son of Jews. And her mother must have known that when *her* mother went into labor too early with her second child, the fumbling doctor at the small, rural hospital missed something and sent her home. When she returned, the baby's heart had stopped beating and she was bleeding so much the doctor had to do a hysterectomy to save her life. The little brother not born. Surely that story was one Neva's mother carried with her always.

How her parents must have grieved for the women they heard about, the girls. Who signed pieces of paper written in someone else's language. Or when they were already under anesthesia. Or who never signed. A girl of fifteen had been told that it was reversible, that when she was ready for more children, they would just change it back.

There were so many stories. When Rhonda, Harker's girlfriend, was finishing her nursing degree, she told him more. Puerto Rican women, she said. Maybe thousands of them. Indian women in South America. Even a story about the Peace Corps—that workers were persuading Quechua women to get sterilized. But no one really believed that.

And no one, her parents thought, would believe what they were hearing. They had to have proof. So much proof that the newspapers couldn't ignore them. Enough to take to Congress. Solid proof to show someone who could do something about it, someone who could stop it.

It must have seemed so simple: find a clinic or hospital and steal their records. The evidence of what was happening. Find someone who cleaned or answered the phone at one of the clinics. Find someone who pushed wheelchairs or carried waste at one of the hospitals. Someone Indian. It took months of planning, months of talking, gathering money. And when it all went wrong, it was a fluke, an accident of the universe. An alarm going off, which the handful of young men who broke into the clinic knew might happen. But what they didn't expect was that in the rush to get out undetected, one of them would trip and tumble down a flight of stairs. Concrete stairs with steel risers. Warren Silverhorn, a Kiowa boy everybody called "Target." He never again opened his eyes.

Neva closed her eyes against the stinging onions she was chopping. Target Silverhorn. He was so young, she thought. Not that much older than the students I teach. But my students are not warriors, and when we choose up sides, they'll be on the other one. She shook her head to stop something like panic threatening to rise up from her belly to her solar plexus to her throat and choke her. Teaching them is how I can stay here. And who knows what I can teach along the way. But I have to stay.

A month, she'd told Deb and Kira. She'd stay a month and they'd agreed. Perhaps the room had already been promised, maybe before she even came. Maybe tomorrow she would wake to see another woman standing in the doorway with a suitcase and a box holding a few books, an alarm clock, and a photograph of a boyfriend named Jason or Milt.

Surely not Milt, she thought, stumbling over a broken place in the tiles of the kitchen floor. She broke two eggs into a bowl and beat them with a fork. She didn't want to leave, but how could she ask? She couldn't ask. She would rather move than endure the moment of asking and hearing "No." But how could she sleep tonight without knowing? Without knowing where she would go. She had been crazy to come here. To move into this house full of people. To get used to it. She checked the house, every room, and looked out the door up and down the street. But no one was home. She called the Mirador, finding their number on her final bill, but heard only a crazy busy signal at the other end, as if the line were broken. She hung up and tried again, then a third time. "El Mirador," a man's voice said, just as she heard Kira's Yamaha outside. She hung up.

She went back to her salmon pie, rolling the dough out and pushing it down into the tart pan, breaking up the can of salmon in a bowl and stirring the eggs in. A month, she thought. She mixed dill and shredded cucumbers into sour cream for a sauce, sliced tomatoes, avocado, and green mango for a salad, squeezing lime over it and sprinkling the top with chopped cilantro.

"What a beautiful meal," Deb said when they were all sitting down, even Jamie who had been lured from his newspaper.

"We need more lime." Neva got up and opened the refrigerator. She stood at the counter with her back to them. "I wasn't sure what might happen tomorrow, so I thought I should make a good farewell dinner."

Neva turned around. Kira's fork was midway to her mouth. "Huh?" she said.

Deb looked tense. "Did you find another place?" she asked.

Neva turned away again to rinse the knife and cutting board in the sink. "I may just go back to the Mirador for a while."

"Why?" said Kira. Deb did not speak.

"Well, we only said a month. I thought you might have rented the room." The limes were sliced and in a small white bowl, the knife and cutting board rinsed and in the drainer. There was nothing to do but sit back down at the table and face them.

"Neva," Deb said. She put her hand on Neva's forearm, but she didn't say anything else.

"God, I hope not," Jamie said. "And they've just gotten you broken in."

"I didn't remember," Kira said, "about the month. Did you remember, Deb?"

"No." Deb shook her head. "At some point you just seemed so . . . permanent."

Neva rose from the table and went up to her room. When she came down a minute later, they weren't talking. Jamie was still eating, but Deb and Kira were sitting, silent.

"Here," Neva said, putting a stack of bills on the table.

"What's this?" Deb asked.

"My October rent. I'm staying."

Kira speared a slice of avocado from Jamie's plate and winked at the look on his face. "You are so weird, Neva," she said.

9

The Farm

There was no echo on the phone line tonight, the first time Neva and Harker had talked without the delay, the weird disconcerting sound of their words repeated and echoed on the line. When this happened, they would wait patiently before responding. What should have been short calls took a long time, cost a fortune.

But tonight the line was clear. Neva told Harker about her job, her students. How they came to her classroom in the morning before school started.

"Why do you seem so surprised?" he asked. "You've always wanted to be a teacher. I knew you'd be good at it.

"Neva," Harker continued after a moment. "You could come back here and teach."

She didn't respond to that. Then Harker said, "Neva, I saw Magruder."

"You went to see him?" Elson Magruder. Her parents' lawyer. Neva was furious. "I thought we agreed."

"I didn't go to see him. I saw him at the Majestic. We ended up sharing a booth."

"When were you in Atlanta?" Neva asked, suspicious, not trusting her brother.

"I went looking for you, before you called."

"Did you see Will?" she asked.

"He wouldn't open the door, talked to me through the chain. He said you had left. That's all. That you had left."

"How did he look?"

"Neva, I couldn't really tell. He's such an asshole. I'm glad you left."

"I'm glad, too." They were silent for a moment. Neva chose her next words carefully. She breathed in shallow quick breaths, sure that if she inhaled too deeply, that if she let her words rush out of her, that

47

something might break, that the tentative hold she had on the bright verdant world around her might shake loose, that the clear mountain sunlight cast through her classroom window each morning might change.

"What did Magruder say? Did you talk about it?"

"He said what he's always said. That we're crazy not to go ahead, declare them dead, settle what little is left." Harker's voice was resigned; he was sure she would never agree.

"What about detectives? Last time, remember, he said we would have to look for them."

"Maybe not. He wasn't sure. It's been so long now." He paused. "Neva, whatever we find out—and we would probably find out nothing—wouldn't it be better to know? I don't like the not-knowing. It used to drive me crazy—I couldn't sleep for not knowing. Not anymore. I had to stop. Stop always thinking about it, about them. Where they were. Now I think a lot about who they were. What was important to them."

Neva felt the heat of her stinging eyes, the effort of holding herself in, not letting it loosen, the knot in her solar plexus, fixed firmly in its place these dozen years.

"Oh, Neva, what are you thinking?" Harker's voice choked on the words. "That they're going to turn up on your doorstep, ready to take their baby girl back home?"

"Well if they did, where would they find me? Where would I be?" It was out, like a rush through her body, as if every cell in her body were weeping.

"Neva—" Harker said, but she could not speak, could not unknot her throat enough to make a sound with it, not a squeak or whimper, not even a long, low whine. It was back now: the stretched-out, sorrowful months after they left her in Alabama, that hardest winter in years, the whole county iced over and wind blowing clear through her as if she wasn't there. Butler City—they should have called it Butler Village. And the farm was miles from what little town there was. A loneliness she now knew she had felt but been unable to understand. The day they told her and Harker—her mother at the kitchen table, waiting for them after school. "When the first trial ended, we all thought we could breathe again, for a while," she told them. "People were in jail; Gus went to jail. We thought it would be over. We thought it would stop, but it didn't stop. We knew it would never be over for some people, but we thought, It is over for us . . ."

Her mother trailed off.

"Meaning what?" Harker said. He looked away as he asked. Neva said nothing.

"We need to get you out of harm's way. Just for a while," her mother said. "Just for a little while."

And then they had disappeared, so completely not even the FBI could find them.

All those years in Alabama: checking the mailbox twice a day, never hearing the phone without adrenaline stirring, her heart racing a little faster. Even after she married Will and moved to Atlanta, she kept watch, sent a new mail forwarding card to the post office every year, wrote cheerful "Season's Greetings!" cards to her grandmother's minister, the people at the next farm who'd nodded when they passed on the road but never spoken, to her parents' friends, doing everything possible to make herself visible, findable, to show up like a blinking dot on somebody's radar screen. Reversing the family pattern, the habits of a lifetime.

If only she had done none of those things. If only she could know they'd tried desperately to find her, but she was the one who had disappeared.

It was her sharpest memory: the back end of the car on the dusty road in front of her grandmother's farmhouse. The car growing smaller. Harker already turning back to the house rather than watch them drive away. Next to her, Bruno, her grandmother's small, fierce terrier, barking sharply. He did not bark out of sympathy but to urge her parents on, away from Alabama, out of her life.

Bruno had no use for her. She remembered his terse, persistent bark and the way—even after he got old and his hips locked up—he could race across the yard faster than she could run. The first time she tried to pet him, reaching out with a "Sweet doggy!" he had drawn back, looking at her with something like contempt. After her parents left, the look turned to pity.

It was Bruno's home, not hers. He was the sneering boy cousin she never had, the one who found her mostly beneath notice but was still hostile at finding her here, in his place. Bruno would come into the kitchen when she was getting a glass of milk. He would look at her as if she were stealing something.

Her parents never called. Her grandmother told her that they would not be able to call. That it wasn't safe to call. Neva didn't believe her—she knew they would call. But they didn't call.

There was little to no news—her grandmother didn't take a news-paper. Neva didn't make friends at school, didn't go home after class to play or study with a girl named Jane or Robin. She listened carefully for any mention of what had happened in Oklahoma, but there was nothing, except the one time when she heard the name Gus Ortega on the radio at the Jitney Jungle and realized it was Uncle Gus.

The sky in the country was so big that beneath it, on any day sunny or stormy, windy or still, Neva could disappear, disappear entirely. She learned in time to love her grandmother, but she loved the sky from the beginning, the sky that erased her. She was surprised years later to discover the terror with which some city people met those skies uncontained by tall buildings, stars not shadowed by streetlights and neon.

After Harker left for college, Neva developed the habit of standing in the yard, then wandering around as if she meant to look at things—trees, animals, her grandmother's flowers. But it was all a disguise for her furtive glances down the road. Her grandmother was out in the yard a lot, too. It was years later that Neva realized her grandmother was following her, that beneath her stoic farmer's wife self, she was deeply troubled: at Neva's parents, her daughter, her granddaughter's future. When Neva would wander in the side yard, her grandmother would weed the patch of summer squash. She would take clothes off the line, hang towels out. After a few days, she began to call Neva over. "Could you hold this basket for just a minute?" she would ask. Or: "Would you hand me a tie? I can't pick up anything in these gloves."

One late afternoon in early December, when the temperature had just begun its evening drop into the high forties, Neva was helping her grandmother bring in what were probably the last of the winter greens. Cars were rare enough on their stretch of highway that they both stopped their work and listened. A blue Chevrolet—not her parents' white station wagon—drove by, dust rising like a banner behind it. Neva turned at the sound of it, watched it go by. She did not cry, but she sat down on the ground, holding her face to her bony knees.

Her grandmother said nothing, and after a few minutes, Neva felt a hand on her shoulder. Her grandmother leaned heavily on her as she stood up. "I get so stiff pulling greens," she said. She tapped on Neva's shoulder. "Look at that," she said, pointing to a hawk on the telephone pole across the road, before she turned back to the house with the bushel basket of kale and turnip greens. The gray hair creeping from its knot at the back of her head. Pushing the blue and silver glasses back against her eyes.

Bruno rose to his feet, sniffed at Neva, and followed her grandmother into the house. Sakakaw, her grandmother's crow, watched them from a cottonwood tree. In the South, it was said that if you split the tongue of a young crow, it could talk. But Sakakaw, orphaned as a young bird and taken in by her grandmother, talked anyway, tongue intact. He could imitate sounds, voices, hoot like an owl, whistle like the postman, call "Bruno! Here boy!" in a voice identical to her grandmother's. Like most crows, Sakakaw was smart and bored. Food came easily enough, and the rest of the day was spent making mischief. His best trick was to call Bruno from the front of the house, then fly over the roof to the back porch and call him again. Bruno raced furiously around, then back around until Sakakaw grew tired and went looking for other means of making trouble. Bruno never figured it out, though once Neva's grandmother had caught Sakakaw at it and scolded him so severely that he flew away in a pout. A few days later he returned, dropping a gold pocket watch at her feet by way of apology. They never found the owner.

"Harker," Neva said. "I didn't tell you the truth. Please don't be mad."

"About what?" he asked.

"About being here. About why I came here," she said as the phone line began to fade, echoing her words back to her.

"Neva?" Harker said.

"I think they might have come here. I'm looking for them," she said. "I didn't want to tell you until I knew something. I didn't want you to be disappointed." But it wasn't true. Even as she said it, she knew it wasn't true. She hadn't told Harker because she wanted it—the trail, the postcard that pointed the way, and any discoveries—to be hers. She wanted them to be hers—not forever, of course, but for a day, an hour, an instant.

"I can't understand you." His words echoed as hers had.

"It's the echo," she shouted. "I could try to call you back. But don't do anything yet."

"No, I mean I can't understand why you would look in Coatepeque, in Central America," he said.

"I found something," she shouted. He did not respond. "I found something in Atlanta. I know I should've told you. Harker?"

But the line was dead. She called back, but his number was busy. So she waited, hoping he was trying to call her back.

"Is the phone dead?" Kira asked. She stood in the doorway.

"I don't think so," Neva said. She picked it up, listening to the click-click-click for a minute.

There had been something inevitable about finding the postcards. When she told Harker—and she was going to tell him before the line went dead—she would describe how she wasn't even thinking about them. That's how she would put it. But she didn't need to think about them—their absence was like an extra sense, an awareness deep in her cells, a hum in the air around her. Would there be a silence one day? She couldn't imagine it.

"Earth to Neva," Kira said.

"Sorry," she said. "No, there's no dial tone."

"A transformer was blown up. There's a paro this weekend. I guess they got the phones, too."

"What's a paro?" Neva asked. But before Kira could answer they heard a clatter outside, the front door opening and closing, Deb coming home.

"A shutdown—it's from *parar*, 'to stop,'" Kira said, as she rushed from the room. Neva could hear them talking in the kitchen, Deb and Kira. She could hear them, but she couldn't understand what they were saying.

Paro, she thought, as she sat by the phone waiting. A shutdown. Well, I know all about that. She sat back, stretching her legs out until they touched the opposite wall of the hallway. Waiting for Harker to call back. But the phone never rang, and each time she picked up the receiver, she heard the dull click-click-click of nothing.

10

El Puerto del Diablo

"I can't dance," Neva said, but the liaison officer was already pulling her to her feet and dragging her out onto the dance floor. "I don't want to." She laughed a little. "Really," she said.

It was as if he didn't hear her. His breath was yeasty and wafted past her left ear. She felt first his belt buckle, then his erection, pressing into her as they circled the room. He spun her so hard her feet left the floor. The lights zigzagged crazily. She felt dizzier and dizzier, knew that if he were to let her go, she would fall, fall at the feet of the women who moved perfectly on their stiletto-heeled sandals, the men who could have taught dance classes in the States.

In the few months she'd lived here, she'd never danced. She always watched. Coatepequens danced before they could read. They danced in complicated, intricate patterns. She hadn't danced once since she came here, not once in all the evenings she'd spent at Mario's with her housemates. She knew she could never chance it: letting her clunky North American movements loose among people who danced as if it were as simple as lying down in a hammock for a nap.

The room was a blur of color and faces. She saw Kira's azure blouse and the bright orange drink she was holding. The room was hot and moist. Among the lights bouncing in the wall-sized mirror, she locked eyes with a man who looked vaguely familiar. When the liaison officer whirled her by the mirror the next time, she saw him again, saw him watching her. Black eyes in a sober, serious face. *Help*, she mouthed at him. Then: *Ayúdame*.

When the music began to wind down, the liaison officer slowed them to a halt. She felt dizzy, breathless. His fingers were locked around her left wrist. "I have to go to the bathroom," she told him, but as the first few beats came over the staticky speakers, he began pacing in the two-two step of the bancha. She pulled against his fingers, feeling them pinch the tender skin on the underside of her wrist.

The black-eyed man was a shape next to them, saying something in Spanish too low and rapid for Neva to understand. The liaison officer released Neva's wrist and took a few steps backward, saluting her by touching two fingers to his lips, then waving them in the air. When she saw him leaning toward a woman at a small round table, Neva turned to the man who had rescued her.

"What did you say to him?" she asked.

"I just told him I wanted to cut in." The man looked Coatepequen—he wore his wavy black hair a little long as was the style here—but his English was almost unaccented, bland as the Midwest where her brother lived.

"You want to dance?" Neva said, a little breathless.

He laughed. "No, not at all. You looked like you needed rescuing."

Her face was hot and she felt her chest tighten with vague shame. Well, why would he? she wondered. You asked him for help and he gave it. He wasn't asking for a date. Still, he stood there. She started to thank him, then said, "I don't know your name."

"It's Tomás." He looked at her as if her face were odd. "I could buy you a drink."

"I should buy you one," she said.

He shrugged. "All right."

They took their drinks outside and sat on the low stone wall surrounding the club. They sat in silence. Neva's back felt cool in the spot where the liaison officer had pressed his damp palm into her.

Tomás seemed preoccupied. Then: "Why are you here?" he asked.

"I teach English at the International School."

"Right," he said. And they were silent for a few minutes.

"I mean," he said, "why are you here?"

"It's a long story," Neva said.

"And one you don't want to tell," he said.

"Not really." She turned to look at him. He smiled and they both laughed.

"Do you want to come in and meet my friends?" she asked him.

"Okay." He drained the last of his drink. "I'm going to the loo. Then I'll come find you."

Neva took her seat across from Kira, who raised her eyebrows at Neva but said nothing when Neva looked away. It was the first time they'd been out since the paro ended, the full ten days of it, while the guerillas tried to shut down the city, blowing up power transformers, disrupting the water supply, and warning everyone to stay home. Linda, one of the teachers at the American School, joined their table. "That girl was hiding guns. Mark told me." She spoke in a low conspiratorial voice, setting down a tall sweating glass and planting herself crosswise in the only empty chair.

"Oh, for god's sakes, Linda," Kira said. "Mark's a fucking military advisor." She pronounced "fucking" with an extra hard *k*.

Linda sniffed, offended. Deb sipped her ginger ale. She rarely came out, and when she did, she never drank. She put a hand on Linda's forearm. "Linda, Allison Lohmann worked for the church. She was raped and tortured before they killed her."

Linda ignored Deb. She pulled her arm away.

"Your boyfriend got bawled out by the state department?" Kira sipped her gin and tonic. "So now everybody's a terrorist?"

Linda had no politics. Her desire to share this piece of information, that the social worker killed nearly two years ago had been working for the Left, was to exhibit how in the know she was since she'd started sleeping with one of the American advisors to the First Army. The state department had ordered an investigation and the tribunal was expected to rule next week.

Jamie called it the "I'm-in-the-know disease." Every expatriate was eager to share the latest, but the Americans were the worst. Neva wondered why Jamie hadn't come tonight. He didn't seem to have any politics, left or right, but a ruthless will to uncover, dissect, analyze. Left or right—every player and act was subjected to Jamie's cutting analysis. Neva was closer to Jamie than to anyone else in Coatepeque and was tempted occasionally to tell him about her parents because, among her friends, he was the one who would find her story interesting rather than tragic. But she kept quiet while he sliced through layer after layer, dissecting the same friends he drank with and bummed rides and cigarettes from.

She still wasn't used to it. At home, people in the news were *in* the news. Here, no one was ever killed or elected to office without someone in the room being related to him, or claiming to be.

Linda and Kira were in a mutual pout, Kira glaring and Linda fiddling with her appearance, winding a lock of her hair around an index finger, scraping smudged eyeliner away with a long red fingernail. Neva had never been able to figure out if Linda was smart. Linda knew things.

Not in-country things—every gringo who paid attention knew what every other gringo did about Coatepequen politics. But things. Facts. She rattled off information like no one Neva had ever met. That Peary's toes had snapped off on the way to the Pole. That vitamin E and iron shouldn't be taken at the same time. That there were stars astronomers called white dwarves. Facts and occasional comments about the size of her own large breasts were Linda's two main contributions to any conversation.

After the shot resounded through the room, they hit the floor, the *crack* so loud the disco music became a pale backdrop to it. A trio of traveling students, recognizable by their backpacks and jeans, were the only people in the room still standing. They must've felt themselves grow suddenly tall, trees on the edge of a clear-cut through the forest. And then, sheepishly, they hunkered down.

"What the hell," Linda whispered.

"Shhhh." Kira put a finger to her lips, and they waited in silence. They could hear a woman sobbing on the other side of the bar. On the floor beneath their table kernels of popcorn were scattered among the hair, fingernails, and grit. The underside of the table was thick with chewing gum.

The single shot was strange. A quick volley from an automatic rifle was not unusual, common enough at parties anyway, when an inexperienced guard accidentally discharged his weapon. Nothing surprising in a country where everyone was armed. Well, *she* wasn't armed. Of course, the guard in the doorway checked all handguns when people entered Mario's. But if everyone at her table had a pistol stowed somewhere, it wouldn't have surprised her. No one wanted to hand theirs over. Guns disappeared here, like everything else. Besides, anything could happen. You might need your gun.

Slowly, people emerged from under tables and began to whisper and talk in low voices. Linda drifted away and then returned. "A marine shot himself," she said.

It was late when they left, nearly two. They had waited, until the police let them leave without questioning them. Security had been really tight since the paro the previous week. Their electricity was back on, but the phone still didn't work.

The students followed them out into the club. "Is there a bus stop near here?" one of them asked.

Deb shook her head. "It's hours past curfew. The buses stopped running at ten."

"How much for a cab?" The student was very tall. He carried a green North Face backpack over one shoulder.

"I don't think you can get one," Deb said. "They don't run much after curfew."

He frowned. "Well, how are you getting home?" he asked.

Deb looked at Neva and Kira. "I guess we're walking." She turned back to the students. "I think you should come with us, crash in our living room. It won't be very comfortable. But the buses will be running at six and it's nearly two now."

The tall student argued with her. "It's not that far to the hostel, only a couple of miles. Jeez, we can walk that far."

Kira let out her breath in a little contemptuous burst and rolled her eyes at Neva.

Neva shook her head at the boy, and Deb said, "It's after curfew. You can't walk around downtown—you'll be picked up."

He was a foot taller than Deb. "Right," he said, "but we won't get picked up walking to your house." The redheaded boy put his hand on his friend's arm, "Jeff . . ." he started to say.

"It's pretty quiet this time of night."

Just leave them, Neva thought. For chrissakes. "They don't pick people up in our neighborhood—" she started to say.

"Jeff, let's just go with them," the redheaded boy pleaded. "They live here."

"You can do what you want," Jeff said. "I'm going back to the hotel." He looked puzzled, unsure which direction to head for.

"Listen to me," Deb said to the redhead. "What is your name?"

"Patrick," he said.

"Listen, Patrick. The guardia cruises downtown all night because that's where the university is. He will get picked up, and whatever happens, he won't like it. Talk to your friend."

The third student stood a little apart. He looked Indian. Neva wondered if he could be from Oklahoma. He pushed his wire glasses into place and said nothing. Patrick, the redheaded student, was talking in a low voice to Jeff. Neva heard him say, "Please."

"All right," Jeff said. "Which way?"

Neva did not realize how drunk she was until they started walking; she felt it sharply when they stepped out into the cool clear mountain night. She could never get used to the night sky here. In Georgia, the summers were so humid, the air hung thick and cloudy between the stars and anyone on the ground. In this country, she drank too much, more than she had ever dared in the past. Every Friday and Saturday night, when she knew that another week had passed and she had learned so little, she drank first beer, and then the drinks they made here from fresh pineapple and mango juice, mixed with tequila or rum.

They had not even been questioned, had been allowed to leave even before the ambassador had arrived. The body lay on the floor covered with a tablecloth, red haloed on the white cloth like a beautiful poppy. Linda said he was one of the embassy guards.

"The walk will sober her up," she heard Kira tell Deb, and felt a brief edge of resentment tighten in her chest. It was a mile and a half to their house, mostly downhill, but she felt hungrier and hungrier as the sugary drinks wore off and hoped they would pass an open pupusa stand, sure the cortido and hot salsa would clear her head, would take the sweet sickly taste out of her mouth. But it was late, dead quiet, a ridiculous time, really, to be out in a country at war. They took chances now she would never have considered when she first arrived. She'd grown blasé, as the war arced out into the countryside and away from the capital.

They walked a half mile or so without speaking. Neva felt flushed and out of breath, her skin damp from the heat and the walking. She realized that Deb was walking a few steps apart from them and turned to look at her, then turned in the direction of Deb's gaze at the carrier driving in their direction and slowing as it neared. She knew from Deb's face that she had been watching the truck a long time before it ever reached them. She knew, too, that Deb, who was almost never afraid, was afraid. She knew it from the way Deb's fingers wrapped tightly around her arm just above the elbow. Neva told her in a low voice, "I'm sober now," and she was, and Deb knew it, too.

"They're presidential guards," Deb whispered. "At least it's not the First Army." At her first embassy party, a pink-cheeked gringo looking to get laid had bragged to Neva that he was an advisor to the First Army. "And what do you advise them to do?" Neva asked, blinking at him in what she hoped was a naive rather than coy manner. He puffed up a little when he told her, "I tell them to kill commies and radicals," and she knew she was filing it away, a funny story to tell at the bar, to people here who knew nothing about her parents or the trial.

The guards were young, and that too was a good thing. When they shouted in Spanish, Deb released her arm and stepped forward. Neva could never follow Deb's rapid-fire vaguely Castilian Spanish. The accent sometimes worked against her, given Coatepeque's complicated class structure. Men of the oligarchy often greeted it with annoyance. For them, femaleness took precedence over everything, even nationality, here where to be American was everything. But the oligarchs had no use for gringa women who seemed uppity. These soldiers, though, were schoolboys, conscripted, she had no doubt, against their will.

And, heartbreakingly, against the wills of their mothers and sisters. The Saturday roundups in the small villages around the capital were terrifying.

Deb was talking to them in earnest now. Her voice was calm, but as she spoke she fingered the hem of her blue skirt. She smiled and shook her head, "Ay no!" she said, laughing. Neva felt Kira's breath on her shoulder even before she spoke: "What? What are they saying?" Neva strained to listen, inferring vaguely that the soldiers thought they needed an escort home.

"Oh great," Kira said. "It's after curfew. No one will know if we don't get home."

"Kira," Neva said, "you know we're safe. You know they don't touch Americans, not after the Peace Corps workers were killed. Not the Right—they can't touch us." When the three workers had disappeared—a young man and woman from the States and a man from the Canadian Amnesty International—the United States had almost cut off all military and civil aid to Coatepeque. American aid now constituted more income for the country than the entire GNP.

"No, no es necessario," Deb said, stumbling a little over the "c," the Castilian creeping into her accent the way it did when she was nervous.

And then several soldiers were climbing down from the truck, waving their guns a little, in the air mostly, as if to show that they were more friendly than not. One of them slid his hand under Deb's elbow and pushed her toward the truck. In his other hand, his rifle pointed toward the clear night sky.

The other soldiers had circled her and Kira, cutting them off from the three students. Deb turned back toward them, just before she climbed into the truck, and smiled stiffly as she said, "They say they want to give us a ride home. That it is not safe here. For women and foreigners. For us to be walking around."

Neva held back, shaking her head. The motion made her woozy. Deb took her arm. "Be quiet," she said. "Get in the truck. If we argue any more, they may get mad. They've been patrolling all night and they're punchy."

The back of the truck had two long benches running lengthwise under a canvas top. There were seven soldiers, and six of them clustered around Kira's blond hair and tall body. Her striking Americanness. The students were on the far side of Kira. The truck was so dark Neva forgot them after a while.

Neva rode in silence across from a thin soldier with a serious expression on his smooth, clean-shaven face. He watched her without speaking, without wavering in his gaze. Kira's shrill laugh cut through the truck. "No!" she shouted, still laughing. "De Des Moines. De estado de Iowa."

The air was stuffy, hot on her clammy face. Neva inched along the bench toward the open end of the truck. The serious soldier touched his rifle gracefully, and she froze, sat up straight and planted her feet on the wooden floor. With every bump and jolt, the sickness was worse, pushing against her throat, rising through her body in wave after wave. She put her hand over her mouth and held the other up to the serious soldier, hoping he would recognize this as "stop, wait," and scooted the length of the bench to the back of the truck where she lifted the canvas flap and vomited onto the rapidly passing cobblestones. Bright, sticky red, like the half-dozen fruit drinks she had sucked down at the Brit Club, the vomit was a long, thin trail behind the truck, a Hansel and Gretel trail, just in case they were headed not for home, but for the witch's gingerbread house in the forest. At the thought of gingerbread, she caught back her hair, leaned out the back, and emptied the rest of her stomach.

The serious soldier was behind her now, with the back of her blouse twisted in his fist. As Neva leaned back into the truck, he released it, smoothing the cloth clumsily. He offered her a bandanna to wipe her mouth, and then he offered her his canteen, and she drank, a long, sweet swallow of water.

"Gracias," she said. She did not look at him. The truck lurched and water splashed the front of her blouse.

"English teacher?" he asked, but then the truck stopped completely and they were swept up, piling out the back to the roadside where a yellow combi sat with its hood up. Neva felt light-headed and leaned against the side of the truck. It was very late, hours after curfew. She wondered if they would ever get home.

A young Indian couple sat beside the combi on bundles tied with string. Beside them, a basket of chickens rustled and fidgeted. Two of the students—Jeff and Patrick—stood together. Patrick fidgeted and

Jeff had his arms wrapped around his middle as if he were cold. The Indian student stood a little to the side, shifting his weight from hip to hip.

She was not a brave person. She had lived most of her life knowing too well the cost of speaking out. She had learned it in her marriage. Smoothing things over. Ignoring. That was not bravery, but a shutdown of sorts. When the part that gets afraid goes away.

Here, though, where fear was shared and not private, it was impossible to shut down, to send the fear away. She was uneasy, as the soldiers motioned all of them together. Uneasy and afraid, as the lieutenant began to argue with the men working on the combi.

She thought of Will, the Americans in Solidarity with the Frente de Coatepeque, the speakers, the talks, the parties. The night they had chanted "El Frente con El Frente." She had no idea what that meant anymore. The day she had taken Susannah to the hospital to get stitches removed from a finger she'd sliced cutting melon, the song had gone round and round in her head. They'd walked past the long row of beggars on crutches, mothers holding children missing an arm or a leg or an eye. Susannah had seen the look on Neva's face and hustled her past them. She thought of factory workers, environmental poisoning, thalidomide. "Land mines," Susannah said. "The Front leaves them all over the countryside."

Neva shook her head, and Susannah said, "I know. And they're the good guys. Amnesty International's been after them for years. And they conscript the healthy ones."

"I thought the army did that," Neva said. They were in the building with its thick smell of antiseptic and overcooked food.

"Everybody does it," Susannah said. "Poor people here get it from both sides."

And earthquakes. And a plot of land that will never grow enough. Stay and starve or go—move into the barrancas, the ghettos around the capital, or lie down finally, into the long wound of hunger that has been their lives.

That night in Atlanta at the solidarity meeting they drank coffee. Miriam's special blend, delicious coffee really, and there was real cream, and turbinado sugar from the co-op. Kevin brought his guitar and played a song he had learned in Nicaragua. He handed out mimeographed sheets of the words and they sang along. Will had insisted

Neva learn Spanish along with the group. "I had two years in college," she'd told him, but he had been adamant, so when Kevin led the group through *estoy/estas/estan,* she recited along with everyone else. Will smiled and nodded at her across the circle.

That was the first night Will's anger had seemed beyond her control. Usually, she could sense the tension early enough to diffuse it, but that night she had been preoccupied. During the music, Miriam's baby had begun to stir in the womb, and Miriam had taken Neva's hand and laid it on her belly, where she could feel the hard knob of an elbow or a heel pushing against Miriam's skin. The baby swam and kicked in motion with the music. She and Miriam had smiled at each other and said nothing.

Will was agitated before they got home, driving jerkily through town and rushing into the apartment ahead of Neva. She caught the door before it flew back in her face. She felt something inside her become solid and brittle.

"Why didn't you sing?" he demanded, as soon as she got in the door. "Everyone was singing. Why didn't you sing?" He paced a little.

Soothing time, she knew. She knew to say: *My throat's been kind of scratchy.* Or: *I'm sorry. I was trying to figure out how to pronounce the words.* She knew the rules. Last week, Will had said to her: "Why don't you do what you used to do? Make a joke or pull a face. Why do you let me get angry like this?"

But she was so tired. She shrugged. "I don't know." She looked down at the floor, noticing for the first time that the gray carpet had a pattern to it.

"God," Will said. He was across the room before she could back away, twisting the sleeve of her blouse into a knot. His face was white. "I'm trying to do something good here. You really piss me off when you act like this."

The Indian student clutched her arm and whispered in English, "Say you know me. Say I am with you." He spoke with an accent, Coatepequen probably, but certainly Central American. This was the first time she'd heard him speak. The faces of the two American students were pale against the ink blue night, and it was quiet on the deserted highway. He wasn't with them, she realized. He hooked his arm through hers and clutched her hand possessively. He was breathing hard and his face glistened with sweat. "Just say I am with you," he whispered.

Why me? Neva thought. She was not at all brave. She began to think, for the first time in months, of the way a fist feels on a body, how a fist might feel on a face. Of what it is to joke with someone larger and more powerful, watching for a sign that he has either relented or grown more angry. She thought she could not know these things with a Coatepequen, would not know how to read these signs.

She thought that a rifle butt would hurt more than a fist. She thought, I do not want to die in this country, on this dark road.

The lieutenant was before them. It would never work. She was too old, late twenties to his teens. "Con migo," she said, coughing as she spoke. "Mi novio."

And then, without warning, he was gone, slipped away into the darkness. The guards shouted, leaving the huddled group of passengers, and chased after him. One of them tripped, and his rifle discharged as it hit the ground. Neva felt the sharp sound through her body, saw Kira run her hands down her side looking for a wound, saw the Indian couple huddle close to the ground.

Miraculously, the guards began to laugh. One of them bent down and helped the soldier up from the ground. "Puta," he said, brushing the gravel from his fatigues. He picked up his rifle. "Puta."

"Your novio seems to have abandoned you," the lieutenant said to Neva. She tried to smile at him, felt her lips catch on her dry teeth. She remembered hearing once that Miss America contestants put cold cream on their teeth to make their lips slide back gracefully into those toothy smiles. She had never been so thirsty. The lieutenant turned away, disinterested.

She was squeezed between the Indian couple and the serious soldier on the ride back to town. Across from her, Kira and Deb leaned against each other. "That was so fucking stupid," Kira said. "What the hell did you think you were doing?"

"Shut up, Kira," Deb said. "Just shut the fuck up."

The wooden bench was hard beneath Neva. Through the canvas flaps, Neva could see one small square of the night sky. She thought she saw a movement across one of the fields and wondered if it could be the boy, still fleeing whatever this week's danger was. She watched the stars receding, trying to pick out the constellations from her childhood, but here, at this altitude, the sky was unrecognizable, the stars impossibly large and bright, so close they frightened her. The moon was a slender crescent and would disappear in a day or two. Its sharp edge pointed down into the gap between Mount Xtapel and Mount Pipile, the place the Indians called the Door of the Devil.

11

Zona Rosa

"You must eat here a lot," Neva said, after they had been seated at a small round table by a window overlooking the courtyard. The room smelled of eucalyptus and garlic. The maître d', then the waiters, had nodded at Tomás in recognition.

"My apartment is around the corner," he said.

Neva looked down at her lap. A parrot screeched, "Cu-cu-cu-cullo!" from the courtyard.

She thought: Well, I guess I know what he's planning. But I'm through with all that. With this. I don't want to love anyone anymore. I don't want to be touched.

"I mean: my apartment is around the corner, so I eat here often."

She felt a faint heat in her cheeks in the cool room, knew she was blushing. Oh, she thought. He didn't mean *that*. Then this wasn't a date? She never knew when something was a date. She didn't know she'd been dating Will until she'd slept at his apartment for a month.

"The calamari is good," he said. He reached across the table and pointed it out on her menu.

"Cujillo! Cujillo!" the parrot shrieked.

"And they make a salad with jicama and lime—you might like that," he said, his voice matter-of-fact.

"All right," she said, nodding. "The calamari and the jicama salad." The waiter hovered. Tomás gave him their order and he turned to go.

"At the same time," Neva said to his back. "I want them together. Junto," she said, looking at the waiter for the first time.

"Okay, Miss," he said.

Tomás said, "After dinner, we can walk around for my car and I'll drive you home."

When she said nothing, he said, "Or I can put you in a cab if you'd rather."

"All right," she said.

The silence was awkward. They both began talking at once: "Did you—" "That marine—"

"You first," she said.

"I couldn't get back inside, at Mario's. They wouldn't tell us anything, and then they ordered everyone away."

"It was a marine," Neva said. "He shot himself."

"I heard," Tomás said. "I heard later. How awful. Were you—"

"No, I was in the other room. I didn't really see it. We got home really late, though. And then these soldiers picked us up and drove us home." She didn't tell him the rest.

"Does that sort of thing happen to you often?" Tomás asked.

She shook her head, then realized he was teasing her. "Yes, all the time," she said. She began to laugh. "I'm sorry," she said. "It was just so awful.

"Really awful, all that blood." She realized her giggles had turned to something else, her eyes wet and stinging.

He handed her a handkerchief across the table. "Really, I'm sorry," she said. "I was so scared when the soldiers picked us up, so glad to get home. I hadn't really thought about him—that marine."

He nodded at her across the table.

"He must have been so homesick," she said.

The waiter brought the wine, and Tomás poured her a glass.

"Or maybe," she said, "he was ashamed. Of what is happening here. Of what the United States is doing here." She gulped her wine.

"I'm sorry," Tomás said. "Are you all right?"

Neva nodded. She didn't see how the evening could save itself. But then he slid his chair closer to hers and reached for his handkerchief. He dried her eyes, then reached down and squeezed her hand where it lay in her lap. "Okay?" he asked.

"Yes," she said. "I'm even hungry."

They talked easily after that, and Neva relaxed a little, knowing at the end of the evening she could get in her cab and go home to her quiet room. She could have this evening, apart from her life, and not look back at it, ever. She could remember how the handkerchief had smelled a little like clove when he dried her tears, how his hand had met hers with kindness, even tenderness. But she didn't have to scrutinize anything for clues. It was here: the present, pushing both past and future away and claiming its own territory.

But after the calamari, the jicama, a plate of cheese, and slices of a green fruit that tasted a little like nectarines; after a conversation about the six different kinds of hummingbirds you could see in the city, E. Nesbitt's *The Enchanted Castle*, a book they had both read as children—In Spanish or English? she'd asked, but he couldn't remember—elephant stories, the way they surround the wounded, she said, an elephant's heart, he said, is a foot and a half of muscle. Not politics, family, where are you from, former lovers, or how hard it was to get good help. They did not talk about the war, about who might be dying, as they fished the calamari from its bowl of butter and garlic. Who might be tired or hungry or hiding. After coffee so good she sighed loudly without meaning to, and when he both smiled and looked puzzled, she said, "We have trouble finding good coffee. You know how it is."

He frowned. "I do. Everything good here is sent away. Shipped north."

"Not just coffee?" Neva asked.

"Not just," he said. "Fruit and textiles. Our best students. They go to American universities and never come home."

"But Americans come here, too," Neva said. "They come and stay."

"Of course," he said. "Even now with a war on, they come. You came."

"I heard that lots of Americans moved here in the sixties and seventies." She looked at him and waited.

"Before my time," he said.

"Activists," she said.

"I don't know," he said. He shrugged and smiled at her.

Neva changed the subject. She would keep asking and sooner or later someone would tell her something. She smiled at the waiter and nodded when he offered her more coffee.

It got closer and closer, the time when they would leave the restaurant, when something would happen or nothing would happen. When she wouldn't know what to do. She found it harder and harder to eat, as if her jaws had clamped down, her throat and stomach grown mysteriously smaller. She felt a drop of sweat run down her belly and clamped her legs together to catch it.

After all of that, there were no cabs. It was cool outside where they stood in front of the restaurant's small, barely noticeable sign. She could smell something—frangipani or jasmine. "We can go back in and call one," Tomás said, "or walk over to Monteverde."

He thinks I hate him, Neva thought. She felt so stiff. Dinner, with the table between them, with no room for touching, she had been so relaxed. Happy, she thought; I have been happy this evening. But now her arms were stiff by her sides. She had never known how to do any of this. How did other girls growing up know to toss their hair? To smile and smile? Sit back while he paid or opened the car door? How did they know how? She was hopeless, Will a fluke, a force of nature, something she could not remember agreeing to. No wonder I held on. No wonder I clung to misery.

"Let's get your car," she said.

And how it had happened she wasn't sure, except that she knew she had leaned toward him, turned her face up toward his and he had stopped, keys in hand, from unlocking the car door. He had looked at her for a long moment, but she had kissed him. Of that she was sure.

"It's up to you," he said when they broke apart. "You must know I want you to come up."

They kissed again and then leaned together. His hair smelled like wood. "Stay or go," he said.

"Stay," she said in a small voice in his left ear.

Jamie was in the kitchen when she came home the next morning. "Juice?" he asked Neva. Neva shook her head. "Is there coffee?"

"Sí, sí." Jamie never said "sí" once. He dipped a cup out of the pot boiling on the back of the stove. "Black, of course?"

They laughed. Jamie found Neva's habit of drinking her coffee black incomprehensible. In Coatepeque the milk was rich and yellow, and tasted like the milk they'd drunk in Alabama. She'd never learned to milk a cow, though she'd tried morning after morning, following her grandmother to the barn, laying her head against the cow's warm side and tugging on its nipples until her hands ached.

"Not with them hands," her grandmother said after each failure, and finally Neva gave up. Food was rich in Coatepeque, as it had been hardy on the farm, a holdover from the days everyone worked from dawn until the sky turned to the brilliant pinks and roses that marked the end of the day.

Sunset, she thought, but through the kitchen window saw the deep pink of sunrise, the light over the east edge of the volcano. Another day, she thought. I am here.

She felt the soreness in her hipbones, the salty foreign smell on her skin, in her hair. A bruised numbness between her legs. How she had fought it, tightening up, holding back, and then, against her will, pleasure rising, *it's coming, coming,* the voice in her head, not her voice, not Tomás's, riding the wave of it, and the moment after, feeling herself relax and open up. She pushed his face from between her legs and curled down to kiss him, tasting herself on his lips. Forgetting for a moment that he was a stranger.

Two days later, a messenger brought a package for her. A five-pound bag of coffee beans, the kind usually exported to the States and Europe. It filled the kitchen with an aroma so rich, Jamie sighed as he leaned over the bag and breathed it in. "Where on earth," he asked, "did you get this?"

She ducked her head so that he wouldn't see her blushing.

"Oh my," he said. She thought he was talking about her blush, but his head was still buried in the bag of coffee beans. As much as Jamie loved gossip, he loved coffee more.

"Let's make a pot," he said.

After that first night, she was with Tomás once or twice a week, but he worked most weekends out of the city. She asked him once. "I think in America you call it consulting work," he told her. And she didn't ask again.

She would stagger to school, dizzy with the memory of so much pleasure. She daydreamed during her prep period, pausing after writing "Work on your focus" on the chalkboard to remember how Tomás would slide his hand between her legs when they were curled up. She would circle a spelling error and think about how she slept after they made love, tumbling into dream and amnesia, her back against the long solid heat of his body.

Here she lived in the present moment, no longer on the fault line between a past she did not know and a future she could not imagine. On a different fault line, though. The first day they'd felt a tremor at school, she had thought she must be ill, dizzy the way you're dizzy when you step off the ferry after a long crossing.

"It's a tremor, Miss!" one of the students told her.

"Are we having an earthquake?" Neva asked, and they shook their heads, no, no, don't worry. Just a tremor.

At lunch, she asked Tony García, one of the science teachers, about it. He held his hands out in front of him, palms parallel to the ground, thumbs touching. "It's like this," he said, shifting first the left then the right up and down slightly. "The plates shift a little and resettle."

She knew it must be the same demonstration he gave his students, but she didn't mind. She could imagine it so clearly, the thick brown puzzle pieces, edges rubbing against each other.

"If they shift a little now and then, it's good," he said. "Otherwise . . ." He threw his hands up in the air. "Earthquake!"

That was it, she thought, the way the past and the future had ground against each other, leaving no room for the present, for the day, the moment, the place you existed. She had sat tight, waiting, waiting, refusing to allow the earth to shift and resettle. Until—she saw again the image of Tony throwing his hands into the air. Until the ground buckled and the fault line opened up, between Atlanta and Coatepeque, running straight through the middle of Alabama, Indian Country—it was all Indian Country—but you had to look a little harder to see it in the South, in Alabama, the heart of Creek country. A map cracking open to reveal red earth beneath it, the way skin might part over the red flesh of the body. The war her parents fought in, she could see it was the same war fought in Coatepeque, where she stood on the sidelines, then as a child, now as an outsider.

There was never any food at Tomás's apartment. Coffee, a small pot for it, and a carton of milk or cream in the refrigerator. But no food at all. When Neva began staying over, Tomás would often get up early and walk around the block for pastries or empanadas, a pint of orange juice if the corner market were open. They ate first at the round glass table in the living room, opening the windows for the slight breeze. It was the height of the dry season; only early mornings were cool. When she knew him better, Neva made coffee and climbed back into bed. "You have crumbs all over your belly," he said once, putting his face to her bare skin and licking them up one by one.

The apartment would be spotless when she came back, the sheets laundered. There was a tall, full bookcase, a desk with a stack of papers on it, a toiletry kit in the bathroom, clothes hanging in the closet. She liked the bareness of his apartment the way she liked the starkness of her own room, with its handful of items acquired in the market: a candle holder, three children's toys painted red and bright yellow. She had never lived without clutter, without years, generations, of objects around her. She and Harker had to sell the farm after her grandmother died, and there was so much she couldn't bear to part with. Her storage compartment in the basement of her college dorm was crammed with boxes of dishes and framed photographs. The chest in her dorm room was covered with her grandmother's costume jewelry and the drawers filled with doilies and scarves smelling of Avon perfume.

When she'd moved in with Will—moved in officially—she'd left the boxes in her storage compartment. It seemed too much, too much of her to bring and ask him to make room for. She hadn't thought of the apartment as half hers, even though she paid half the rent. Not even when Will wasn't teaching so he could write his thesis and they'd practically lived on her tutoring money and what his parents gave him. She left the boxes, put a combination lock on the wire door of the storage bin, and put them out of her mind, until months later one of the resident advisors had called and told her they'd be cleared out if she didn't take them.

Here, she had nothing. As she put dinner on the table, she realized there were objects she was fond of: the yellow bowl with the orange stripe, two dark wooden spoons they always used for salad, the mismatched glasses—Jamie had the blue one this evening. But nothing attached to her. Everything was landscape, a part of the view, like the volcano from the kitchen window. Nothing would trail after her or need to be packed up, taken, stored. The art of losing, Neva thought, like in that poem. Not so hard to master. She wondered if she would miss the yellow bowl when she left, when she finished what she came here to do.

They were eating early. From the sink where she sliced a tomato, Neva could just see the sun behind the volcano. The phone rang and Jamie jumped up.

"You, Neva," he said sitting back down and pouring himself a glass of wine.

When Neva came back to the table, they all looked at her expectantly.

"So, who's the guy?" Kira asked. She stabbed her fork into a drumstick and ate it like a Popsicle.

"Oh, Kira, how couth," Jamie said. "Yes, when do we get to meet him? Is he meet-able? Or will he just honk for you late at night and you run out to the car?"

"You know, Neva," Deb said, "if you're going to be spending a lot of time with him, we won't know how to find you . . ."

"Listen to Mother," Jamie said. Deb looked at her plate frowning, then made a face at Jamie when she realized he was watching her.

"Well, it's true," Jamie said. "You just can't be too careful with all those mean guerillas around and those awful death squads." He exaggerated the words.

"I don't know why I like you," Neva said to Jamie. She realized she meant it, that in the States she would not have broken bread with someone who always made fun, who only made fun. "You act like it doesn't matter, like it's just something someone made up," Neva said.

"I'm just joking," Jamie said.

"Don't look at me," Kira said. She reached for the platter of fried plantains.

"Come on guys," Jamie said. He seemed upset.

"There's a war here," Deb said. "Maybe you joke too much."

"There's a war everywhere," Kira said. She forked the beans on her plate into a tortilla, rolled it, and stood up. "I don't know what I'm talking about," she said, "but I gotta go. I promise, promise, promise to do the dishes tomorrow, okay, Deb?"

"I'm not in charge," Deb said, but Kira was gone, leaving the way she always left, so fast you hardly saw her, the buzz of her Yamaha trailing away.

"Yes, you are," Jamie said. They finished the meal in silence.

12

The Indian Summer

It had happened once, a few months before she left Atlanta, and then it didn't happen for a long time. The phone rang one evening. It was Will. "I'll be late," he said. "A meeting and then some things to do at the office."

"Okay," Neva said. "Maybe I'll go to the movie. *Five Easy Pieces* is playing and you probably don't want to see that."

There was silence on the other end. Then Will said, "I'd rather you just stay home."

"I'm just going to *Five Easy Pieces*. They're showing it at the Tara," Neva said. "You know I love that movie."

"I don't think it's a good idea. I don't like the idea of you running all over Atlanta at night."

She went anyway, distracted when she stood in the ticket line, glancing at her watch from time to time. It's just a movie, she thought. He'll be mad, she thought. Midway through, she gave up, knew she couldn't concentrate, and left early. The apartment was stuffy. Will didn't come home for hours after, and she finally gave up and went to bed. She woke when she heard the door slam, the refrigerator door open and close.

She could smell him in the doorway, yeasty with all the beer he'd drunk that night. Pretending to be asleep, she heard him lurch away, bumping into the doorway. She stretched out, relieved. He turned on the stereo, and the music he loved, vintage seventies, blasted through the apartment. She lay, still as cotton, through one song, then another. He stood in the doorway, the light behind him outlining his body.

"Oh, come on," he said. "You're not asleep."

Neva had never been so still. She breathed through her nose in tiny, short breaths.

"Oh, right," he said. "Like you've been home all night." He turned on the bright overhead light.

Neva opened her eyes and looked at him. "I'm really tired, Will," she said. Pleading.

He looked at her. She knew that look. He looked at her while he thought of the next thing to say. He was so drunk it took a few moments, during which Neva knew anything could happen. He could change his mind, lurch back to the living room and pass out.

"And just what made you so tired?" When Neva didn't answer, he said, "Huh? What made you so tired, Neva?" He pulled the covers off the bed. She lay like a dead woman.

"Huh, Neva? Huh?" he said. He wrapped his fingers around one of her ankles and started pulling.

Still, she said nothing. She said nothing while he dragged her out of the bed entirely and onto the floor. She refused to look at him, to make eye contact.

He left, but before she could get up, he was back, leaning in the doorway, with a beer in one hand and a sandwich in the other. He ate a few bites and took a long drink from the beer. When she still didn't move, he stood over her, tearing the sandwich into pieces and dropping them one by one. They landed mayonnaise-side down and stuck to her skin. He took one last swallow of his beer and poured the rest on her.

She lay there. She refused to speak. It was her way of fighting back.

Other things had happened—she saw that now. He had cleaned out the closets, insisting she gather up clothes she didn't wear, old magazines, a toaster that only toasted the bread on one side. In a frenzy, he loaded boxes into the trunk of the car and took them to the Salvation Army. A week later, tagging along with Miriam who hunted for vintage jewelry at all the thrift stores, Neva found a sunflower print set in a pewter frame so like the print she'd kept from the farm.

"That looks like the one you used to have," Miriam said.

"I know," Neva told her, tilting the print away from the window's glare. She paid the shop owner a dollar for it and hung it back on its nail in the hallway. Sometimes everything seemed like an accident. If she and Miriam hadn't gone into that shop that day. If she hadn't knocked the print off the wall. If.

The night of Will's lecture at Georgia State. She'd waited while he accepted congratulations from people, first going to the ladies' room, then lingering in the back until there were only a couple of people standing around with him. When she approached, Will continued talking to a tall woman with red hair cut in a short shag like Jane Fonda's.

Neva walked to Will's side, but he stepped away from her. "Oh, hello, Neva," he'd said, the way one might speak to a student or a secretary. The way you might speak to someone you didn't know or someone, as she could see now, you'd been fucking. He stepped farther away, glancing at her once but intent on the tall woman. Neva waited a few minutes not sure what to do, where to look. She sidled away.

"You could've waited in the car," he said.

She only realized it now, so long after, the way your body realized something before your brain did. Stomach hardening, heart racing, palms sweating. Will must've been sleeping with that woman. Maybe she didn't know about Neva or maybe what she knew about Neva was all wrong. That they led separate lives. That she was old or ugly. That they never touched each other. That she mistreated him. Maybe she had mistreated Will. But she wasn't the only one who placated him. Miriam and Brian tiptoed around him until they couldn't, and Neva all but lost touch with them. She knew that whatever solid thing lay beneath her sternum hadn't dissolved or softened in the years they'd lived together. It sat, hard as a block of granite waiting for the right chisel.

"Neva," Harker said. "Are you still there? Hello," he said, a little louder.

"No, I'm still here," she said. She didn't tell him about Tomás. She couldn't. But it made her awkward on the phone, the knowledge of a new life lived nearly every day since she'd met Tomás. The Spanish restaurant where they ate paella and he licked the olive oil off her fingers, the way he would put his face in her hair and breathe her in after sex.

What could she say to Harker? I don't know what Tomás does for a living, or where he's from. I don't know anything about his family. I don't know if he hates Indians. So many people here do, though they call that hatred by other names. Even people whose skin isn't white. People who call themselves Spanish. The first morning she had woken before Tomás, she had stretched her arm across him as he lay sleeping. His arm, her arm, his belly, her breast—variations of color, like a paint card you might collect from a store if you wanted to paint a room. His skin felt familiar to her like a map she'd been studying before undertaking a long journey. Something tugged at her body, skin calling to skin, and Tomás woke and pulled her hand to his mouth and kissed it.

Because on that score, she and Tomás were almost even. They talked about the wine they were drinking, the books they had read. They talked about Americans and the strange lives they led in Central America. He shrugged off politics, seemed to have no opinion on the election, the peace talks due to start next month. But there never seemed to be time to talk about where they'd been, only the present: this moment, this wine, this food, this body. The black volcanic beach where they spent a weekend, rushing inside once, skin burning, to make love until her belly was raw from the sand caught between their bodies.

"Harker," Neva said. "I've been trying to tell you. I found something."

"You found something?"

"Some postcards. They were hidden in a picture I brought from the farm. Tucked into the frame."

"Postcards? Who sent them?"

"They were all from Coatepeque. Sent to the house in Atlanta—"

"So you thought the parents might be there? That doesn't make much sense, Neva."

"No, listen," she said. "They were sent after we left. Months after. The first in August. Addressed to the parents. But get this: signed Herman and Lily."

"Oh, Neva, I don't know."

"It's got to mean something. Herman and Lily. I think they were trying to tell us where they were."

"Neva, they laid a lot of false trails. You can't imagine the ups and downs. Magruder's firm hired a private detective and he was always turning something up—Canada, even France."

"You never told me," she said.

"You were too young. All those dead ends. I didn't want you to have to live with them."

"What about you? You're only three years older than me. If I was too young, you were too young."

"I *was* too young," he said. "But there was no one else."

"Why are you saying this, Harker? Don't you want me to find them?" She burst into tears. "I'm sorry, Harker. I don't mean it." He was still too young. All those years and she had no idea what he had lived through. What he had spared her.

"I don't want you to be disappointed. Of course I want to know what happened."

"Harker. It's okay about Magruder. Let me know what he says when we talk next week."

"Yeah, I will," he said, his voice relieved. "You're okay, aren't you?"

"I'm fine," she said. "I like it here, despite everything."

"I miss you," she said, into the pause.

"Me, too. Neva—" but the line crackled and the connection was broken before he could finish what he started to say.

Neva's classroom was on the second floor of the skinny, L-shaped school building. The windows overlooked a green field of yucca and bright violet flowers no one knew the name of in English. She day-dreamed in class more and more. When her students read their essays aloud, she felt herself drifting, hovering for a moment, then easing out the window. At first she floated, face toward the sky as if rocking on a bed of warm air, but lately she had begun to fly, arms stretched out, body flat as an eagle's, across the fields of flower and yucca, the smells rising to her as she scanned the ground, until the sound of the bell or a student's question yanked her back into the room.

Grit covered her desk, the yellow dust that was everywhere, on everything, during the dry season. There were faculty meetings, teachers arguing about issues she didn't understand. The American teachers argued that they should make more, even more than the Coatepequen teachers. Did she make more? Neva wondered. It was hard to imagine anyone making less.

She remembered her mother and father talking about the patients at the Free Clinic. "I don't see how they manage," her mother had said. She had spent the day signing in patients when the regular receptionist was sick. "How do they pay rent?" And an argument Harker had gotten into with their father, when Neva was too young to understand. His fists clenched, he shouted, "Why do we live here, then? Why don't we live where they live? If it's so unfair! If it's so unfair!"

The American teachers used terminology unfamiliar to her: "career ladder," "objectives," "lesson plan." Neva whispered to Susannah: "Is that the same as a plan for a lesson?" But at lunch or in the lounge, they talked about food, the hired help, packages from home, going home. They planned outings, inviting each other as if Neva weren't there. Once, Linda Sachi had said: "It's for families—couples only," as if that would make Neva feel better. She tried to imagine Will at her side, but she could no longer imagine Will at all. He was like a shadow, sometimes, in the corner of the room, a faint smell, a feeling in the pit of her stomach. But his face could not be summoned.

She tried to imagine Tomás there with her, awash among the International teachers, but they had never been with other people. Their time always seemed short, rushed even. When they were apart during the week, she would think about the last night they'd spent and everything seemed sped up, like a movie montage collapsing years and years of story into a few images—the shimmering black beach, restaurant tables of buttery food and Chilean wine, his fingers in her mouth, his fingers in her, his teeth on her earlobe. She knew at some point he would come to the house, to one of their large parties. But it had never come up between them—other people. He was her secret. She wondered if she were his.

They kept their lives separate from *their* life. She didn't talk about work, though she rushed away early on weekday mornings. His work only touched them once, when the phone rang late one night when they had just turned the light off. He spoke briefly, in Spanish, then hung up and began to get dressed. "I'm so sorry," he said. "There's something at work I have to sort out."

"It's so late," she said.

"I know." He bent over his shoes, tying the laces. "And I have to go to Santa Maria. I'll try to get back as soon as I can, but it could be a while."

"Are you sure you aren't meeting one of your other girlfriends?" Neva asked. She meant it to sound light, like teasing, but it didn't come out that way.

He lay back down on the bed with her, the buttons of his jacket pressing through the sheet and into her bare chest.

"I'm sure," he said.

When she didn't respond, he put his mouth close to her ear and whispered, "I only have one girlfriend."

He kissed her throat and whispered in her other ear, "And no, I'm not married, in case you were worried about that."

She felt her body stiffen beneath his, felt the slight edge to her voice when she said, "I wasn't worried." She knew he thought she was jealous, but how to ever explain the real reason her muscles had, for that brief moment, tightened around her lungs and rib cage, around her heart. It wasn't that she had forgotten that she was the married one, but she never thought about it. She had made it disappear.

"I'll try to get back before morning," he said. "But it's a couple of hours up there."

When Neva kissed him, she knew she had betrayed him somehow, in some small way. "Be careful," she said.

She wondered if all the single people she knew had lovers stashed away somewhere. If everyone had a secret. A bed in a downtown apartment. A marriage in another country. Her Tomás-my-lover-secret made her smile, her cheeks flush, a throbbing start between her legs. But her Will-my-husband-secret gave her a stiff face, pounding heart, sweaty palms.

Was it like that for her parents? She remembered, in the last few days before they left, her mother's shaking hands as she filled the kettle for morning tea, how wrinkled her father had become, his face, his suit.

Was there more? More than she and her brother had ever been told? She wanted to ask Harker—What did he know? What did he remember?—but the phone was in the hallway of the house, and words echoed off the stone walls.

She was too young then; she couldn't remember. Her parents had seemed so happy before the trouble—joyous even, despite the long hours. Gus's cousin Robert Blue visited from Oklahoma and told the story of trying to take some supplies into Wounded Knee the year before. He was headed back to the Rez, to Pine Ridge, and Neva's mother got the idea that they should load his car up with food for the elders there. For days their living room was filled with boxes of Cheerios, canned tomatoes, a case of MoonPies someone had found on sale at the Jitney Jungle. They hadn't talked about it much, but looking back, Neva could see that her parents thought change was around the corner. That human beings craved justice, would reach for it. Nothing else made any sense.

And later, they worked and worked to raise money for the people who needed lawyers. The people they thought needed lawyers, not themselves. Because they hadn't been there. They were in Alabama when the clinic was broken into. When the boy fell down the stairs. In Alabama, all four of them, visiting her grandmother, a thousand miles from Oklahoma. From the break-in, the stolen files, the panic when Target Silverhorn fell, the sorrow when he lay in the hospital dying.

All those dinners. People showed up earlier and earlier, the women drifting into the kitchen to help, except for Mrs. Winstead—Neva had never heard her first name—who had a full-time housekeeper and didn't know how to cook. She sat at the kitchen table and smoked while the other women roasted and sautéed and broiled.

There were people around all the time. On Tuesdays, when her father ran a free clinic, things were quieter at the house. Her father always came home late, usually after Neva and Harker were in bed, though once or twice her mother let them stay up. Her mother always waited up, a plate ready to go in the oven. The glass of wine ready to be poured.

That was after they'd moved to the house in Decatur, when the Atlanta apartment could no longer hold them. On the edge of the park—what was the name of that little park? She never drove by when she moved back to Atlanta. She couldn't bear to see another family there, the children's bicycles abandoned on the lawn, the pansies replaced with marigolds. She couldn't bear it if the windows were dark or if the windows were lit with the yellow light of early evening. She couldn't bear to see the house empty or abandoned. She couldn't bear to see the silhouettes of mother, father, brother, sister through the curtains.

She shook it off; she tried not to think about her parents, about those years, but leaned back into the warmth of the house she now lived in. It was rarely empty. There was almost always someone to talk to; someone was usually cooking something. She could sit at the kitchen table and grade papers, while Deb read and Jamie caught up on a week-old *New York Times*. She had fallen into a routine with Tomás—one weekday night and one weekend. Friday or Saturday, sometimes both. He called and she went, but he never seemed to expect it. He seemed surprised and grateful, and he courted her with paella and figs, with a concert downtown, with fresh flowers in every corner of his apartment.

She could've brought him home, but she wasn't ready yet, to see him here in this kitchen, in the room upstairs which was hers and hers alone. Meeting him was like taking a trip out of town. His apartment, bare as a hotel room except for the vases of lilies or roses, the large double bed, all meals eaten out, except for coffee and croissants from a bakery on the corner. There were books, papers on the desk, but not much more than you could haul up in a large suitcase. She found it restful. She never imagined a future, because vacations have no futures. They happen and then you return to your life. To the work of being who you are, who you've become whether you wanted to or not.

She licked the drop of sweat beaded on his left nipple and then ran her face down the soft strip of skin on his side from beneath his arm to his hip, a long plain of tenderness. His skin there was impossibly soft. When they were apart, this was what she thought about, more than fucking, even more than the feel of his mouth pushing between her legs. Hunger for skin that was the same as hers. Sometimes the longing was palpable.

"Coatepequens do read, Neva," he was saying. "We know about Neruda. We read him in his own language. In our language."

"It isn't that. You know a lot. You know more than the teachers I work with. You know things . . ." she trailed off. It was pointless. Some something she couldn't quite identify. Him. Tomás. A man she met at a bar one night when someone died. Someone whose head turned into a red puddle of sorrow. Death didn't seem so strange when it happened like that. Not like when you sat by the bed of someone whose shallow breaths grew farther and farther apart until they stopped. Who was alive at 10:01 but dead, emptied out, at 10:02. The body in the same position, the bed sheeted and calm. Nothing changed except that one minute she was there and the next minute gone. Or death by disappearance. It happened over and over here.

But Tomás—lying down with him felt like a kind of homecoming.

He was getting dressed. "Do you want some dinner?" he asked.

"Sure," Neva said. They looked at each other for a moment, the subject hovering in the air. Who he *was* didn't seem to fit with who he was. She sighed. This country. She knew nothing. She didn't know enough. She reached for her blouse.

13

Burning the Letters

Mail never came for Neva. No one knew where she was for months until she called Harker. They talked every week—on Thursdays at seven, or Fridays at four if he couldn't get through. But they never wrote. "You must get your mail at home," Nina Prescott said, as she ripped open a brown paper package one day in the teachers' lounge and shrieked, "Fig Newtons!" to the rest of the room.

Coatepeque was a foreign country; every mother, brother, sister, cousin knew they did things differently there. Relatives imagined their children, their siblings, or nieces camping out, as if the whole country were lush green jungle. They were surprised to hear about indoor toilets or cars. But they would not have been surprised by the houses in the barranca, ten-by-ten shacks of plywood and tin, with dirt floors and no plumbing. Most of the barranca shacks had electricity: orange extension cords running from shack to shack for lights or a small cookstove.

Packages arrived from the States, when the mail came in just before midmorning break. Flashlights and plastic rain ponchos. Cookies or tampons, shampoo or ketchup. Susannah's mother sent her six pairs of Hanes white cotton briefs. Someone's ex sent coffee, a round tin of Maxwell House, which had made them all laugh. They had given it to the housekeepers, for the cupboard under the stairs where they prepared their own coffee.

Everyone shipped their mail in and out through the school's Miami courier service. It took about ten days. Coatepequen mail took three weeks or three months or forever, depending. Packages might not arrive at all. Her students said: "Miss, my father can take your mail to Miami in our airplane. Just give it to me." But she had no mail to give them, nothing to send north. Throughout the Alabama years, her brother wrote her every couple of weeks. She would check the mailbox at the end of the dirt road each day when the school bus dropped her off. From the front porch of the barn, Bruno would bark at her as if she were a stranger. It startled her at first. Then she ignored him. On a day when her collar was a solid itch around her neck, her skirt stained where she had spilled ketchup on it, she dropped her books and ran at him, waving her arms and yelling, "Booga, Booga, Booga." He faced her down for a moment, then hesitated, backing up a few steps and tucking his hindquarters under before he turned and ran, looking back at her once in disbelief. Their relationship was never the same.

She lived for the letters, but each time she found the one letter with its Wisconsin postmark—but no other letters—she sank a little, feeling her sweaty feet in her shoes, her hair snaking out of its hair band, mouth thick with the starchy school lunch.

After the first month, she started reaching into the mailbox and feeling around to make sure there wasn't something she'd missed. One day she felt something scratchy against her fingertips and jerked her hand out. She started for the house but turned back, stooping down until she was level with the open end of the metal mailbox. It was a bird's nest, a small messy basket shape set into the far end.

"You've been leaving the door open?" her grandmother asked. "It's those wrens again. I'd better move the nest before they lay eggs."

Letters with New York postmarks came for Jamie, but he only smiled and took them to his room. Deb received letters from a handful of friends with ordinary midwestern names—Mary, Susan, Barb. For Kira it was postcards, often from travelers who'd passed through Coatepeque on their way to South America or Mexico. Kira would be thick with them for a few days or a week and then they would head on. She never seemed to miss them, but when the postcards arrived, she would shriek, "Oh my god, Harold broke his ankle on Machu Picchu!" or "Marcus got a job in Bolivia!"

Harold, Marcus, and the others blurred into each other—Neva could never remember which was which. They carried backpacks and wore socks with their sandals. She would find them at the kitchen table drinking coffee after Kira had left for work. They might ask: "Isn't there any real cream?" One had seemed awkward, a little embarrassed to be drinking their coffee, but the others had left their dirty cups on the table or counter without a backward glance. One morning, after Neva had slept badly, she came down the stairs to find the coffeepot dirty and a Luxembourger at the table smoking. As she rinsed out the pot and began to scoop coffee into the basket, he said, "Could you make that a little stronger?"

Neva nodded, too foggy to argue, but she measured out the coffee exactly as she did every morning. "Ah!!! Much better," he said, sipping it. "You Americans and your pale coffee." He pronounced it "pell." "My Italian friends call it 'the dirty water.'"

Neva did not respond, but he talked on and on, in a dazzling blur that began to blend with her dream from the night before. Finally she put her head down, cradling it on her arm, as she chewed the last bit of toast. From this angle, she could see the fine white hairs on his fingers.

"You Americans!" he said. "Not so good at drinking!"

Kira was ruthless with them, warning them not to hang around while she was at work. Once she'd rushed through the kitchen on her way out the door to find a young man from France still sitting at the table. "What did I tell you?" she asked. She did not smile. France-boy gathered his belongings and slumped out the door.

One wrapped himself around Kira as she rose to put up the orange juice. He pushed his face into her neck and wedged his crotch against the side of her leg, humping it a little. Neva couldn't make out what he murmured in her ear. "Hans," Kira said, her voice rising slightly. "No, I can't. Some of us work for a living." She pushed him away, making a face at Neva over his shoulder, the kind of face you might make at a wedding if you ate too much cake.

Kira seemed to like them better in their postcards than in real life. They could spend the night, but they were never invited to dinner. She never let them interfere with trips with Neva and Deb to the beach or taking the bus to Guatemala to shop or find a decent restaurant. She wasn't home that much. She had gigs across town that lasted into the small hours. Once when Neva and Susannah were on the Tesoro bus, stopped at a traffic light in Santa Tecla, Neva watched three people bent over a pile of papers on a café table. One of them seemed angry, flinging his hands up, then bringing one of them down to point. The woman at the table leaned back, throwing her pencil onto the table. As she turned her head away from the men, Neva sat up. The nose, the blond hair snaking out from under a blue bandanna. Kira. But Kira was in Guatemala City, playing all weekend at a piano bar.

As the bus whipped around the corner, Neva twisted her neck, but the woman had turned back toward the men, the pile of papers.

Her parents burned letters, late one night when Neva and Harker were supposed to be asleep. They were in the living room, crouched before the fireplace. A small pile of kindling and paper smouldered, but it was June, too hot for the chimney to draw properly, and the room was filling with smoke. Her mother turned when Neva came down the stairs, and Neva could see tears running down her face.

"It's just the smoke," she said, wiping her eyes. "I'm not crying, I swear!" she said, laughing in a way that was supposed to be gay. Neva's father did not laugh.

"Open a window," he said. "Let's just throw them all in."

Her mother rose and began tugging a window open.

"No, wait," her father said, rising. "I don't want the neighbors to smell smoke." He pushed at a window on the other side of the room. "Crap," he said, leaning his weight against it until it popped open. He held his arm in front of him as if to ward off something.

"Neva," he said, "go to the upstairs bedroom and bring the tweezers and some rubbing alcohol."

"What is it?" her mother said. She and Neva moved toward her father. A splinter the size of a small chopstick stuck out of the heel of his hand.

"Get some cotton, too," he said.

Her father's hand was bandaged and useless for days. He sat at the kitchen table, listless and sweaty until he wrote himself a prescription for penicillin and sent her mother to the drugstore to pick it up. "Did they say anything?" he asked her mother when she came home with a bag of groceries and the medicine.

"What would they say?" she asked. Her hat tilted to one side and there were gray circles beneath her eyes. She set the groceries on the counter and gave a small sigh. Neva had not noticed that her mother was beautiful. Maybe they had been too happy before. That all you could see was happy. But now her mother was tired, tired and sad. Neva could see the sharp bones of her face, the black eyes, the reddish-black hair knotted loosely at the back of her neck.

What were those letters, the ones that had filled their living room with smoke? She had never asked. They had moved beyond ordinary by then; events had their own unquestionable logic. She would have to ask Harker, but why would he know? He had never stirred that night, though when Neva had taken the tweezers out of the medicine chest, she had knocked the soap dish on the floor where it bounced and clattered. It unsettled her, even now, so many years later, to think she and Harker had not shared this story. And then it occurred to her: What did he know, what had he witnessed, that she had not?

After sending her to bed, her parents had pushed two chairs together under the floor lamp, and her mother took her father's hand into her lap and put on her reading glasses. Neva had turned back once to see her father wince.

Was it so much, what had they done? And what had she done to cause this absence, this long dark hole in the center of her life? What had she done to change it? She wondered if other people were dogged by every mean or petty thing they'd ever done, if they thought about them when they woke in the middle of the night. If they woke. If they'd ever done the kinds of things she'd done. You could never ask, though, because what if they hadn't? What if they stared at you in shock to know that you had put your cousin's favorite book in the dishwasher for no other reason but that she loved it, a pale blue book about some animals going to a party? That in the eleventh grade you had avoided your best friend because a boy you liked didn't like her? That you had let your grandmother do the dishes, when you knew she was tired, because a book you were reading called to you like a drug?

And that you never stopped, never ever stopped, wanting a car to pull up outside and take you away, take you back to the people you were supposed to love? Would I have been happier if they had died?

She felt the shock of that thought separating her from the teachers lined up on the couch, stirring their coffee, passing around the pictures from Alice Coffman's niece's eighth birthday party. No one said anything to her as she left the room. She climbed the concrete stairs to her classroom, taking them slowly. Grit had collected in the grooved tread on each stair—hair and gravel and old chewing gum. But when she reached the top, she saw that the hibiscus was blooming, pale lavender against the stalky green and yellow flowers of that plant that grew everywhere here. She must remember to ask someone what it was. She locked the door behind her and sat down to grade the last of Friday's quizzes.

14

The Madres Office

Deb drove, skirting the edge of the city where the shanty towns went as far as you could see, then turning back into town. "You can get here on the Number 10," she told Neva. "Take the Downtown and get off at Calle Los Parques, then take the 10 west. Or, if you want to walk half a mile or so, you can get the 10 at Benitez and Juarez." She leaned forward when she drove, her thin back never touching the seat, whipping around curves so fast Neva had to hold on to the dash. "It lets you off right there," she said, pointing, then turned the Peugeot into a dirt parking lot and waved at a guard pacing before a long low building.

It was a large, bare room. Fluorescent lights and long foldout tables. Boxes of files on the floors. The wall to the left was covered with corkboard painted white, and tacked to it were pictures, hundreds of pictures. Deb introduced her to a chubby, white-haired woman whose dimpled fingers rested on a stack of manila folders. "Cecilia, I thought Neva could help you with the files," she told her. "This is Neva."

Cecilia was in her fifties. She wore so much jewelry, she made a continual little clinking sound. She started firing questions at Neva in a rapid mix of Spanish and English—"Spanglish" her students called it. Cecilia didn't seem to mind that Neva didn't answer any of them and would answer them herself. "Are you a professora?" she asked. "My daughter is studying to be a teacher pero ella . . ." "How long have you lived here?" "We have so many friends Americanos." "You call me tía Ceci," she said, finally releasing Neva's hand.

Most of the volunteers were foreigners, but there were a few women from the Coatepequen middle class. They used only their first names, not out of fear of the army, as Neva had assumed before Deb set her straight, but of their husbands. The morning strained her limited Spanish. Deb showed her the desk where she usually worked, the one cheerful spot in the room, with pots of succulents and a crayon portrait of Deb their nine-year-old neighbor Regina Vides had drawn. She didn't see Deb for hours. She had gone back outside to talk to the guard about a car that had been parked there for a couple of days. In Ciudad Coatepeque, abandoned cars sometimes held car bombs. When they walked, they looped around parked cars and transformers. Either could blow up, and passersby could lose a limb or a life.

After a while, she realized that if she tried to keep up with tía Ceci's endless chatter, she'd be too exhausted to work, too drained to respond to the women who came in in what seemed a constant but not particularly heavy flow through the door. She smiled and nodded, following the pace of tía Ceci's words but not their meaning. That tía Ceci's youngest daughter wanted to be a doctor and refused to learn to cook. That her best friend Veronica was moving to Miami and what would she do without Veronica to talk to. That everyone wanted their children to go to New England universities but what did Neva think? Weren't there good schools where it wasn't so cold?

After that, Neva came every Wednesday after school. She told Deb that she wanted to help, and it was true. But she wanted something else. The Madres office collected expat Americans the way her Atlanta peace group had collected twentysomethings who liked coffee and were learning to play the guitar. She always sat next to tía Ceci. Tía Ceci seemed to know everyone, and each time Neva came, she asked her something. "Have so many Americans always lived here?" she asked. "It must've been so different ten years ago," she said a week later, "when there were hardly any Americans living here." Little by little, Neva picked up information. How American hippies tended to end up in Guatemala. How a whole colony of them were living around Lake Panajachel. Young politicals went to Nicaragua to pick coffee; some of them stayed on.

But tía Ceci's information about tiny Coatepeque was scarce, or scarcely given. There was a town up in the mountains, La Loma, where Quakers had settled, but it was difficult to get to now that the guerillas controlled the only road that led there. One of the women used to come to the city, sometimes to the Madres office, but not lately. Ellen. She thought her name was Ellen. What did she look like? Neva asked, and to tía Ceci's puzzled look she explained: I've never seen a Quaker. But the woman, Ellen, was fair. She thought that when the war abated or lumbered its heavy body to another part of the country, she might go up there. It was her only lead. There were so many false trails, as she and Harker found out in the years after the disappearance.

Small towns in the desert or mountains. Miami. Brooklyn. But Magruder, Harker had told her, was sure they had left the country, crossing the border into Mexico or following the path laid by draft dodgers during the war, to Canada, where there were networks for American dissidents who no longer felt welcome in the United States. Neva began to ask around, to mention La Loma at the Brit Club and once in the teachers' lounge at the school.

Each Wednesday, Neva straightened and sorted. Mostly she listened as the women came to the Madres office. They carried photographs; they came by themselves, with their children, with other women. Three women in the traditional black kerchiefs of mourning linked their hands throughout the interview, like a chain of grief. Their sons or husbands were gone, into the army, into the Frente, or dead. Sometimes all they wanted were the bodies.

The woman who came in sobbing one afternoon took them by surprise. The stoic Coatepequens usually lined the room like flowerpots. Their stories—no matter how desperate or sad—had to be culled from them. The woman was young, her face bruised, her arms and legs covered with purple welts. At the next table, Bill from New York rose, reaching for the woman, who waved him away from her body and sat in the metal chair facing him. Tía Ceci stopped talking. Neva saw Bill lean forward, his face creased with concern, then shift into an expression she couldn't read. His sigh was loud enough to be heard at their table. The woman rose and moved toward them, her shoulders pulling into her chest in a half C. Bill rose, too, and both of them began talking in Spanish to tía Ceci—the woman's voice rising and falling, Bill's loud and uninflected. Neva had never understood how Americans could live here for years and not hear the language they were speaking. Bill said "yo gusto" a lot, which he seemed to think meant "I want," but which meant either "I please myself" or "I am delicious." Neva listened to Bill and the woman, but she could only figure out that they were disagreeing about something. Deb came out of the kitchen and sat down next to the woman. Neva saw her lean in toward her and nod as the woman spoke. Bill inched toward Neva, looming over her end of the table, his voice vexed:

"It's got nothing to do with us. The soldiers didn't do this—she and her husband had a tiff."

Neva looked down at her feet in her brown sandals.

"This is private," Bill said, his voice aggrieved. "Jesus Christ there's a war on here. We don't have time for this." He scratched his nose.

"Entendes?" Bill had a habit of punctuating sentences, even in English, by pointing his index finger and querying, "Entendes, entendes?" without waiting for a reply.

Neva's toenails were edged with the yellow dust of the dry season. When it was dry here, it was so dry.

"Neva." Bill's voice was insistent. "Entendes me or not?"

From across the room, Deb was motioning to her. "No, Bill," Neva said. "I don't entendes you. Not at all."

"This is Virginia," Deb said, then introduced Neva to her in Spanish. Deb turned away and asked Neva, "Could you get her some coffee? She probably should go to the hospital, but she's afraid."

"Is she afraid she'll be sterilized?" Neva blurted.

Deb looked at her in surprise. "No, I don't think so. Where did you get that idea?"

Neva shrugged, embarrassed. "I'll get the coffee. I'll be right back." She walked into the kitchen and leaned against the cool front of the refrigerator, the only cool spot in the building. What had she said? That word, so old, so thick in her history. She remembered when she had first heard it. She and Harker on the upstairs landing, eavesdropping on their parents.

"What does that mean—sterilize?" Neva whispered.

Harker put his index finger to his lips to shush her. The voices rose. "It's just so hard to believe," her father was saying.

"No, it isn't," her mother said. "The Nazis did it."

"Stop comparing everything to the Holocaust," her father said.

"I'm just trying to make you see this for what it is." Neva heard her mother's voice crack, as if she were about to cry.

"You have to give me a minute, Frances. It's just so hard to believe." They moved into the kitchen, their voices too distant for Neva and Harker.

"It's when a woman can't have more babies," Harker told her. "She wants to, but she can't because someone does something to her."

"You mean, hits her or something?" Neva asked.

"No, in a hospital. A doctor does it."

What did she really remember and what had she filled in later? Who could say? Memory was a canny trickster, as full of mischief as Rabbit, who stole fire and nearly burned up the whole world. Remembering was like that. You had to be careful what embers you fanned to life; memories could rage out of control. They could leave your world bare.

Neva poured a cup of coffee and brought it to the woman. She broke a stalk off the aloe plant in the front window and squeezed the thick gel out onto her fingers. "Sí," the woman said, and Neva smoothed it over the welts on her arms.

Later, of course, Harker told Neva everything he knew about what had happened in the hospitals, in the clinics the Bureau of Indian Affairs ran. Thousands of women, he said. At least. And all the children they did not have. And the ghosts of their children's children. "I know you hate them for leaving us," Harker said.

"I don't hate them," Neva told him. "I don't."

"But you wish they had chosen us, chosen safety. But Neva, they thought it would be so simple and their part in it so small. Steal the records from one of the clinics. Leak them to the press. End it. How could it go on, once people knew?"

"Harker, I know all this," she said. There was so much more, Harker found out after he started college. Women everywhere. In Puerto Rico. Quechua women in Peru. She realized she was holding her palm flat against her belly, in the space between her hipbones. She felt it there, but she did not know how to tell him what she felt. Less than a knife, but more than mere emptiness.

She looked down to see her hand on her belly, Deb looking at her with a puzzled expression. She touched Virginia gently on the shoulder and went back to the table where she'd been working. Bill from New York was in a pout. Neva realized how surprised he'd been when she'd snapped at him, how foolish he'd felt, when the woman came in crying and he thought he'd be first on the scene for another village razed, its inhabitants tortured, a roundup in one of the smaller cities to the north, something important in the war they were here to fight. But Bill didn't know anything about women. Someone at the Brit Club swore Bill came to Coatepeque because he couldn't get a date in the States. He claimed to be writing a book, but British Timothy said, "Trust-fund baby," and Neva believed him. It wasn't that Bill did no work at the Madres Office. It was just that the mundane aspects of it, sitting, listening, writing, stacking, filing, filing, filing, seemed beyond him. He was restless when there wasn't enough going on in the office, up and down in his chair, talking to anyone who would talk, getting coffee, but never making it. He'd tried once when none of the women came to his aid, and when the coffee had leaked out all over the table, he'd thrown up his hands in dismay.

Trust-fund baby. He went out with Coatepequen women, tiny women wearing high heels. Sometimes he brought one of them to the Brit Club. She would laugh when he laughed, stir her drink with a straw, long, painted fingernails like graceful weapons on the side of the sweating glass. Paulita, who went with Bill for a few months, never really talked. She pretended not to understand much English, not to be able to speak it at all. But Neva thought she was faking it. That it was a way to keep Bill—and all of them—at a distance.

. Don't do it, Neva sometimes wanted to say to her, imagining living with that pout day after day. There is no answer good enough for a pouter. No concession large enough. No mood good enough to lift his spirits. But perhaps, for Paulita—or the Paulita before her or the one after—the trade-off wouldn't be that bad. So many people here wanted out, wanted out desperately, and Bill, self-centered and childish as he was, still seemed a better alternative than the waiting, the endless waiting, while they worked in shops or restaurants, mending their only pair of dress shoes, which the buses and the broken streets wore down.

Bill from New York was a big guy, and his sulky mood took up a lot of space. Usually, when Bill was in one of his moods, the other women teased him out of it or tía Ceci fussed over him, giving him an extra cookie or fetching him coffee. Today, though, everyone seemed tired, disheartened. The beaten woman had jarred them. Last week's assassination of Rodolfo Umaña, the head of the new human rights agency, still hung over them. Neva heard on the radio this morning that the students had finally released his body. They had carried it around the city, from downtown to the university and back again, day after day, with placards saying, "Se noticia, el mundo." There were always reporters here, reporters from the States, occasionally someone she'd seen on TV. At first she thought that the news would shock people at home, but when she talked to Harker during their weekly phone call, he'd heard nothing about most of the events that loomed so large in daily life here: assassinations, arrests, disappearances, bombings. He scoured the international pages of the *Times*, the *Tribune*, but there was nothing.

"Maybe there's some sort of news block," Harker said one evening.

"Maybe no one cares," Neva said. "Maybe it's not really news if it happens in Coatepeque."

"The land that time forgot?"

"Something like that," she laughed. But sometimes she felt an acute despair, as if her whole body might tear up. Once when she was teaching English to her youngest students, high school students who came in the late afternoon when their own school was out, they heard what she took to be a round of gunfire. When she crouched low, the students laughed. "Miss," they said, "those were firecrackers."

They could tell, though, that she didn't quite believe them. Francisco, the class leader and the class clown—an unusual combination in the States but common here—said, "You have to listen for the whistle. Firecrackers pop; bullets pop, then whistle."

All the students nodded. Eduardo made a pop sound with his lips, then a high descending whistle following it. Neva looked over at Irene, always her checkpoint as to whether or not she was being teased. Irene was nodding. "Okay," Neva said. "Next time I'll listen for the whistle."

Francisco was on his feet. "Miss, you were so funny!" He imitated Neva crouched over, eyes big. In the States she would've been offended, but the teasing from these students never seemed mean spirited. They all laughed, Neva with them.

She had been unsettled by their laughter at first, their asides in Spanish too low and quick for her to understand. They teased her about her clothes, about dozens of imaginary boyfriends, including all her male coworkers, about her inability to roll her r's. "No, no," they would say, "put your tongue in the middle of the mouth." They teased her by drumming their feet on the floor, so that it vibrated with the tremor of an earthquake. They remembered the last earthquake, in which a few of them had lost family members. One girl from their school had died when a brick wall toppled over on her. Most of the damage had been in the northern part of the city, but they remembered the fear, running from the building, not being able to talk to their parents for hours.

They were wealthy students, extremely wealthy by Coatepequen standards. She was surprised to like them so much when everything was wrong about them—their privileged selfishness, their parents' whispered connections to death squads. She had tried hard to despise them and keep her distance, but after the day they explained the difference between bullets and firecrackers, a difference they had known since they were children, she felt a lurch in her stomach that she realized was pity.

Some of them drove new cars. They believed the government had stolen their family land and given it to ignorant, undeserving peasants. They believed the Americans had helped the government do this, but that when the Republicans were back in the White House, the land would be returned.

Yet they had no concept of property, and might walk off with a paperback Neva was reading and had put down on her desk without thinking. A few of them took her out for breakfast on her birthday, and they opened salt packages, unscrewed the tops of ketchup bottles, and misbehaved like fifth graders, spoiled fifth graders. They shouted at the women in their stained white uniforms. Neva felt powerless, so flattered they'd taken her out she couldn't bring herself to intervene. As they started out the door, she said, "I forgot something!" and went back to the counter, apologizing to each woman in turn and dividing among them the little bit of cash in her purse.

They lived in castles, were waited on hand and foot, and punished only for bringing home bad grades. Some of the boys were beaten by their fathers; Andres came in sometimes with bruises. After that, she never gave him lower than a C+. Sometimes she wondered if everyone got hit sometime, by someone in their life. She looked for bruises. She examined bare arms in the grocery store, stole furtive glances at other women in restrooms. When any of the women teachers called in sick, she wondered. So many of the girls got their noses fixed as soon as they turned sixteen, and they came to school bandaged, then bruised, wearing sunglasses. After they recovered, their noses were smaller, straighter, more Spanish. Neva tried not to look at them.

Neva knew Bill from New York was right in some way. That they had to remain focused on the war, on human rights. All day she sat at her desk, listening to tía Ceci with half her attention. Still, even if it weren't as important, the woman's bruises were real, her fear palpable. When she heard how the guards woke prisoners in the middle of the night to shine bright lights in their faces and question them: *What do you know? Who helped you?* she thought of Will coming home from the bar, turning on all the lights in the bedroom, and dragging her out of bed by an ankle. *Who? Who was with you?*

No, no, not the same, not ever the same. She thought of her friends at home, eager for news about torture in Central America, the letter-writing parties for Amnesty International. How embarrassed they would be at the news of her torture. How they would turn away, wondering: What was wrong with her? But Will loves you, they might say.

If that was love, then did the death squads love their victims? Or when a doctor took care of you so that you never had to have a baby ever again, what kind of love was that? Her head hurt, and she thought: I should go home. Not the quiet room at the top of the stairs, but home.

Somewhere where, when you go there, they have to take you in. But where was home? Not with Will. Marrying him had been a way not to think about the past. Never to think of it and never to leave it.

Would the woman with the welts go back to her husband? She had family in Alcalá and thought she might try to go there. But there was often trouble on the roads between Ciudad Coatepeque and Alcalá, the guerillas stopping cars to look for recruits, the army stopping them for guns. Caught between husband and war. Neva wished she knew the Spanish for: "If it's not one thing, it's another." She gave the woman some money, all she had in her purse, enough for bus fare, food for a few days. The woman didn't want to take it until Neva said: "I wish someone had done it for me."

She was so busy, keeping up with her classes. She graded papers on the bus, waiting for the bus, during her lunch hour. She put a stack on her bedside table and graded three or four before she got out of bed in the morning. She went to the Madres office once or twice a week and filed or typed or listened—whatever they needed; but she always listened. She saw Tomás every weekend, on Saturdays when they met for dinner and once for the whole weekend when he took her to Tesoro, the black volcanic beach whose name meant "treasure." It arced in a curve around an aquamarine inlet of ocean, the fierce sun making the sand rainbow the way asphalt roads lit up in the south in July or August.

When she thought about it later, it seemed a scene straight out of a travel brochure, the happy couple frolicking on the impossibly beautiful beach. She wondered: Am I happy?

But in the weeks that followed, she was too busy to answer her own question. She made a list, the things he might do or say that would make her know to walk away. She made the list on the back of a mimeographed handout, then decided to walk to Kismet and buy a notebook. She wrote the list on the first page, leaving an extra page so that she could add to it as things occurred to her or as memories came back. She started keeping a journal, the way she had as a teenager. She thought the first entry should only be questions. She wrote her first question: *If you have to keep a list, how can you ever be happy?*

What other lists, she wondered, should I be making?

Lost articles of clothing and places they might have been lost.

Every poem I memorized growing up. Season of mists and mellow fruitfulness. Ah love let us be true to one another for the world. The singers and workers that never handled the air. Only here and there an old sailor, drunk and asleep in his boots, catches tigers in red weather.

What my parents might say when I find them, to explain their long silence.

What I was thinking all those years. The years I was disappearing.

15

Red Weather

Neva met Will when she was twenty, a student in his political science class at the university. He did not notice her. On the few occasions when she put her hand up to answer questions, he never called on her, focusing, instead, on a handful of young men who sat in the first row and clustered around the lectern when class was over.

Toward the end of the term, when Will asked them to hand in topics for their term papers, Neva tried for a week to catch his eye after class, but she always stood just outside the circle of male students, who talked about capitalism in high, excited voices. Sometimes Will would nod at one of them, "Right," and sometimes he would resume lecture mode. He was young, still a graduate student, and very tall. When he spoke, the students standing nearest to him had to crane their necks to look up into his face.

So she went to his office, knocking on the glass window of his door. When he opened it, he was laughing at something one of the students on his couch had said. He did not seem to recognize her. "I'm in your poli sci class—Critiques of Capitalism?" She said it as a question.

"What can I do for you?" he asked, his eyes grazing her face, her breasts and legs, her feet in their rope sandals.

"I wanted to talk to you about my paper—"

"Nothing like waiting till the last minute." He cut her off. "Topics are due tomorrow."

"I tried—" she started to say, then shook her head and turned to go.

He looked at his watch. "I can give you fifteen minutes. Just a minute." He closed the door. She heard more laughter and then the door opened and the two students from her class spilled out. They didn't seem to notice her, even when one of them brushed against her as they headed down the hall.

Will held the door open and gestured to a chair under the window.

There were mice where Will lived. Neva heard them in the walls when she slept over. She couldn't actually sleep. She didn't know how anyone did it, curl up next to a stranger and sleep, fall into that other world. Sex was different. She could hold back, contain her pleasure. Some nights he was impatient, so it didn't matter.

Will slept with his back to her, his legs crossed, the feet knotted together. He bunched the pillow into a hard knot under his head, and lay in a straight column on the far side of the bed. Neva could spread out her arms, turn over, curl up as much as she wanted. But she did not sleep.

She had his full attention. For a month they spent most nights together, except Thursdays when he had his seminar and sometimes when he would call to say he was working too late to see her. Each time he said he would miss her . . . *but*. He would miss her *but*. The words trailed off, and Neva said, I have some work to do, anyway. The right response, she thought, to keep him close. She never called, though, to say she had to work late. Or that she was going out after her seminar.

Yet she didn't mind those nights. When she was around Will, she watched herself carefully, terrified of saying something foolish, asking questions instead of making statements. She wanted to win him. She didn't want to do anything to drive him away. But the nights they weren't together were a relief. She could lie in her bed and read. Her roommate subscribed to *Glamour*. She could lie in the bed and turn the pages, thinking about lipstick, the new pink shades, or cowl-necked sweaters.

Will had been dismissive of her during that first meeting; she didn't know when she caught his eye. When she picked up her paper, after the semester was over, he had made only a few comments and given her a B+, adding "Almost an A-." But none of his comments suggested what she might have done for that A-. When she asked about the grade, he said, "If you want an A that bad, I can give you one. You didn't strike me as that kind of student."

Neva was puzzled. "I don't know what you mean," she said. "What kind of student?"

"Grade-obsessed. The ones who are here to get A's, not to learn."

After they were married, she found the Silverhorn case in the index of a book in Will's library. In the text, it was mentioned only in passing, in a long list of incidents. Resnick's edited collection. The source he'd told her to check for her term paper in his class. Had he checked it, too? She never asked, never told him anything about her parents. Though it finally became obvious he knew. Had he known all along? She could not imagine what would have happened if he had been in the dark, if he had stumbled on the information, one more secret she had kept from him.

When she lived with her grandmother, it took her a few months to figure out that her grandmother didn't like TV. She and her grandmother would sit in the living room, Neva on the couch and her grandmother on the yellow recliner. Her grandmother would ask: What do you want to watch? But Neva didn't know. They hadn't watched TV at home. Her parents would linger at the dinner table, there were so many guests, and sometimes someone would play the piano. There was talk. About what they were reading. Politics. "Your father's a Red," Uncle Gus had teased her one night, tugging on a lock of her hair. "That's why he likes Indians so much." Her mother had hushed him.

"I really hate that," her grandmother said one night.

"What?" Neva asked.

"When you hear one of those loud bursts of laughter," she said, gesturing toward the television. "It's fake." She looked at Neva.

"I hate TV," Neva burst out. "It's stupid."

"You don't like TV?" Her grandmother raised up in the yellow recliner.

Neva shook her head.

"Then turn it off. I can't stand it either."

In the evenings they sat. Her grandmother tatted, moving the silver spindle with a quick twist of her wrist until the strip of lace piled in her lap. She sold most of it, but some she put away for Neva. Neva did her homework—there wasn't much and it was easy for her—and then she read.

Neva helped her grandmother in the evenings—it stayed light until eight or so in the summer and early fall. It was too hot in the middle of the day, and her grandmother let her sleep in. On weekends, too, after school started. Her grandmother asked the same question each time Neva came to help: "Are you done with your studies?" And Neva always said yes.

She found the schoolwork too easy after the schools in Atlanta, a good year behind in math, maybe two in English. Her biggest problem was drifting away in the classroom, gazing out the window. She saw herself hammocked in the high branches of a live oak, the hollow trunk of the huge tree a secret only she knew about. She saw a path leading farther and farther into the green woods, mossy banks, caves made from the curling fronds of ferns. She saw a dozen resting places.

But the sound of books closing, of notebooks pulled out, always brought her back to the fluorescent-lit classroom, its linoleum floor, and forty desks lined up in exact rows. Then, she would scramble to figure out the assignment, glancing at the notebook on the desk next to her, sometimes having to ask someone to explain it to her.

She hated asking. She was already a weird girl, and she was becoming a space cadet. "Spacey girl," Wes Dowdy said, from the desk in front of her, when Sandra, who was nice, had to show her how to do it.

An assignment so simple, Neva couldn't understand it. Finally she said: "You mean she just wants us to copy the Bill of Rights?" And Sandra nodded. "Yeah, but you have to number them vertically, not side by side."

She sat in her classes, bored, restless. She cultivated contempt for the teachers, for their dull monotones or for their chirpy brightness. She noticed every slip that hung below a hemline, every stray hair, dandruff snowing the shoulders of their not quite dowdy dresses.

"I wanted to get more schooling," her grandmother said one night when Neva closed her thick blue English book—*Adventures in American Literature*. She set her crochet hook down in her lap. "You know I only finished the sixth grade."

"Why did you stop?" Neva asked. "Did you get married?"

Neva could count on one hand the times she saw her grandmother laugh out loud. This time she laughed so long, she had to take her glasses off and wipe her eyes.

"Lord, Neva, I was twelve." She sighed. "No, you had to buy your own books in those days."

She looked up. "It doesn't seem like much, does it? But on a farm there's never much for extras. My family was poor but not as poor as your granddaddy's. And there were hard times ahead." She turned her chair to face Neva.

"That's why I never blamed your mother. Wanting to change things, same as her daddy."

"What do you mean?" Neva asked.

"They used to go up to Ashville to meetings," her grandmother said. "Communist meetings. Your granddaddy and your uncle JT. Everybody was so poor. You can't imagine what it was like. But then your uncle got so sick."

"What was wrong with him?" Neva asked.

"The TB," her grandmother said. "Lots of people had it back then."

When Harker came for Christmas, Neva cornered him. "Granddaddy was a Red," she said. Harker rolled his eyes. "I don't want to talk about this," he said.

Neva followed him up the stairs. "But they went to meetings. There were meetings here. Not here, but near here. With Uncle JT."

He wouldn't talk about it. He went in his room and closed the door against her and her questions. But a few weeks after Harker had gone back to college, he wrote her a letter. Dad's family called themselves Democrats, but they were practically Republicans. When he joined the Party, they blamed *her*. That's why his family abandoned us, why they wouldn't take us.

"Native Americans?" Will had asked that day she went by to see him in his office. "You mean Alcatraz or something? That's what you want to write your paper on?"

"No," she said. "Not the stuff that made the news. Smaller protests after the occupation of the Federal Building. There was something that happened in Oklahoma . . ."

"You mean when that kid was shot?" Will asked.

"He wasn't shot. He fell down a staircase—"

"Oh, right," he said. He was half listening, half shuffling through papers on his desk. "Pushed, wasn't he? Did they find out the kid was pushed?"

"The FBI said he was pushed. And he wasn't a kid. He'd just started college—"

He interrupted her: "What's your point exactly?"

What was her point? She didn't know exactly. Didn't know what she'd find. "I don't have a point yet," she said. "Communism, maybe. How much that had to do with the FBI investigating people." She looked at her hands folded over her notebook, the left one clutching a blue fountain pen.

"There's not much written on it," he said.

"That's why I want to write on it. That's my point, I guess."

Her grandmother never again talked about her parents' politics. She seemed fond of Neva's father but never spoke emotionally about her mother. Her love for her daughter seemed a thing unnecessary ever to state but rather something anyone could take for granted. In her grandmother's bedroom the bureau was covered with framed black-and-white photographs: her parents' wedding, hands clasped over the white cake Neva knew her grandmother had made herself. Her mother was pictured at nearly every stage of her life—annual school photos, her mother in an Easter dress when she was seven or eight, the crinolines fanned out around her, her feet in white patent-leather Mary Janes crossed at the ankles.

Their parents never taught them directly. But during dinnertime conversations, every news item, every anecdote, was evaluated in terms of class struggle. Once when Harker had brought home a history book and read her father a definition of anarchism—trying just once to prove their father wrong about something—he had sat both of them down and explained the term, first breaking the word down into its different parts on a white legal pad.

"But it's in the book," Harker said, furious.

"Harker," her father said, "you have to think about who wrote the book. Who paid for the book. Why do they say what they say?"

"It's history. You can't just make up history." He clutched his book, unwilling to give an inch.

But their father just shook his head. "You can make up anything. If the money's good enough, you can make up anything."

Her grandmother never talked about them except to report anecdotes or habits. That Neva's father would get up early when they visited, could sit at the table and drink cup after cup of coffee—black, two sugars—waiting for Neva's mother to get up. How they would walk after dinner, hand in hand, down the red dirt farm road. Her grandmother never again mentioned their politics. Maybe she didn't know anything, but Neva suspected that her grandmother, a fierce pro-union voter in a right-to-work state, knew a lot more than she was letting on.

They married. Will asked, and it never occurred to her to say no. They went to the justice of the peace. Neva wore a flowered skirt and cream-colored sweater, suede boots. Harker came and Will's friends Miriam and Brian. Miriam brought flowers, and just before the ceremony she took Neva into the ladies' room and wove some baby's breath into two tiny braids on either side of Neva's face. After the ceremony, they went to Miriam and Brian's house for lunch, running from the courthouse to the car, from the car to the house it was so cold. Will's friends arrived, some of them bringing gifts, a handmade pot or wind chimes, and Miriam spooned out couscous and salad, Brian poured wine, and late in the day they offered coffee and a slice of a rich dark chocolate cake Miriam had baked for the occasion.

Will and Harker did not warm up to each other. Will wanted to impress Harker, monologuing at him about Cambodia, waiting for Harker to acknowledge him in some way. But Harker seemed to want to just eat his cake. Later, when Neva walked him out to his cab, he asked her, "Does this guy know you're smart?" Don't ruin it, she thought, but she didn't say anything, not even when he put his arms around her and hugged her so tight she felt the air go out of her chest in a rush.

"You need to come up to Wisconsin," he said, opening the door to the taxi. Harker was in his second year studying tribal law at the university. "You'd love it."

Neva nodded, but of course she couldn't go now. She was married. There was her job at the bookstore, the peace group, her tutoring. Still, she felt a little wave of panic as the taxi door closed and her brother rode away. *You come back here*, she wanted to say. *Here*. The word was a silent weight in her mouth, smooth and round as a pebble.

She went back into the house where Miriam was stacking plates and Brian and Will were sitting on the sofa talking about a demonstration for tax day. Neva started gathering dishes up, but Miriam said, "Uh uh, it's your wedding day. Put your feet up." She drifted into the living room, but Will and Brian didn't make room for her on the couch, and the chairs were filled with presents and coats. She looked out the window to where the snow had almost covered the spirea bushes lining the sidewalk. It rarely snowed in Atlanta, but this winter had been harsh and cold with little sunlight and five snow days in a row.

Miriam came and stood beside her. "It's beautiful, isn't it?" She put her arm around Neva's waist. "But so cold! I feel like I'm back in Minnesota."

Neva felt stiff inside the half circle of Miriam's arm. No one touched her like that anymore, and she wished she could lean into it. She wanted Miriam to like her. She wanted all Will's friends to like her.

"How are you doing?" Miriam asked. "You must be tired."

"A little," Neva said.

"I'm going to run you guys out of here. I'll go tell Will." She caught Neva's hand and squeezed it.

"I loved the cake," Neva said. She wanted to say: *Thank you for doing this. Thank you for everything.* She missed everyone at that moment. Her grandmother. Her brother driving away.

Miriam smiled at her. "I'll tell Will," she said.

They settled into routines, and for a while it was good.

Well, it wasn't. Neva paused on her walk to the Supermercado. It wasn't ever good. Not really. I was always so nervous. For a couple of years I liked feeling chosen. For a couple of years, he seemed to approve of me. Will taught his classes, Neva worked at the bookstore. They had a close circle of friends, the overlapping groups from the food co-op and the activist group with its shifting names. But he began to ignore her in public, though always insisting she go—to meetings, to lectures.

There was a picnic in the park one September. A "Picnic against Hunger," with speakers and a folk band taking turns on the grandstand. They wove their way through the crowd, looking for a space big enough for the blanket they'd brought. Will stopped to talk to George Meadows, a law professor at State, and Neva stood, holding the cooler with both hands. The sun burned on her shoulders, and she thought, I hope we can find a place in the shade.

"Neva," Will called. She started toward him. "Just find a place you like. I need to talk to George about a couple of things."

She stood, ill at ease in the sea of strangers, in their plastic lawn chairs, on their patched quilts, tupperware filled with baked beans and cole slaw. Will looked back at her. "Go on." He made a shooing motion with one hand and said something to George over his shoulder. "I'll find you."

She found a spot sandwiched between a college-student couple and a family with three children, the youngest a baby who kept crawling toward Neva until his mother snatched him up with an apologetic smile. The family ignored her mostly, but the students kept glancing her way as she sat cross-legged on the blanket, pretending to listen attentively to the speaker. The family unpacked their lunch and offered Neva some.

"Oh, no thanks," she said. "I'm waiting for my husband."

More students joined the couple, splaying their feet out so that Neva had to retreat to a corner of her blanket. The family finished eating, the plump father dropping the last deviled egg into his mouth as if it were a peeled grape and sighing with great pleasure.

She stood up and looked for Will but saw him nowhere.

"Do you think your husband got lost?" the mother asked her.

"I don't know," Neva said.

"We can watch your stuff if you want to go look for him." But she didn't. She wished she could just go home. She had been hungry when they arrived, and now her stomach was cramped way past hunger.

And then Will was a long shadow across the blanket. "Sheesh," he said. "Why'd you set up over here? Miriam and Brian are over by the

103

stand." He gestured toward it. "I indulged in a little of Miriam's hummus," he said, rubbing his belly and grinning as if Neva would enjoy his pleasure. "Let's go over there." He began folding up the blanket, tugging on it so she had to get up.

"Will," she said, then stopped.

"What?" he asked her.

"Nothing," she said.

"What, Neva? You know I hate it when you start to say something and then don't."

She hesitated. How to say it? "You were gone a long time."

"Christ," he said. "You always do this. You're a grown woman." He stopped and faced her, the blanket draped over a shoulder.

The cooler was heavy, the underside making a wet spot on her skirt.

He started walking again. "You always ruin things," he said.

16

The Courtyard of the Yellow House

Neva left the market with a broad-brimmed straw hat, a bag of limes, and a round mirror framed by a ring of painted wooden dancers. She headed for the row of shops on Boulevard Calderón, hoping to find a metal hook for the back of her bedroom door, where she could hang the blue embroidered robe she'd inherited from the never-seen Cristina. She lived in Cristina's room, wore Cristina's clothes, kept a small, tightly woven basket on top of the chest, a basket she knew must've been Cristina's. On hot days, she thought she could smell a faint scent different from her own, a scent that had to be Cristina. Cristina should've been a ghost hovering in her room, at the kitchen table, but she wasn't. Pale yellow flowers ran up the arms of the robe, every stitch tiny and exact. Neva could not imagine the person who would leave it behind. She could no longer imagine the person who left her luggage on a dusty road just north of the border. The room could've been so full of ghosts there was no room to breathe. But it wasn't. It was clean, like a body pared almost down to bone, and in it there was plenty of room for Neva. More room than she had ever had. She hadn't known it was possible to have so much room.

The shops were busy. They were a little like the shops in Butler City. Most people did their big shopping at the central market, the way everyone in Butler City went to the Piggly Wiggly in Springville. But if you had to pick up a few things or wanted to be sure to find something, you went to a shop. It was the same here. Neva needed a towel, and the only ones she found in the market were beach towels, thin with ugly scenes in orange and blue, one that looked like a giant coke can. There was a row of shops halfway between their house and the school where she sometimes stopped for pencils or paper clips—they never had enough of them at school.

In Butler City, the shops were small, tiny even, and the customers and owners knew each other, knew what you might buy, knew your habits. Her grandmother never went to the Springville Piggly Wiggly. On Saturday mornings, the first Saturday of each month, after her social security had come, she and Neva went into town where they bought thread or yarn or candles at Jemison's, salt, flour, eggs at Sisemore's. Once, buying wire tie-ups at the hardware store, Neva saw two women look at her grandmother; then one whispered something to the other. "Mrs. Clare," her grandmother said, nodding to the whisperer, who nodded back and left the store. Her grandmother sighed. Mr. Dowdy, who ran the hardware store, came over to them and said, "Now Lila, you shouldn't be putting in these tie-ups yourself. One of the Crocker boys can do it, won't charge you much."

Her grandmother nodded but said nothing. "You don't need to pay any attention to Lessie Clare," Mr. Dowdy said. "Nobody around here ever thought of Martin as an Indian, and if we had, we wouldn't have cared no way." He tied the stakes together in a bundle. "Lord," he said, shaking his head. "It weren't like he was colored."

Red, Neva thought, not colored. She shook her head at the memory, shifted her shopping bag to the other hand, ignoring the growing clamor behind her until the whip caught her on the left shoulder, stinging a little. She turned to a mad face, bearded and filthy, a mouth open and shouting at her in garbled Spanish, lips crusted with white and working over the words: "Gringa," "Puta," "Chingada." She ran.

She ran, and the people around her scattered, some of them touched by the whip, too, but only women and a girl of about eleven or twelve holding her mother's hand. She backed into a doorway, a shop that sold cloth. "Venga!" she heard, and turned to see two girls crouched behind the counter. She scrambled to join them. El Loco loomed in the doorway, shouting, whip still in his hand. One of the girls giggled, but Neva's palms soaked through her skirt to the fronts of her thighs. El Loco turned back to the breezeway as two old women came at him, shouting and brandishing brooms as if they meant to sweep him away. He dropped his whip and ran.

Neva's mesh shopping bag had turned over on the floor behind the counter. She crawled after a lime that had rolled away, set the mango gently back into the bag, and stood up. The women with brooms were deep in conversation with the two shopgirls. They were laughing, and the girls were arm in arm, the way girls touched each other here. Neva stood uncertainly with her bag of food, but no one turned around. They did not notice her leaving.

Deb knew all about El Loco. "I wish people wouldn't call him that," she said. "It's cruel. He's a human being, not a thing." She put Neva's food away and poured her a glass of juice. "You better drink some. You know Kira will guzzle most of it when she gets home."

"And the rest when she gets home from the bar." Neva took her sandals off and pressed the soles of her feet against the cool tile of the kitchen floor.

"I don't think anyone knows his real name. He's been El Loco at least since I moved here."

They heard the front door slam and Kira came in.

"Neva had her first encounter with El Loco, today."

Kira opened the refrigerator and took out the jar of orange juice. Neva and Deb exchanged looks.

"Did you tell her about the kitchen window?" Kira pointed at the window over the sink with the jar.

"What?" Neva asked.

"Oh, it's nothing," Deb said. "El Loco looked in one night."

Kira started laughing. "It was really creepy. I came in here one night to get something to drink, and his face was pressed, really mashed up against the glass. He looked like a monster."

"What did you do?" Neva asked. She was glad her room was upstairs.

"I screamed, of course. Then I saw the face grin a little. I mean, he still had it mashed up against the window. But when he grinned I got mad. I mean, I could tell that's what he wanted me to do, so I ran over and pounded on the glass and he ran away." Kira drank straight from the jar. She licked her lips when she had emptied it. "I hate crazies," she said.

Deb took the jar from her and rinsed it in the sink. "I guess it depends on the crazy," she said.

"My mother took things," Deb said, later that evening. They were sitting side by side in the tiny courtyard in the center of their house, backs against the fountain in the center, their legs splayed out like a Mercedes Benz hood ornament.

"What kind of things?" Kira asked. Their voices went straight up into the night. It was late, but none of them felt like going to sleep.

Deb ignored Kira's question. "Not like a kleptomaniac, but like someone who had a right to things. To everything she came in contact with."

107

"Like what?" Neva repeated Kira's question.

"Oh, the usual things people take—hotel ashtrays and towels. All our towels were from hotels. We had a lot of ashtrays, too. But nobody smoked, so we used them for candy dishes—there was one on the coffee table with butterscotch in it. We each had one on our dresser—a 'catchall' my mother called it."

"Yuk, I hate butterscotch," Kira said. Neva didn't say anything.

"But not just hotel stuff. The silverware from restaurants. Once my mother put a water pitcher in her purse."

"Why do you say she wasn't a kleptomaniac?" Neva asked. She wasn't sure what to say.

"Because kleptos take things they don't need. They take things to take things. My mother furnished our house."

"What about your dad? Did he know? What did he think?" Neva thought of her parents shopping together. How they ordered the towels and sheets from catalogs, the dishes from a potter in North Carolina.

"I don't think he ever noticed. He traveled so much. And then he died when I was twelve."

"Yeah, but not your whole house. Surely she bought some stuff," Neva said.

"You'd be surprised." Deb sighed and looked out the window. "Once she pulled up in front of this tavern that was downtown, and my sister and I had to go in and carry chairs out."

"Chairs?"

"My mother had seen them—bentwood chairs with cane seats. She thought they would look good with our kitchen table." Deb took a swallow of water from the bottle next to her. "Which had come from somebody's front porch."

"You just carried them out?"

"My sister was trembling. My mother said: 'No one will notice. Just act like you know what you're doing.' She waited in the car, and we put them in the back seat."

They were all quiet. The sky was cloudy, the light of a few stars leaking through the milky clouds.

Neva had stolen makeup and earrings when she was ten. She and her best friend, Allison, giggled out the door of Gayland's, the area department store, where they had switched the wigs on the mannequins, put a frilly blue dress on a little boy mannequin, and each pocketed a handful of costume jewelry. No one caught them, so they stole stuff every week—nail polish, cheap perfume—until they got bored and started going to the movies instead.

"Did the chairs match the table?" Kira asked.

"Oh, yeah. They looked great. We sat in them every morning and had breakfast. You know what was on the table?"

Neva shook her head in the dark. "No," Kira said.

"A bowl of sugar and salt packets. Those tiny plastic packs of jelly—they only had grape and mixed fruit at Hardee's, which is where my mother got that stuff. We hated the mixed fruit and it would pile up, untouched." Deb sighed. "When I went to my friend Mary Louise's house, there was grape jelly in a jar in the refrigerator. God, how I loved that. And nothing written on the towels, just plain store-bought terrycloth."

"Wonder where they got their chairs," Kira said, and they all laughed, the fountain rocking a little against their backs, but Neva felt a wave of sadness. It was a story she would've distrusted or thought exaggerated if anyone but Deb had told it. She thought of Deb and her sister rooting through the jelly packets or drying their faces with towels that said *Holiday Inn*, guests at the nonexistent hotel of their mother's making. Did everyone have a shadow life? A life of ghosts and red weather?

"What's with this fountain, anyway?" Deb said. "It looks like someone's been digging around it."

"I don't know. The gardener's weird, always changing things," Kira said. "I'll ask him about it." Then she turned, as if it were an afterthought: "He's touchy, so let me do it."

After Kira had gone inside, Deb elbowed Neva. "What's up with Kira and the gardener?"

"I don't know. You think he's her new boyfriend?" They both laughed. The gardener was over sixty.

"Or maybe they're spies," Neva said, rising.

17

If Lightning Was Desire

That last night with Tomás: the strained silence over dinner. She wondered later what to unsay, but it had been building between them for weeks. Maybe it had been building since the first morning she awoke in his bare studio apartment and looked around. His secrets. His other life. Her life must've seemed an open book. Maybe that was the attraction, that for once she was not the one in hiding. She shouldn't have asked. She should never have asked.

Did she see it clearly now, months later? What she should or should not have done? Or was it just a history rewritten because, the truth was, nothing had seemed any different. Rewritten the way adjectives and nouns were erased, so that everything could be described as good, doubleplusgood or bad. Maybe he'd just been tired, preoccupied. Maybe she had been. Maybe the strained silence she now remembered had felt companionable, comfortable to him, to both of them.

"I'll be out of town until Tuesday," he'd told her. They parted at the bus stop. He lingered until the Number 7 pulled up. They had drifted in and out of sleep the night before, waking each time one of them turned over. Once when they were curling back around each other, Neva felt Tomás hard against her and opened her legs a little, reaching back for him. He came quickly and began to stroke her, but she pushed his hand away. "I'm too sleepy," she said.

"That's your bus," he said. The sky was a milky washed white; it had been storming all week. She shivered and pulled her jacket closer. "Be careful," she said, her mother's line. No one ever said that here. It was too silly. He buttoned her jacket and kissed her on the mouth. "No, really," she said. "Be careful. This week feels . . . weird."

She didn't look back as the bus pulled away. She'd already taken papers out of her bag and was marking comma splices and sentence fragments. It was the week after she'd asked him about her parents. She didn't call them her parents. Distant cousins, she said, very distant, David and Frances Greene. He shook his head. She wasn't sure he was really listening to her. Some people called them Herman and Lily, she said, desperate. That got his attention. Some people? he said, his eyebrows raised.

"Have you ever been to La Loma?" she blurted.

"La Loma," he said. "A long time ago, maybe. When I was a kid."

"I just thought they might have gone there."

"Nobody goes up there, Neva. It's way up in the mountains, on the lake. Even during the cease-fires, no one goes up or comes down."

"A long time ago, I mean. Ten years ago, maybe."

"I don't understand," he said. "Are these people you heard about here?"

"No, I came wanting to find them. They went into hiding. They were in some trouble." It was too hard, too much to explain. "Just a crazy goose chase," she said.

"Goose chase," he was frowning. "What is that?"

"Nothing," she said. "Just an expression. It was just a notion I had. Nothing really."

"I have to get to work," he said.

"I know." Neva picked up her sweater, put the strap of her briefcase over her shoulder. "Me, too."

He didn't call on Tuesday or Wednesday. He didn't call Thursday. She tried to call, but there was no answer. On Friday, she stayed in, worried, though things had been quiet and there were no reports of trouble on the highways. Saturday afternoon, she let Jamie lure her to the lake, where she swam all the way across and back, hesitating only once when she looked back and saw how far she'd come. I could drown, she thought, panic tightening up in her throat.

And all that week she didn't know whether to worry or curl up, rejected. She did both, as she wrote on the chalkboard or sat at her desk during her lunch hour. She took the bus to his apartment and knocked. She went back the next day and left a note, but he didn't call.

"Couldn't you ask at the embassy?" Susannah asked.

"He's not American," Neva said.

"What about—"

Neva cut her off. "I don't know anyone who knows him. I can't just start asking questions, you know. Not here." They were in the teachers' lounge, talking in bursts in between arrivals and departures. The door would open and someone start for the mailboxes, take one look at Neva's face and leave. Except Ted Christian, who sat on the couch across from them and started telling them what he'd had for dinner the night before, the White Meat Half-Chicken Special from Pollo Loco, with yucca chips and black beans.

Neva and Susannah didn't respond. "Jeez, what's with you guys?" he said, picking up a magazine. He thumbed through, his lips moving once or twice. "Wellup," he said. "Free period over."

"Hey," Susannah said. "I bet Ted's available."

The night they'd met, he'd asked her who she was, why she was here, but let it go when she didn't want to answer. He never asked again—because he knew asking meant he had to answer, too? To answer for himself? There was some part of her that didn't want to know, that wanted to go on, in this country apart from the past. A step out of history, a neutral zone where time and loss disappeared and she could again live in her body, without fear of reprisals.

If she had thought about it then, she would've thought: we both keep our secrets. But she didn't think about it. He said, "I'll be gone for a few days," and she never said, "Where?" He asked, "Have you ever been to New York?" and she said, "Yes, once," but he never asked, "Why? Who did you go with?"

He existed only in her memory. No one, none of her friends, had met him. Kira had answered the phone once when he called; Jamie remembered the coffee. But when she tried to get them to remember him from Mario's the night they'd met, they shook their head. The marine's suicide had eclipsed everything. The amnesia of shock erased not only the moments that followed but the moments that came before.

It was the way an alarm clock could work its way into a dream about a school bell that wouldn't stop ringing, or a cat outside the window into a dream about a baby left uncared for. But how? She'd always wondered. The baby story was long and involved, ending perfectly in the cry that was the cat's cry from the yard. But how? It made sense that it could start the dream, but how could it end it? Unless things didn't have to go in order in dreams. In which case, there was no time there. None. Just something someone made up a *long time ago*. Probably some white guy in England.

Her own life separated neatly into No Time/Not Time. There was No Time before They came, not enough time to pack, to say good-bye.

When she looked back, she seemed always to be in motion, but she knew it wasn't so, remembered the first few months at her grandmother's when time was Not Time, when each day was like the one before, and they did not come back, did not send news. Or before. Before Uncle Gus was arrested, before her parents did whatever they did to make them hunted people. Real Time was what other people lived by. But she had been too young to notice. She'd had nothing to compare it to.

Tomás did not call. Once she took a bus downtown and sat on a bench outside his apartment building.

In the evenings, she graded papers until nine or so and then went to the Brit Club. Sometimes Jamie would go with her, but his car was broken and waiting on a part from the States. He hated the mile walk, especially after they'd been there a while, drinking beer or scotch in the smoke-filled room. Jamie caught rides back—he had a knack for spotting someone headed out the door and a knack for getting people to drive him way out of their way. At first, Neva went, too, checking for messages as soon as she got home. But there never were any, and she would sit down at the kitchen table wishing she'd never left the bar, the distraction of beer and company.

There were stories about roundups, about arrests, torture. Student demonstrations. That Ramirez had ordered the university closed. A village the United States had bombed. But nothing showed up in the paper. There were more beggars on the street and in the market. Once she had given some pesetas to a woman whose left arm was missing. When the woman tucked the coins into a fold of the bright rebozo she'd wrapped her baby in, Neva saw that the baby was missing both its hands. She got off the bus halfway home and vomited while she waited for the next one. Deb brought her crackers and ginger ale at home and asked, "Did you eat something at the market?" But Neva only shook her head.

She found she could no longer cut open fruit. She waited until Kira or Deb had left a bowl of cubed pineapple or cantaloupe in the refrigerator. She gave up papaya entirely. Once she opened the refrigerator door to half a papaya with its rows and rows of mucusy black seeds and had to shut the door and go to her room and lie down for a while. She ate nothing with seeds or pith. Nothing with bones. Chicken only when it was cut up and cooked into small white unrecognizable pieces.

She stayed later and later at the Brit Club. She couldn't bear to leave the room, to lift her body from the wooden seat. At a table with a beer in front of her, she could feel that time had stopped. That it was still the Thursday they had parted in Tomás's apartment, the Wednesday her parents drove away, the day she sat outside Will's office to ask for advice about her term paper, the day she might have become tired of waiting, the day he might've been too busy to see her.

One night Susannah was crying into her beer. Her boyfriend, Henry, a volunteer for Amnesty International, had gotten into graduate school at UC–Irvine and left a few weeks before. Susannah had been making plans to cut her time here short, join him as soon as she could, when he told her not to. "I just feel I want something different out of a relationship," he said. Susannah had joked about it when she first told them: "Yeah, and I know what he wants different, too," she said. The part that made them all cackle with laughter was what he said to her as she drove him to the airport: "I hope we can stay in touch, if it's not too painful for you."

Neva had never really liked Henry. He was too nice, all the time, to everybody. She thought he didn't want Susannah to have opinions about anything. He would apologize to the group for her—"That's my Susannah," he'd say, shaking his head fondly if Susannah said she didn't think American teachers should be paid more than Coatepequen ones, or rolling his eyes if she complained about Mr. Kremer, the school director, a loathsome man they all despised, a boss they all complained about.

Susannah's role was to be difficult so that Henry could be in contrast a "super-nice" guy. After meeting Henry, someone would always say, "He's such a nice guy!" But Susannah wasn't particularly difficult. She was the friend who'd spent hours after school showing Neva how to grade her papers quickly, who'd come to her classroom one afternoon the second week, after Neva had had a particularly tough day. "I have to go to Santa Tecla," she'd said. "Come with me and I'll buy you a beer."

"How did you know?" Neva asked later. "You'd only just met me."

"Second week's the worst," Susannah told her. "And you were so quiet at lunch." If you were female you had to be nice, and then some, just to be okay, just to be not a bitch. Henry smiled at everyone and bought the beer; he was an heir. But once when he and Susannah had given her a ride home, she'd heard Henry, who must've thought she was asleep, ugh-ing everyone at the table. "That guy—ugh," he would say, "his paintings are awful." "Clarise—ugh. There's a woman looking for a man to have a baby with."

Once at a party at their house, Henry had exclaimed, "Susannah thought Farabundo Martí was Cuban!" One person had laughed, but everyone else looked uncomfortable. Susannah's face bloomed scarlet.

But after Henry had been gone a week or so, Susannah stopped wisecracking and began tearing up at the slightest provocation. Henry seemed unworthy of all this suffering. Neva remembered how often he interrupted Susannah, how he wanted to go home when she was in the middle of a conversation with someone else, how he kept his hand on the back of her neck during parties. "Stay," they'd asked her once or twice. "We'll get you a ride." But she always said, "Oh, it's okay." Once she confided in Neva: "Henry's last girlfriend really hurt him. I know when he feels safe with me things will be different."

Kira ran a slice of lime around the rim of her glass and said, "You'll get over it. People always do." Neva wondered what Kira had ever gotten over, had ever had to get over. There was silence while everyone at the table except Neva and Susannah nodded. After a few moments, Susannah looked up and said, "No, sometimes people don't get over it. That's what I'm afraid of. What if I feel like this in a year? In five years? When I'm forty?"

What if? Neva thought. She had spent too much of her life on a dirt road in Alabama, watching her parents' station wagon disappearing around the bend. What if in five years I still want to take the bus downtown and sit on a bench across from his apartment? What if I want to peer in the window of Mario's at the table where we sat? What if this is it, the rest of my life, loneliness for someone I know nothing about except the tender skin running down his side—skin that maybe only looks like my own—how he would take my hand to cross the street, the way his face clenches when he comes.

They were eating cucumber spears sprinkled with chile from a bowl in the middle of the table. Neva's mouth burned. She sipped her beer and ran the cold mouth of the bottle over her stinging lips. It was late, and she knew she would be exhausted if she didn't go home soon. She had never been able to sleep late. The pile of student papers she lugged home Friday was enormous, the papers growing a little older each weekend, a reproachful mound next to her bed. Her students had stopped asking. They would linger briefly by her desk, saying "Miss, you look tired."

Deb told her, "They don't want you to leave. So many teachers burn out the first year here." She sipped her coke. "They'll do almost anything to keep you."

Peter joined them, asking Neva if any of the boys were giving her a hard time—they had many students in common—and if he should speak to them for her. He did not understand her relationships to her male students, that their crushes were embarrassing but inoffensive. He always couched his questions in fatherly concern, even though he was only a few years older than Neva, as if to cover up some vague jealousy. She'd never figured out if he didn't like her buddying up to his students, the ones he struggled to keep up with through frequent visits to the gym and after-school basketball games. Or if all he was doing was lifting his leg and spraying a wide—if figurative—boundary around her and every single gringa living in Coatepeque.

Peter was said to be on the prowl among their students, and a couple of the girls had asked Neva if she and Peter were an item. Neva thought she might be the only single American woman in the city who hadn't slept with Peter. He was not unattractive, but she suspected that if she did sleep with him, their relationship would change, that he would go from treating her like someone who was smart to someone who'd been stupid enough to sleep with him. She had heard that once when he was drunk, he'd pointed his beer bottle at one woman after another in the crowded bar. "Had her, had her, had *her* . . ." until Mario, the boyfriend of one of the women pointed to, had asked him to leave. She knew she didn't want to be pointed at—by him or anyone.

Kira came in from the back room. "Pool?" she asked their table. Peter got up. Neva drank. "Get up," Kira said. "I need two more. We're playing these kids from the PanAmerican School." When Neva and Susannah still didn't move, Kira picked up their beers. "Come on," she said. "I'm taking your beers."

"Keep mine," Susannah said. "I'm going home."

The three boys had impeccable manners. Still wearing their high school uniforms, they introduced themselves and shook hands all around. They were lousy pool players and didn't flinch when Kira gloated over every ball she sunk. They did not drink. Out of their group, Neva was the only one drinking.

British Timothy, so named not because he worked for the British Embassy—he was Australian—but because of the hours he spent here at the Brit Club, lurked behind her, his gin-and-tonic breath on the back of her neck. "Do you know who they are, then?" he asked her once after she'd sunk the seven ball in a side pocket after banking it twice. She shook her head, leaned into the table for her next shot, missed and stood up. British Timothy was at her side. "The Major's boys," he said, nodding, his face dewy and flushed with gin.

Neva turned to look at him. "You can't be serious."

"Yep," he said. He suppressed a burp. "The Little Major's sons. Those are the uniforms from the PanAmerican School."

The Major. Jesus. Mr. Death Squad himself.

"You better not win, then, had you?" British Timothy drained his glass and lurched around the table to whisper in Kira's ear. Neva wondered if Kira even knew who the Major was or would care if she did. She had told Jamie—who had told Neva with great relish—that a few weeks before Kira left the States to come to Coatepeque, a friend had asked her, "Aren't you worried about the war?" Kira loved to tell this story. She hadn't even known there was a war! But no, she hadn't been worried, and she didn't seem to worry now.

Still, she knew Kira would like this. A story to tell the friend back home who'd asked her about the war. Exciting not because of the Major's death squad connections, but because he was a character in the movie *Death by Government Order*, played by the same actor who had been one of the Indians in *A Man Called Horse*.

No one in-country would be impressed with this anecdote. "Oh yes, Bobby and Tico. Can't remember the other one's name. Nice boys," they might say. Or: "Oh, everybody knows them. Tico plays squash with my neighbor's son." There was a certain chic currency to hanging out with the right wing here. Something manly and authentic in showing how little you had in common with American liberals and their bleeding red hearts.

At the Brit Club, no one seemed to have any politics. An AID wife, who came in with a group after an embassy party, started ranting at Neva and Susannah, ranting about the students they taught, their parents' whispered death squad connections. There'd been a hush at the party as the woman's voice got louder and louder and people moved away, not because of the danger, but because of the bad manners.

But no one else. It sucked her in, the relief of apolitical life opening up like a green field she could lie down in. She was that tired. When Neva told her brother about the pool game during their weekly phone call, he laughed and said, "Well, they say the children of mafia dons are also polite and well behaved."

Neva switched from beer to gin gimlets, a strong drink she usually stayed away from. She found herself leaning back against Peter. Found herself in his car, him asking, Did she want to come over for a drink? Shaking her head too much, No, I can't, I'm too drunk, but when he pulled up at her house and leaned across to unlock her door, he began kissing her neck. She found she was considering it. She'd always believed that stupid men made for stupid fucking, but she felt the tip of his tongue touching the skin behind her ears, the back of her neck, biting her lip between his own even as he ran his hand down her belly, between her legs, and held it there.

She was willing to rethink the correlation between stupid men and stupid sex but not willing to imagine he was much smarter than a brick. She worked with him—she knew. But then his hand reached down inside the elastic of her underwear. "You're so wet," he said, stroking her into a hard knot. He put his mouth on hers and sucked her tongue into his mouth.

Oh, why wasn't he some stranger she'd met in a downtown hotel, she thought as he ran his hands over her breasts. Would he think they were a couple? Would he want to go out on dates?

The drive to his apartment was a blur. He kept his right hand between her legs, unbuttoned her blouse when they stopped for a red light.

She followed him up the twisting stone stairs to his apartment, to his bedroom where two twin beds were pushed together. Undressed, he was pale, muscular, his penis, not yet fully erect, bobbed a little. She realized that he was skillful rather than passionate and felt both disappointed and relieved. When they lay down, his body covered hers entirely. She felt swollen between her legs, but her skin remained cool.

The sky was streaked with pink, backlighting the half-finished building down the street from her house, the scaffolding around it glowing rose. The cab let her off at the corner. The chill morning air cut through her thin dress. She hoped no one was awake.

But Deb was up, sitting at the kitchen table with a cup of tea, writing a letter. "I'm just finishing this," she said, not looking up. She scribbled her name, folded the pages in thirds, and sealed them in an envelope. "The coffee's ready to go," she said. "I just have to turn it on."

Neva was tired and sore. Her skin itched, her crotch itched. She wanted her bed, she wanted a shower. She wanted to sit in the kitchen and drink coffee with Deb. She didn't want Deb to ask her anything. Deb fussed over the coffee, poured Neva a glass of orange juice. "This is the last of it," she said. "We're out of oranges, again."

They sat in silence. The coffee spit and gurgled on the counter. "Neva," Deb said, "you have to stop. You can't keep doing this." She put her hand on Neva's. Deb's hand and forearm were a uniform light brown, tanned from being outdoors so much, working door to door in the city, driving out into the countryside to interview families, make reports on the fincas, the people who worked them. The underside of her arm was pale as buttermilk.

"I haven't done anything wrong," Neva said, pulling away. She rose from the table. "Kira does it. She does it all the time. Do you have these little talks with her?" She poured herself a cup of coffee and started toward the door to her room.

"No," Deb said, shaking her head. "I don't. But you and Kira are different people."

Little Miss Superior, Neva thought, looking at Deb in her denim skirt, her hair chopped off like an afterthought. What would you know about it?

Who would date you? she thought, slamming her bedroom door. She opened and slammed the drawers in her bureau. Treachery rose in her throat smart as a lemon. She sat down on the bed—everything sour and smarting. She cried until she couldn't breathe out of her nose at all, until her left sleeve was a mucusy smear. Some things you could never take back. If I will always be this person. If I have to be who I am right now. Always.

She could feel Deb, solid as a sofa in the room below her. My friend sits at the table worried about me. Some people have so much less.

She thought he would be furtive, avoiding her, refusing to meet her eyes, worried she'd want something from him. Instead, he greeted her with a proprietary manner, fetching her coffee in the teachers' lounge. She remembered how quickly he had tongued her to orgasm, then entered her while she was still tight and pulsing, so that he had to push a little too hard. At first she thought she had misjudged him, what he felt, what he wanted from her, and she accused herself—user, cold, cold, user—the way she used to when Will's weeping and remorse no longer stirred any tenderness in her. When his red-rimmed eyes made her turn away. When she held him to keep from looking at his face.

But when she saw Tony García glance between them as Peter handed her a cup of coffee, standing a little close as he did so, she understood. When she saw that Tony saw, she felt embarrassed. More embarrassed than she would've believed, because Tony was a smart man whose dedication to his students was second only to his dedication to an adored lawyer-wife. Peter was a buffoon, but a clever one who made sure somehow—Neva had never understood just how until now—that everyone knew each and every woman he'd slept with.

It wasn't the sex, which had been passionate and eager. His techniques were so studied, she wondered if he'd taken a class in it. It was after, when he'd curled up around her, sighing into her hair. She should've left, but was still too drunk, then when she sobered up, too embarrassed. She woke just as it was getting light. The place where the fronts of Peter's thighs touched the back of hers was wet with sweat, and the room smelled sour. She left without waking him.

All day she had trouble teaching, thinking: They know, they know. Everyone knows. She stayed in her room during lunch, eating a pack of cheese crackers and drinking a bottle of Sidral. She wanted to go home sick, but if they knew, what would they think? She scrutinized the faces of a handful of girls in her classes, the ones who wore a lot of jewelry and brought French *Vogue* with them to class. Had they? Was it possible to have this in common?

She walked home instead of taking the shuttle, crossing the bar-ranca on the swinging bridge, stopping in the middle for a few moments to watch clouds gather over the tin and cardboard houses on the ridge behind her.

She was so tired, she ate dinner early, reheating some beans and rice from the refrigerator, slicing an avocado and seasoning it with lime and salt. She crawled into bed without brushing her teeth, leaving her clothes in a wad at the foot of the bed. She woke once, hot and sweaty under the covers, and threw them off. Rolling over into a cool spot in the bed, into a patch of grass on the green hill behind her grandmother's farm. Bruno curled into the small of her back, licking her hand once. Bruno was a sweet dog, she thought, though he disliked me so. Her mother, her father, her grandmother, her brother were on the grass near her talking, and she thought: I should go over there, since they will be gone soon. But she was so sleepy. The wind was picking them up, lifting them; they hovered just off the ground near her, then a little higher. Like kites. I never knew they were kites. I should go. I should go up there. Soon it will be dark here, everyone flown or drifted away. In a few minutes, she thought; I will just rest for one more minute. And the kites rustled as they rose in the wind, until the rustling woke her, and it was not wind at all but rain.

She had slept late. She opened the shutters to find the whole world changed. The rain was a gentle steady downpour—female rain, they called it in Alabama—and everything was green, the air cool and smelling the way it does when you've hiked up a mountain.

She felt as if she *had* gone up a mountain, the way the air changes suddenly halfway up a trail. The trees change, the colors change.

It had started, the rainy season. Even the air felt different.

18

The Rainy Season

It rained every afternoon. It was nothing like the rain in the States. For two hours, everything was dark green and black; then trees, lawns, houses—it all turned to pale green, to yellowish green, especially where the sunlight broke through the dense trees. Green as a forest. And when the rain stopped, the air was fresh, crisp as autumn in Alabama. Now there was mud everywhere instead of the gritty yellow dust Neva used to wash off her desktop every Monday morning. She wore skirts instead of pants, carried an extra pair of sandals, a hat instead of an umbrella—a useless item when even the air seemed to be made of water.

It rained, but no one missed the dry season, when it was hot and dusty, when the water was dirty and anything could make you sick to your stomach. With the rains, Neva stopped wondering about Tomás. She had—without realizing it at first—walked through a door into a different world, where the light was so different he might as well have been an actor in a film she saw one afternoon, a character in a dream someone narrated over the lunch table. She thought: All I wanted was to escape. All I wanted was to live. To come home and lie down in a bed no one would drag me out of. To wake up to a face marked only by sleep and dreaming.

I never really thought I would find them. That I would find out what happened.

She returned to wanting only what she wanted before.

She rearranged her room so that the light woke her in the morning. When she came home in the afternoons, she made a pot of tea and drank it instead of beer. She sat in the kitchen grading papers, surprised that these were the same students whose awkward sentences she had so struggled with a few months before.

She never planned the future, but little by little she began to piece together the past, to try to figure out when it happened—the moment she began to go under. She thought about that Neva in the third person. She remembered when Miriam's five-year-old niece Neva, who had never met anyone with the same name as herself, started referring to her as "that other kind of Neva." In the dark green forest of the rainy season, she began to think about that "other kind" of Neva, lost in the dry world. The broken, cracked-open world on the other side of the forest. A Neva who could be remembered with regret and tenderness, but never rescued.

She wanted to be the clever girl in the fairy tale, who took a gold ring, a tiny wooden chair, and a lock of her dead mother's golden hair on her journey. Who night after night wove a jacket of stinging nettles, though her hands burned and though she was not allowed to speak. The girl who solved the riddle, who outlasted the witch's impossible task. She wanted to guess the secret name of the little man, who spun straw into gold, who wanted to take something precious and irreplaceable from her. The clever girl who waved a cutoff finger at her robber bridegroom, not the one searching for her shadow, which had slipped away one day when she wasn't paying attention.

That "other kind" of Neva could not be rescued. She was lost in the ogre's castle, in the giant's lair. There was no secret wardrobe, no rope of hair out of the tower, no underground tunnel. Maybe she had known all along that her search was futile. Maybe it had just been an excuse. In a distant room, someone was reading that story aloud, but she could no longer hear the ending.

Her brother called. He and Rhonda, his girlfriend, were talking about getting a house together when the estate was settled and wondered if Neva might want to live with them for a while.

"I don't want to go back," Neva told him, her words echoing back to her as if she were sending them down a dark well instead of across a continent.

He knew what she meant. He knew she didn't mean she didn't want to come back to the States. "I don't either," Harker said. "But that would be the point, wouldn't it? To stop waiting for them. To make our own family."

She could finish college in a year. Harker wanted to stay in the Midwest and keep studying tribal law. Somewhere they'd never lived as a family. Where the past would never catch up.

"Neva," Harker said, "you have to get a divorce. You have to do it before the estate is settled."

"I know," she said. "I know I should. But it will be easier when I'm back there." She could almost see the house: brick, two-story, its arched front door, oak with iron fittings. The snow a clean white field surrounding it. She had heard that snow made everything quiet.

She thought of the mornings her parents had left the house early and Harker made her breakfast. His forced cheerfulness, white dish towel over one arm, asking if she wanted eggs, pancakes, oatmeal. How did she want her eggs—fried, scrambled, raw? In a glass or a cup? Grits or potatoes with those, Ma'am?

Not yet. She thought. Not just yet. That life would wait as long as she needed it to. It had become peaceful in Coatepeque. Everyone seemed to soften with the rain. I have to be here a while longer, here where people know me only according to what I make of myself each day.

Her grandmother died just before Neva's eighteenth birthday. Eight months earlier, Mr. Gresham, the minister, had found a lady who lived just outside of town and would come each day to help take care of her grandmother while Neva was at school. Her grandmother's heart was failing, though she never seemed sick, just weaker than she'd been. Breathless, as if she'd just run a mile. Herself, but different in some way Neva could never identify. Sharla came every weekday, and during the last few weeks she stayed over sometimes and checked on them during the weekend. Sharla and her grandmother fought a running battle over names, since her grandmother didn't like to be called "Mrs." and Sharla didn't think she ought to call a white woman by her first name. They finally settled on "Miss Lila," as if the farm were a plantation in the old South and her grandmother a young belle. Neva asked once, "Why don't you call her 'Miss Sharla'?" and her grandmother, cranky with pain and weariness, snapped at her, "That would make me comfortable and her uncomfortable. But I guess that would be the right thing to do."

Harker came for the funeral. Neva hadn't seen him since Christmas. He had filled out a little, was thicker through the shoulders. He no longer stooped over, but stood up straight, so that his thick brown hair, always weeks past a cut, no longer fell in his face. He claimed to go home for holidays with friends, but Neva wondered if, since he'd started college, he just stayed on campus and read through Thanksgiving or spring holiday. There was something loosened up about him, something that had stood up and spread out, the way corn unfurls in the summer fields.

There were hardly any women at the funeral. The Delacort twins, who had gone to every funeral in the county for the last forty years, Mrs. Ollar and Miss Preston. Neva's two friends from school were the only girls. The room was full of men, husbands without their wives. The women minded in some way the men did not, about her grandfather. Neva could see that now.

Mr. Gresham, the minister, was red-nosed and teary. He choked a little as he read the prayer over the coffin. It was cold. The small church had been like an oven, so hot she thought: I am going to faint and every-one will look at me; everyone will ask, "Are you all right now?" or tell me, "It's no wonder." I won't faint, she thought, and didn't. But the wind cut right through her as they huddled around the mound of dirt, the open grave, flowers so carefully matched and arranged they didn't look like flowers. They sang "Amazing Grace," a song Neva had insisted on because her grandmother loved it. But only a handful of them sang, and in the sharp wind their voices were the wail of a restless ghost, someone caught between death and an unfinished story.

The minister had asked two of the ladies to take charge after the funeral; so they went back to the farm for cold ham, beans baked into a sweet, stiff paste, deviled eggs and watermelon pickles, potato salad, green bean casserole, and scalloped tomatoes with biscuits browned on the top. The sideboard held coffee, a pitcher of half and half, sugar, and a bottle of saccharine tablets. Next to it were peach pie, apple pie, sweet potato pie, cherry crumble, pecan tassies, blond brownies, red devil cake, coconut cake, and ugly duckling cake, a cake made by mixing a large can of fruit cocktail into the batter. Neva felt so ashamed to be hungry that she hid her first plate after eating everything on it and asked Harker to get her seconds.

Everyone made a fuss over him. Cindy and Lana kept glancing at him while they were telling Neva their good-byes at the cemetery. They said they had a project to work on that was due the next day, but Neva wondered if their mothers didn't want them coming to the house.

The three ladies, who ignored Neva except for Mrs. Ollar tucking the tag of Neva's dress back under the collar, couldn't stop asking Harker questions about college, what he was studying. Mr. Gresham took Harker into one corner for a serious talk, stopping every few minutes to wipe his eyes or blow his nose. Neva saw Harker pat his arm. Who needed comfort? I hope, she wanted to say to Harker, she knew I loved her, thinking of how hollowed out she'd been most of the years she'd lived here. How busy she was waiting, too busy to notice when one life ended and another began.

"What?" Neva said when he came back. They had spoken in shorthand their whole lives.

Harker picked up his abandoned paper plate and began pushing half an egg around, rearranging his cole slaw. "He just talked about how Grandmother loved having you here. How lonely she was before."

The summer garden always had tomatoes, corn, yellow squash, zucchini, bell pepper, melon. Midsummer the zucchini grew so fast you had to watch it. Tiny one evening, it could be loaf-sized by noon the next day and so seedy and fibrous you'd have to stew it instead of pan frying it with butter and onions, the way Neva and her grandmother liked it.

Midfall her grandmother planted greens, red-top turnips and collards mostly. Neva helped her grandmother pick and clean the turnip greens, though her hands itched for hours after. There were always vegetables, plenty to eat, some to sell, and some to can for the winter months when nothing grew. They put up tomatoes, froze squash, black-eyed peas, and yellow corn, the kernels scraped from the cob with a sharp knife. She grew zinnias, bright orange tiger lilies, gerber daisies; tiny pink roses climbed the trellis and bees buzzed around the purple bougainvillea.

If anyone had ever visited her grandmother, they would've been arrested by the riot of color, rooted into place at the scent of rose, crepe jasmine and wisteria, the honeysuckle that grew in a long ramble behind the house.

But hardly anyone visited. The postman came by or waved from his red Dodge Duster. Mr. Gresham made his monthly call, sometimes staying for dinner. Her grandmother always sent her to her room to do homework, but Neva thought it was to exclude her from their conversation, the low voices drifting down the hall to where her bedroom door was cracked, but never loud enough for her to make out the words.

Neva did not want to cry in this room of strangers, among the gladiolas and funeral wreaths. In her family, they had always toughed it out. Her mother, no matter how late she sat up wringing her hands at the kitchen table, heart racing over a dream she couldn't shake, ironed a dress and put on a bright smile when she and her father left the house the next morning. They smiled but shook their heads at reporters. When her father's patients stopped showing up for appointments, they shrugged. Her father said "Oh well" once, but that was all. When they dropped her off at the farm, they acted as if nothing were really wrong. They talked about the crops along the way—"Look, Neva, that's cotton!" They stopped at the same diner where they always stopped, ordering chocolate milkshakes for Neva and her father, a strawberry one for her mother. "These are the best milkshakes," they said, the way they always said it, except this time Neva didn't say it with them. Her stomach was too knotted up. She kept the straw in her mouth to keep up the pretense of enjoying it.

Her mother's lipstick was smeared in the left corner of her mouth, and there were two tiny vertical lines between her eyes. But otherwise you would never have known there was anything wrong. Never known the phone rang all the time now, night and day, that a reporter had climbed the fence to knock on their door, look in their windows. Never known someone hated them enough to leave a bag of shit on their front porch—"excrement" her father had called it. That they could be forced to choose between lying and telling the truth, between themselves and their closest friends, their children and their friends' children, between life and life without enough sunlight or books. Without each other.

"Neva," Harker said. "Will could take a lot of the money. That's the law."

And would, she thought. He would say it was for some cause. He might even say it was what her parents would want.

One day she ducked into a doorway to wait out the sudden downpour. Through the rain, she saw a man's face in the passenger window of a van and thought for a minute it might be Tomás. When the rain stopped, she took her time walking home, walking into shops to look at ugly polyester dresses, cassette tapes of Abba or Yes, bright plastic dishes in primary colors. She walked and walked, until the unease in her muscles turned to fatigue. Until she had to use all the hot water in the house to shower the chill from her bones.

She did so much waiting when she was with Will. She would go home, knowing he might come home any minute or not for hours. It didn't start that way. She used to keep her own schedule, and if he came home before her, he was never angry, only hurt. "I missed you," he would say. "I was worried."

She began calling if she were going to be late. She began telling him her plans so that he wouldn't worry. She began telling him her plans with a question mark at the end of every sentence. She began asking permission. She began staying home. More and more she stayed home.

Things had been quiet for a month—no paros, no bombs. Their lights never went out, and there was plenty of hot water. Sometimes Susannah came home with her from the International and stayed for dinner, or Mario and Greg, who played in Kira's band, but the loud autumn parties, the feverish conversations and drinking, went on the back burner. Even the Brit Club was quiet. The few times she went there, nothing exceptional happened. People drank. Someone went home with someone. They ridiculed their students fondly. They talked about missing Hershey bars or Cheetos. The men talked about American football or soccer; the women swapped the few novels written in English they had among them.

She thought about her parents sometimes, wondering how, in their own safe lives, they had known there was so much terror in the world. Surely they were dead. She had always known it. Knew Harker had known it, too. Had known it and waited for her to admit it. But she had had to come here, into a life so different she was a different person, a person who could step far enough away from the past to see it, to say, Of course. They are gone and it is time, it is past the time, to grieve. Soon, she thought. But not just yet.

She wanted, someday, to know. She was so tired of wondering, of speculating. She had always known that her parents could never have been silent so long. How she had wanted to keep them alive: driving cross-country, flying to Brazil, tucked into a cabin in the mountains of British Columbia where they read books and planned the day when the government would come to its senses and they would be reunited with their children. But to keep them—flying or driving or hiding—made them into different people: betrayers, the one thing they could never allow themselves to be.

There was a half-finished building down the street from their house. One morning, Neva and Kira decided to take the early bus to the beach at Tesoro. Neva woke early, and just before dawn she took her coffee outside to watch the sky turn from dark rose to a pale wash of pink. She saw the silhouette of a man on one of the second-floor balconies, a blanket around his shoulders like a cape, his hair and beard wild around his head. El Loco, she realized with a start. He must live there. His profile was black against the dark rose sky. And when he stretched and threw the blanket off his shoulders, he looked like a stone gargoyle, a rough beast, shaking itself into life before flying over the city, looking for weak souls to consume. She shivered, and when she looked back up, he was gone, and the sky was already the pale blue of mornings here during the rainy season.

She told Kira about it, when she came outside, but El Loco—if it was El Loco—never reappeared, and she could tell Kira didn't completely believe her. The building was rough and craggy. It could have been anything—a trick of the eyes in the odd pink morning light. That episode of *The Twilight Zone* with the monster on the airplane wing, never there when the stewardess came back down the aisle after the passenger with fear of flying had pushed his call button. The show had so scared her and Harker that they told their parents they would never, never, never fly anywhere. They were children, and they knew that when the monster appeared, the stewardess would never believe them either, no matter how many times they saw it, pulling the wing apart, while the plane bucked and spun out of control toward the ground.

That last month before her parents left, there were monsters in the fig tree outside; they were under Neva's bed, behind the door. There was a furry monster in the hall closet, which turned out to be her mother's old coat with the rabbit collar. There were monsters in dreams; there were men chasing her; there were parents with twisted faces, her mother hateful and foreign, her father putting her up for adoption. "It's for the best," he told her and the judge while she saw her mother and Harker through the window, eating peach ice cream from cones made of newspapers, their hands smeared with ink. That last month everything was a monster: the curtains with their folds and shadows, clothes heaped on the floor. When she woke at night, she was so stiff with fear she couldn't reach for the switch on the bedside lamp. Harker gave her a flashlight, which she clutched under the covers, waking sometimes with her hand cramped into a grip around it.

They were looking for a school for Neva; Harker would be going to college anyway. There were Quaker schools in the Midwest, a school in Appalachia where students worked for their tuition with area families and learned to build dulcimers. But by then there was little money and Neva was only fourteen.

Neva's mother had her own bad dreams. Her nights of rising, afraid to sleep again. That last month, sometimes it was all Neva could remember, and she had to force herself to recount by categories her childhood—vacations, dinners, the way her father read them the Narnia books chapter by chapter, violin lessons, the elaborate treasure hunt her mother organized for her ninth birthday.

Since the rain started, the days seemed endless, the routine of them comforting as a blanket. She stopped reading and instead lay on her bed as scenes from her childhood played out like a novel. She wondered how much of what she remembered had ever happened. What details had been lost or changed—a red dress becoming a purple sweater, a chocolate birthday cake blossoming into lemon, the hired clown a pony instead.

She floated on the quiet, knowing it couldn't last, but still she floated, as if the damp air, the lulling sound of the rain, were enough to hold her steady forever.

"Neva," Kira called up the stairs.

"What?" She came halfway down.

"Some friends of mine are playing at one of the cabanas this afternoon. Deb's coming. Do you want to?"

Neva shook her head. She didn't want to do anything but lie on the bed and listen to the rain.

"Come on," Kira said. "It's not some big drinking scene. It's open air, lots of families. We'll only stay for a couple of sets."

Neva still hesitated.

"The band is really good," Kira said.

"Okay," Neva said.

They went to La Ranchera, a cabana on the south side. "Linda is Rolando's latest stupid girlfriend," Kira said. "She'll want to sit with us unless there are other girlfriends here. Then she'll sit with them."

"Linda?" Neva asked. "What happened to her boyfriend the military advisor?"

"His wife decided to move down here," Kira said. "Tee-hee." She and Deb smiled at each other across the table.

They ordered a pitcher of beer and a pitcher of margaritas. The waitress brought them on a tray with bocas, little plates with a mouthful of guacamole or pico de gallo on a chip.

Linda joined them. She signaled the waitress to bring her two glasses, holding her fingers up in a peace sign in case the waitress didn't understand the word 'dos.' She raked three of the platillos over toward her and scarfed down the bocas. "You think she'd bring more?" she asked.

"Linda," Kira said. "You want to pitch in? The liquor's not free, you know."

"Rolando will get mine," Linda said. She sat with her back arched, twining a lock of her long black hair around her finger. She drank like a thirsty woman, like someone just in from the desert.

Rolando waved Kira onstage, but she shook her head. He jumped down and came over to their table. "Please play bass on this one. Jack is totally fucked up." Kira climbed onstage and picked up the bass.

"Kira plays bass?" Neva asked.

"Kira," Deb stirred her margarita, "plays everything."

"Big deal," Linda said, arching her back a little more and flipping her hair down her back. Linda was already drunk, Neva realized. She sucked everything in through a straw, even the beer. The straw gurgled like an old man clearing his throat each time she finished a glass.

Kira and Rolando pulled two stools to the front of the stage. Rolando changed his electric guitar for an acoustic. Kira set the bass on a stand and picked up a microphone.

"Don't slurp, Linda," Deb said. She pushed Linda's glass away.

"Bitch," Linda muttered.

"This is a John Prine song," Rolando said.

"Play 'Feelings,'" someone shouted from the front row.

"You guys are gonna have to be quiet for this one. I almost didn't talk Kira into singing it."

"Yeah, Kerri!" the same voice said.

The song surprised Neva, a ballad about an old woman living in Montgomery, Alabama. Montgomery, of all places. Neva felt something twist deep inside, and her eyes stung, even though she'd never been there. The town Hank Williams came from. He was part Cherokee, people said. The thin, hard-boned face on his albums had always reminded her of her grandfather's.

But Kira's voice surprised Neva more. She'd imagined a deep, even rough alto, but when Kira sang, it was in a clear bright soprano.

The band took a break. Kira came back to their table.

"You're better than their bass player," Neva said. "Why don't you play bass with them all the time?"

"Birth defect," Kira said. The waiter brought over a tray of bottled beer. He gestured to a table of men who waved eagerly at Kira. "Thanks fellers," she said, giving them a little salute. "Oh brother."

Neva was too embarrassed to ask her. She was what her grandmother Greene would have called "mortified."

"Neva," Kira said. "I meant the lack of a penis. Boy bands don't let girls play bass. They're always trying to get me to sing, but I hate it because I'm not very good at it."

"But you sing at the piano bar, all the time."

Kira shrugged. "Drunks don't care. Put scotch and blond hair in front of them and they think it's art. Besides, I'm not terrible. I'd just rather play bass or keyboards."

Rolando was weaving among the tables, talking to people. Linda fidgeted in her chair. "So, Neva," she asked, still twirling her hair, "do you have a boyfriend?"

Neva shook her head.

"Come on," Linda said, "there must be somebody. Don't tell me you just do without it."

"Jesus, Linda," Kira said.

"Neva is very pretty," Linda said. "A little exotic." She trailed a finger along Neva's forearm. Her words slurred a little. "She could have a boyfriend. Unless—" she hesitated. "Unless you're a nun or a lesbian," she said with a little laugh. "Maybe you and Deb are lesbians."

Deb didn't say anything. She pushed a bit of onion around with a straw.

"I am, Linda," Kira said.

"Whut?" Linda asked. She slurped the last of her beer.

"A big old lesbo," Kira said. She watched Linda's face. "And I think you're real cute." She leaned in close.

"Fuck you, Kira," Linda said. She stood up and wove her way through the tables toward Rolando.

Deb stared at the table, her cheeks flushed.

"Deb!" Kira jumped to her feet. Deb looked up, startled. "Let's get some guacamole, a family-size order of it, and some chips and salsa. Come with me, in case I can't carry it all."

Deb rose and followed Kira. Neva watched as Kira put her arm around Deb, giving her a sideways half-hug. Kira said something to her that made Deb shake her head, then laugh.

It was time, Neva thought as she watched them laughing, as she thought of how they had taken her in, how they were family to each other. How they would be family to her if she would let them. Wherever she went from here—deeper into her life in Coatepeque or back to the States to build a home there—she had to know she had tried everything. She could see how she had waited and watched, waited for someone else to fix things, to find them, to figure out what ought to happen. But it was time, time for what she had to do. She saw Deb and Kira coming across the grass, their arms loaded with food, a pitcher of beer sloshing back and forth. *If I never go up there, to La Loma, I'll always wonder. Harker is right; it's not even a long shot. But the country is so quiet now. If I am ever to go, I should go now.*

She looked up as Deb and Kira sat down. "I have to go up to the mountains," she said. "To a town called La Loma."

Deb frowned, but she said nothing as she refilled their glasses.

"You think Tomás is there?" Kira asked.

"No, it has nothing to do with Tomás," Neva said. She shook her head at their skeptical faces. "No, really. It's something else. A family thing. I don't want to tell you. I'll tell you when I get back."

"La Loma," Deb said. "I've never been there. Sometimes people call it 'La Paloma,' The Dove, because of the Quakers settling there. I hear it's beautiful up there. Do you want one of us to go with you?"

"No." Neva shook her head. "I need to do this." As she said it, she felt something lifting away, something she had always carried. She reached for Deb's hand. "But be there when I get back," she said. She looked across the table. "You, too, Kira. I need you to be there when I come back."

19

The Heart of the World

They kept climbing. The air was clear, so thin that gravity pulled at her ears. It was nearly midmorning, but still she heard the roosters crowing, the last a little plaintive, as if desperate to be heard. Up and up they went, passing little clusters of houses, a few signs, and then nothing but the narrow road, the rock and scrub falling away to the valley. At the first glimpse of Lake Chichool from the bus window, she felt it. Something still and perfect settled in her. The indigenous people called the lake the Heart of the World. Yes, it had to be here, in this perfect blue place. Everything else fell away in the face of it. She understood why it had called them, why it called to her.

Neva took the first launch leaving the dock. The small boat roared through the bright sunshine, then slowed to a chug-chug as they came into the fog covering most of the lake. It was chilly, and when they crossed the wake of another boat, the spray rushed into her face. When she shivered, she felt it in her bones. She zipped her jacket and listened, but there was nothing: a hint of voices behind her, the bow of the boat slapping down on the water, but nothing else.

The boat pulled in at a small wharf. A boy rushed to tie them up and then reached for Neva's hand to help her out. "La Loma?" she asked.

"Arriba," he said. "Mas arriba," pointing to a path leading up the hill.

She went up and up. She climbed until the backs of her legs burned. It was like climbing into the sky. When she reached the village, she stopped to ask a grandmother sitting on the steps of her house, "What street is this?" The woman shook her head and called back into the house, a word Neva did not recognize.

A young man appeared in the doorway. "My grandmother doesn't speak Spanish," he said. But he knew where the gringos lived. "Directo." He pointed straight up the road. "Una casa rosa."

No, not far, he told her.

The woman who answered the door of the pink house was her mother's age, the age she would be now, and she was Native, black hair shot with gray, a silver turtle pendant on a string of green and yellow beads around her neck. But she wasn't Neva's mother.

And the man in the garden—white, tall as her father—wasn't Neva's father.

"Sit down," he said. "You must be out of breath. It's quite a climb."

"I'll get some tea," the woman said. She came back with a pitcher and three tall glasses.

"You've come to the right place." She poured a glass and handed it to Neva. "Oh no," she said when she saw Neva's face. "I didn't mean that—they're not here."

Neva couldn't swallow. How had it happened, the thing she had sworn would not happen? A moment of such joy—how had she allowed herself to feel it?

"We sent the postcards," the man said.

Neva was surprised at her own furious weeping, at how long it went on, at the way the man and woman waited, quiet and patient. "My grandmother's name was Lila," she blurted.

"Lily," the woman said. "I'm Lily."

"We knew your parents," she said. "I shouldn't say 'knew.' We'd met them. And later we heard what had happened. Tim and I were headed down here to pick coffee—"

"The coffee brigades," Tim said. "You probably don't know about those."

Neva nodded. She had trouble looking at them.

"Someone asked us to bring the postcards, mail them from here," Lily said.

"We always wondered if someone would come, but we thought it would be someone else."

Neva looked up. She could imagine the someone or someones they had expected. "Thank you for what you did," she said.

"You are so like your mother," Lily said. "When you came to the door, for just a moment I thought you were Frances. But then I knew who you had to be."

Neva spent the night on their sofa, and even so, she was late getting home the next day, past curfew. But she didn't care. She wanted her own bed enough to risk it.

"Neva?" She heard Deb's voice as she started up the stairs to her room.

Deb came into the kitchen in her pink bathrobe. "Are you all right?" she asked.

Neva nodded. "I'm glad I went. I'll tell you tomorrow. When we're all here tomorrow night, I'll tell you all everything."

"You look exhausted," Deb said.

Neva nodded. "I'm so tired," she said. "Is Kira here?"

"Asleep," Deb said. "You know nothing ever wakes her. Are you going in tomorrow?"

"Yeah," Neva said. "I'm going to set two alarms, but wake me if I'm not down in the morning. Goodnight, Deb."

"Goodnight," Deb said. "Neva—"

Neva turned back from the stairs. "You look changed," Deb said. "Sadder, but not so worried."

"Tomorrow," Neva said. "It will be good to talk about it." She wished she had known all along that it was possible to survive such sadness. That the work of keeping it at bay was more work than you could manage and still live your life, live *in* your own life. She was full of sadness—every cell, every molecule. Full of it. But it no longer felt like a part of her was standing apart, waiting and watching. Lily and Tim had wanted her to stay, and they talked through dinner, late into the night, until Tim nudged Lily, who said, "You're exhausted, Neva." She made up the sofa for her and said, "Call us if you need anything."

What a relief to talk openly. To say anything without fear. Neva had washed her face, drunk the tea, then told her own story, why she had come here, what she had hoped to find. She knew she must've been incoherent at first. But they listened, without interruption. It was only over dinner that they talked about themselves, about their time in Atlanta. No, they shook their heads, they weren't there that summer.

"We only lived in Atlanta for a year, and we really didn't live in the city. We were working on a project to set up these marketing cooperatives with small farmers in the Black Belt. But then the grant ran out, and someone we knew had just come back from working on the coffee brigades."

"I miss that life," Tim said.

Lily laughed. "Yeah, but you don't miss that life and I don't either. I like remembering. But I couldn't do it again."

"Where did you meet?" Neva asked.

"We met at Dartmouth," Tim said. "Lily's Abenaki."

136

"You're a long way from home then," Neva said, looking at Lily.

"This is home," Tim said. "This is our home now."

Bright light woke Neva the next morning, flooding the window behind the sofa. She had slept straight through, so deeply she couldn't remember dreaming or even turning over. She felt purged, a little tired, but relaxed to the core.

Neva could smell coffee. She pulled her jeans on and joined Lily in the kitchen. "Stand here, Neva," she said, motioning her to the spot where she herself stood. "It's the one place in the house where you can see the lake."

The fog sat on it in patches, like small clouds.

"I can see why you've stayed here. I've never been anywhere so beautiful," Neva said.

Lily did not respond. She poured another cup of coffee and handed it to Neva.

"I'm going home soon," she said. "Back to Vermont."

"To stay?" Neva asked.

"To stay. The tribe's been trying to get recognized. I only know a little Abenaki, but I think I could learn it, maybe teach. I can't really explain it—I just feel this tug, this need to go home."

"What will Tim do?"

"He'll stay. There's a five-year grant for the school, but he has to be here to administer it. The foundation says they have to have someone with a master's degree, but it's hard not to think they just want someone white, someone from the United States."

"But—" Neva said.

"What?" Lily asked her.

"Won't you be sad? Won't you miss each other?"

"It will break my heart," Lily said. "His, too, I think. But at some point you realize that your heart has so many claims on it."

"And how do you choose?" Neva said.

"And how do you choose?" Lily echoed her.

20

Shifting Ground

It was impossible to talk over the noise of backhoes, helicopters, and men shouting. Neva could only communicate by pointing and gesturing, as she dished up soup and handed out corn tortillas to a dazed mother and child. The little boy's head was bandaged. Each person received one bowl of pork soup and two tortillas. Neva was so hungry that every few minutes her stomach would cramp and bend her over. Once she turned away and stuffed half a tortilla in her mouth, turning back to the endless line, every face watching her jaws working, her throat swallowing. It was three days since the earthquake. Flies buzzed over the warm food. She had been standing for four hours.

It was hot, Alabama hot, Atlanta asphalt on an August day hot. From time to time a slight breeze lifted the stray locks of dirty hair around her face, but with the breeze came the smell of the bodies they were still uncovering from the rubble of what used to be downtown. Her hands were so dirty she tried not to touch the food, but as one layer of dust then another settled over everything they were serving, it seemed ridiculous even to try. All day the sweet breeze had gagged her. She knew if she didn't eat soon, she would faint. She was afraid if she ate she would vomit.

Three days since Kira woke her up from a dead sleep. Four since she'd returned from La Loma. She'd been dreaming. She and Harker at the state fair, spinning crazily in one of those rides that turned from side to side. The machine made a grinding sound that hurt her ears, vibrated uneasily in her jaw and molars. She was turning to Harker to tell him she had to get off—she was too dizzy—when there was a bright light. And then the light was over her head and Kira was shouting from the doorway. Her bed moved from side to side, and around them was the sound of the earth grinding against itself, of buildings trying to go down.

How instantly the world had changed. A few days ago, she had come down from the mountain filled with her story. "It's so hard to know how to begin," she'd said to Deb and Kira at dinner the next night. "And I have to ask you not to talk with anyone about this." They had nodded, but then Jamie had come in with a boy they didn't know, and the moment had passed.

She was covered with mosquito bites from sleeping outside. They'd run out of repellent the first night, and there was none to buy. There had been dengue fever in the city last May, but no one seemed to worry about it now. She was sure the hospitals were choked with people. No one knew how many had died, how many were dying, how many had been found. The worst damage was downtown, in the stacks of apartments and office buildings. The offices had been empty, but the fast-food places collapsed instantly under the floors stacking overhead. The Pollo Loco had been crammed with students from the university. When they pulled the bodies out, some of them were clutching chicken legs in their hands. One boy's jaws were clamped together on a wing.

Sleeping outdoors seemed oddly safe. They had not seen their vigilante since the quake, the young man they paid protection to. Before the earthquake, they would hear the two quick toots on his whistle as he strolled by their house on his nightly rounds. They didn't know if he was dead or stranded in the countryside, but the Vides family next door had their guards out patrolling most of the night. Once Deb had cried out in her sleep, and all three of them had rushed over. After that, none of them could sleep, and they spent the hours until dawn teaching the guards to play hearts. They carved up the last watermelon and ate it in the dark. Everyone was afraid of running out of water. When they'd scooped the last of the red pulp from the rind, Tino, the youngest of the guards, tipped it back and drank the juice that remained.

"Gracias! Gracias!" the next woman in line was saying. Her eyes were teary. "Los Americanos, gracias a ustedes," she said, and Neva realized that she thought the United States had sent aid, that she, Neva, was here to save Coatepeque, from this, the emergency in the country of emergencies.

Neva turned to the woman next to her. "I have to go to the bathroom."

Frowning, the woman checked her delicate silver wristwatch. "Can't you wait?"

Neva shook her head. The need was suddenly so urgent, she wasn't sure she would make it. She ran, but the line was endless, even for the two Port-a-Potties set aside for volunteers, so they could get back to work quickly, so they wouldn't have to share with the people they were helping.

"Miss Greene"—it was Marta, one of the students from the school—"my father has a trailer."

"Is it close?" Neva asked, thinking that she could not go on, could not walk, that if there were anything, a tree, a wall, a road sign, she would squat down, but everything had been leveled.

"Air conditioning," Marta's father told her when she entered the RV and couldn't help sighing at the cool air. He was watching the news from a reclining chair. At the sight of it, Neva felt the tug of gravity on her sleepless body. On the TV screen, men shouted in Spanish and hauled rubble out with large steel cables. The RV was huge and immaculate. Everything was in miniature, from the beige dinette set to the Naugahyde love seat where Marta's father lay at a forty-five-degree angle to the floor like an arrow that had missed its mark and sunk into the ground. Entering the narrow room, Neva felt she'd entered a book from her childhood, a cool green wood in the ravaged downtown landscape. Lucy in the wardrobe, the wool coats scratching her cheek and turning into the twigs and branches of Narnia. There was no smell. The air was cool. Marta opened the door to the bathroom, and Neva had barely closed it behind her and sat down when she began to pee in a gush, trying to hold back, sure that they would hear her.

She had never lived with earthquakes before, or tremors. Her students had joked about earthquakes, teasing her about her uneasiness when the ground moved. They didn't have earthquakes in Atlanta or Alabama, though the tornadoes in Alabama were fierce. One March, the roar of one had sent Neva and her class into the basement of the schoolhouse. The school basement was damp, and once Neva saw a rat scuttling along the pipes over her head. She told no one, worried that one of the boys, Walker James or Wes Dowdy, would do something: knock it down with a stick, threaten her with it. She hated rats, felt her palms dampen at the sight of this one. From the basement you couldn't hear the wind, couldn't know what was happening until the principal came to the doorway waving them back upstairs.

Most of the windows in their classroom had popped out of their frames. Broken glass lay everywhere: on the sills, the floor, the tops of their desks. Mrs. Burroway was sweeping, raking the pieces into a large metal dustpan and tossing them with a clink into the trash. The yellow school bus lay on its side in the yard. Walker and Wes were the first to the open windows.

"Whoa, look at that!" Walker said.

"Cool," Wes nodded.

But Neva worried how she would get home. Then she worried about home, her grandmother, the fragile farm buildings. She imagined Bruno swept up in the twisting winds, the fury of his yelps turned to terror. She felt only sick at the thought, not satisfaction. She remembered her mother's story about Mrs. Henderson, the fifth-grade teacher who had humiliated her once for doing her homework wrong, for numbering across the page instead of up and down. When her mother told the story, she would scrooch her face up and tap Neva's forearm with an imaginary ruler.

For years, Neva's mother told her, she dreamed of the day she would see Mrs. Henderson again, when she would exact some sort of revenge. But it turned out to be a luncheon at one of the nursing homes where Frances, Neva's mother, volunteered. Mrs. Henderson was in a wheelchair, and she wore pink bedroom slippers on her swollen feet. "It wasn't the bedroom slippers themselves," Neva's mother said, "but the fact that they were dirty." Her mother shrugged. "All those plans— wasted!" Neva could still remember the shrug, the ironic twist of her mother's mouth. And she could remember how cowed she'd been those first few weeks in Alabama by Bruno, a tiny Yorkshire terrier whose greatest weapon was a disdainful look.

"Stay against the walls, boys and girls!" Mrs. Burroway told them, pausing to push the wispy gray hair back from her forehead. The sweeping made a raking sound. Neva leaned against the wall and waited.

Cars were pulling into the schoolyard. Wes's father, Mr. Dowdy, stepped from his maroon pickup truck and put his head in the door a few minutes later. "I'm gon take Wes home, Miz Burroway," he said. He took off his hat. "If school's out for the day."

Mrs. Burroway nodded and continued her sweeping. Mr. Dowdy looked at Neva. "Neva Greene. I'm supposed to get you, too. Your grandmother asked."

Neva felt rooted against the wall. She couldn't do it, get in the front seat of the pickup and sit next to Wes, her torturer. Mrs. Burroway looked up. "You go on now, Neva," she said.

"Your grandmother's fine," Mr. Dowdy said, after he cranked the truck and pulled out onto the asphalt highway. Wes, balanced in the middle, had leaned hard against her when they made the turn. "Oh, sorry, Neva," he said. She ignored him. They'd passed Branchwater when Neva felt it: the tips of fingers under the edge of her left hip. She shifted closer to the window, but the fingers were in pursuit, digging under her, burrowing toward her crotch. She pinched the skin on the top of Wes's forearm as hard as she could, twisting it, hoping it would make him stop, would hurt enough to sting for days.

The arm jerked out of her fingers as the truck pulled onto the shoulder. Mr. Dowdy opened his door and yanked Wes out onto the gravel of the road's shoulder. He pulled the leather belt out of the belt loops of his jeans. He held Wes by his upper arm and began whipping him with the belt with slow patient motions. With each strike, Wes leapt into the air a little. When he returned to earth he would hunker down a little farther. When Mr. Dowdy was finished, he threw his belt into the back of the pickup and hitched up his jeans. Wes stood by the road, his back to the truck. "Come on now, boy," Mr. Dowdy said. "Sit in the middle, Neva," he told her.

Neva saw Wes wipe his face with his sleeve. When he turned to climb into the cab, his eyes were red and a cloud of green snot hung between his nose and upper lip. She looked away.

Her grandmother was wearing work boots and gloves. When Neva climbed out of Mr. Dowdy's truck, she put an arm around her shoulders and smoothed her hair back into its ponytail. "I'm glad to see you, girl," she said. She waved at the truck. "Thanks, Weston," she shouted at Mr. Dowdy.

"The house is okay," she told Neva as they walked toward it. "Some of the fences are down, and everything out in the yard has blowed away."

Bruno was in his basket beside the stove, trembling. When Neva came in, he refused to look at her.

The next day they found the washstand nearly half a mile away. School was cancelled, and Neva and her grandmother spent the day gathering and cleaning, deciding what should be kept, what could be mended. The sky was bright blue, the air still, as if there had never been a storm in Butler City, Alabama.

Neva washed her face, her hands, her forearms in the tiny RV bathroom. When she came out, Marta said, "My father wants to know if you want a Pepsi—but there's no ice."

Neva nodded. "Sit down, Miss," Marta said, motioning to one of the benches adjacent to the dining table. "I'll get it for you."

Neva leaned back. It seemed impossible to rise, to return to her station, spooning soup to the endless line of mouths, of hands reaching out.

"My father says you can take a nap in one of the bunks if you want," Marta said, but Neva shook her head. She had to go back.

The warm Pepsi filled her up, made her head clear. She leaned back. Mr. García spoke to her in Spanish. "My father says you should go home, Miss," Marta said.

"I understood him," Neva nodded, "but I can't—the lines are too long; they're short volunteers."

"No, Miss," Marta interrupted. "He means you should go home to America."

Mr. García spoke in halting English, "The guerillas will come now. Not safe. We will fly you to Miami in our airplane." He nodded, as if it were a done deal.

"Miss, they will come here. Through the barrancas. You have to leave."

Some mornings when Neva had been too tired to rise for the seven o'clock bus, she walked to school through the barranca, the deep ravine that ran between Colonia García and the school. Its sides were stacked with makeshift houses. Half the population was in the capital now, fleeing the war in the countryside. The barranca was crossed by a swinging bridge. Far below, a stream of sewage eased along. There was little garbage, since everything—plastic bags, bits of old tires—could be put to use. The bridge swung a little when Neva walked across it. It required a certain rhythm, and if Kira or Deb were with her, they had to take turns crossing.

Once, halfway across, she had heard the crack of a rifle and seen three soldiers below shooting crows. The people who lived in the barranca shacks turned away when Neva and the others walked through. They washed in front of each other at the spigot set in the mud center of their cluster of cardboard and tin houses, but they turned away, casting their eyes down, when the gringas passed through. Real privacy was clearly impossible here. Instead there seemed to be some understanding among them that they did not see each other, did not look. But the North Americans weren't in on the agreement. Isa and her cousins, the girls who came to their house sometimes for food, lived in this barranca, but Neva had never seen them when she walked this way.

The soldiers shot at the crows, and the crows rose startled, squawking in furious voices. They settled on another bank, picking at the garbage tossed over the side. A soldier raised his rifle and fired again, a quick volley that made dust plume in the air above the crows but missed them again. The crows squawked and resettled. The soldier with the mirror sunglasses aimed his rifle, steadying it against the limb of a tree, and fired a round. The crows simply lay down, as if they were resting, and stopped moving. There was nothing to mark their deaths—no stray feathers, no telltale circle of red, only the three black bodies lying in a semicircle, the yellow beak of one touching the clawed feet of another.

How did they live? Isa and her cousins, their dresses clean and pressed, mended. One day two of them had shown up wearing headscarves, shaved scalp barely visible around the edges. Jamie was horrified. "It's head lice," he said. He didn't want to let them in the house. But Deb had insisted. Isa was twelve. She did not accept her lot in life, complained that the clothes they gave her and her sisters were too big, told them that they were rich. When they disagreed, she pointed to things in their house. "Rich," she would say, "rich." She never seemed to worry that she would offend her benefactresses.

They took the girls to the movies, Disney films dubbed in Spanish—*Snow White* or *Pinocchio*. Going in, they bought orange sodas, yucca chips, and chocolate stars. The theater was always freezing, so they brought blankets and wrapped the girls in them. The first Saturday they took Isa and her little sister Dora with them. The next week Isa showed up with another sister and two cousins, the week after with more cousins. She was brusque as a seventh-grade schoolteacher: taking charge, ordering food for all of them and dispersing it equally, covering them with the blankets.

Isa. Neva watched her eat a few bites of her peanut butter sandwich, then wrap up the rest to take home. How she must hate us. Once, going into the movie theater, the man taking tickets had said, "Not so much for you, eh?" and Neva hadn't understood.

She found herself easing out of the missionary position. She felt sad, but sometimes she felt something that could only be shame. One Saturday, even though they'd promised to take the girls to *Sleeping Beauty*, they left early in the morning for El Paradiso, the resort on the west coast's black volcanic beach. It had always been so important to her. She remembered racing home one morning after spending the weekend with Tomás. How hard it had been to ease away from his sleeping body and dress and go.

She remembered the day she was harsh with Chita, a woman who lived in the barranca and did alterations for a living. She was sick with it, with Coatepeque and the endless negotiation between politics and comfort. The little time away from a job that drained her, as the war accelerated, as her students became more agitated, more needy. As their parents left or made plans for the whole family to flee to the United States.

More and more she found herself irritated when things weren't exactly as she wanted them. She knew the man in the movie theater had been right; it was nothing to them to take two or three or nine or thirty children to the movies. But she sometimes thought, Couldn't they have said thank you, just once?

Thank you for what? she knew Deb would say. It's their country.

They had not seen the girls since the earthquake, but the barranca was intact—most of the damage, the casualties, downtown. Once the aftershocks died down, they would move back into their house. The garden wall had a long horizontal crack running nearly the length of the front yard, but otherwise the house seemed undamaged.

They had run out of medicine; they had run out of coffins. They sprayed the ground, the mud, with chemicals to ward off typhus or cholera. Some of the children had rashes from the spray, but they had run out of ointment. They heard that Switzerland was sending an entire shipload of coffins, that French doctors were coming, that all the bodies had been found. But there were also stories of families digging with spoons for their still missing relatives. That the government was considering mass graves.

Every night when she went home, her eyes so full of grit she blinked constantly, her hair, her clothes, smelling the way the piles of garbage smelled when they burned them on the farm, every night, she thought, That's it. I won't go again. I won't. I won't. But she went. It wasn't charity; it wasn't an apology for everything she'd taken for granted. It was a restlessness that made it impossible to sit still, to sit and look out the window at the angry ground. Restless with what she had found out at the pink house near Lake Chichocol. Restless because she had readied herself to tell—to tell all of it. And the moment had been interrupted. It might never return. Now there was nothing but the earthquake.

They went—she and Kira and Susannah—everyone they knew; Deb, but Deb had always gone, had always filled the spaces between ill-prepared relief agencies and what they found here. They called for anyone who was bilingual, even people like Neva with her smattering of Spanish. "Jesus Christ!" Kira had said, aghast at what Deb was telling them. "The United States sent workers who don't speak Spanish?"

Neva had never known Kira noticed things like that or that she knew how to bind a wound, pour plasma on a burn. She had disappeared into the medic tent the first day and stayed there. Neva had to remind herself when she crawled home filthy, back and feet aching, that at least no one had vomited on her, no stranger's blood was crusted beneath her fingernails.

21

Limbo

They were in Peter's Cherokee, four of them in the backseat sitting
two forward, two back, the way the cousins did summers at her Aunt
Moss's house. The road went up and down hills, curving to the left, then
the right. Peter kept his foot heavy on the gas pedal, laughing as they
careened toward the Supermercado in Santa Ana. They were out of
everything. The power was back, the water. But the store near them still
had no rear wall, and Deb, the only one of them with a working car, was
gone from early in the morning until late every night. She would come
in dusty, her eyes raccooned with fatigue. "I'm not hungry," she would
say, but when Kira put a plate of food in front of her, she would pick up
her fork and begin to eat. She would eat straight through, sitting back
and panting a little with the effort when the plate was clean. "Beer?"
Kira always asked her, but Deb didn't drink and always shook her head
no.

They'd been waiting for Rolando to take them shopping, when
Peter pulled up in front of their house with Susannah and Lianna, the
new teacher from school. Rolando's Land Rover was acting up, so he
asked Peter to take everyone shopping after school. The car twisted
and turned, the fruit-shaped auto deodorizer dipping and bobbing
around the rearview mirror. It smelled like cherry cough drops. Perched
forward, Neva had nothing to hold onto. She felt her head lurch with
every movement the car made.

"Stop," she said, and everyone shrieked, "Stop, stop," and they went
up a steep hill and down so fast, she thought her stomach might come
out the top of her head. The cherry scent was strong, sweet over a faint
odor of mildew. Change rattled in the ashtray.

"Kira," she said, but Kira ignored her, her blond head bent over a
score she was marking up with a pencil. Kira could work anywhere. She
dug her nails into Kira's forearm. "Kira, I'm sick," she said.

"Peter, stop the fucking car," Kira said in a low voice, barely glancing up from her work.

Peter pulled onto the narrow shoulder. He turned around, irritated, but Kira ignored him. She reached across Susannah to unlock the door. "Go," she said, and Neva stumbled out onto the side of the road.

Neva went behind a clump of waist-high grass. She leaned over, supporting herself with her hands on the tops of her thighs. She breathed slowly, counting: *eight in, four out.* She remembered when Will decided to learn to meditate. Energy in, toxins out. She stood up, queasy and panting, but better, her face cool with sweat in the slight breeze.

Everyone was out of the car, except for Lianna, the new teacher, who sat in the front passenger seat and stared straight ahead. Lianna's husband had come down with one of the relief agencies, and she had been hired to teach eighth grade when Jackie Reznick, a twenty-two-year-old from Cleveland, had finally given in to her parents' pleas to come home and take a job in a safe place.

"Okay?" Kira asked Neva. She was leaning against the Cherokee, still studying the score.

Neva nodded.

"Lianna," Kira said. "Neva needs to sit up front."

Lianna did not move. She was enamored of Peter. Her husband was out of town, traveling with a group into the Escazú region where AID thought the farmers might raise goats. When Peter made a joke, Lianna laughed longer than anyone else. She asked him lots of questions.

Kira opened the passenger door and waited. Lianna gathered up her things, a large pocketbook and a pale blue sweater. Kira said something to her as she clambered out, too low for Neva to hear, but she saw Lianna's face flush.

The store's shelves were half empty, bags of sugar forlorn next to canned juice in weird flavors, quince or pomegranate.

"It's like this all the time in Nicaragua," Susannah said, "because of the American embargo."

"An earthquake or a government," Kira said. "Either way you're drinking quince juice." Susannah and Neva walked up and down the aisles, filling their red plastic baskets. They bought extra for the beggars outside.

"What I would give for something spicy," Susannah said. Neva nodded. She remembered this same sinking feeling when Will would send her to the co-op for food. The co-op kept a small storeroom in the basement of the Unitarian Church, where paid members could shop on the honor system from the coolers of yogurt and tofu, the bins of millet or black beans. Staring at the shelves in the Supermercado or rooting around among the wheat germ, the whole wheat pasta, the salt-free cheese—both made her feel hungry in a particular way she could not describe. She remembered Alice in the boat on the dream river, picking beautiful white lilies that melted as fast as she plucked them. The Duchess offering her a biscuit for her thirst, tea when she was hungry. There seemed to be plenty to eat when you went in the door, but it melted as you rooted around. You wanted something salty or pungent for your taste buds. You settled for quince juice or the sweet bland Bimbo bread.

Food choices at the co-op were largely dictated by Paul and Janice Radison, who began every sentence with "We think" and were so circumspect about what they put in their mouths Neva wondered how they ever kissed or had sex. Once, the Radisons brought cookies, passing the plate around during the meeting. As Neva bit into hers, Janice Radison exclaimed, "These don't have any sugar or butter in them." Neva swallowed hard.

"What makes it a cookie?" Jerry, the new guy, blurted out. He held his untouched in his right hand.

When everyone turned and looked at him, he settled back into his chair, holding the cookie down in his lap. Neva pushed hers around in her mouth, glancing up once to see Jerry smiling at her. She smiled back and had to look at her lap to keep from laughing out loud. It wasn't a cookie. It wasn't even a very good cracker.

Later, Will said, "What were you and that Jerry smirking at each other about?"

"What?" Neva asked, startled. "Oh, that cookie thing."

Will made a face. "People who don't care about their bodies. The poison they put into them . . ." Will drifted into the bedroom. He had forbidden ice cream and sugar, meat, of course, anything made with white flour, butter, whole milk. Neva left a baggie of fudge on the kitchen counter once, a gift from Mrs. Nicolas, one of the students she tutored. Will paced around the house until he left for his evening run. Neva found the baggie of fudge in the garbage can.

Tuesdays, when she had the car to run errands, were her chocolate days. She would pull the car into the parking lot of a Jr. Food Mart and buy Milk Duds, a Butterfinger, a 3 Musketeers bar. It started when she stopped for gas and bought a bag of peanut M&Ms on impulse, wolfing them down in the car on her way to the bank. She bought gas there the next Tuesday and the next. She could tell the cashier remembered her, saw him noting her habit. She could tell from the way he said, "Will that be all, Miss?" She changed stores. First it was M&Ms, then a Butterfinger. Soon it was both. Then lemon drops or candy corn to offset the chocolate. She would eat until she was queasy. It was hard to eat an entire week's worth of candy in one day—a Baby Ruth, a Milky Way, a bag of Sweet Tarts. It was more than a meal.

And meat. Red meat. She stopped at Hardee's for a chili dog with onions and mustard. She ordered a side of fries and a Dr Pepper. The first time she wolfed it all down; later, she pulled onto a side road to eat a leisurely lunch with the radio turned up loud. All that awful food—the enemy of my enemy, what that kind of thinking could lead you to do. She lived a double life: bringing home steel-cut oats and kefir from the co-op, but carrying a toothbrush and a roll of dental floss in her purse whenever she had to run out to the store or the bank. She brushed her teeth in bathrooms all over Atlanta.

"She's a meat eater. You can always smell it on them," Will said one night about Elspeth, who had worked the room, flirting with every man there except Will. Will she consistently ignored. He began to find her politics "increasingly suspicious." He pointed out that she wore makeup, that she shaved her legs.

"But Will, I shave my legs," Neva protested. "You like it that I shave my legs."

She started thinking about food, bad food, all the time. Hunger gnawed in the pit of her stomach, in her throat. She bought cheese curls from the machine at the center where she tutored, hurrying in case someone came around the corner and saw her. She stowed them in her purse and ate them in the car on the way home. Once, when Will was driving, his fingertips grew orange from clutching the steering wheel. She held her breath, but he didn't notice until they were home from the party and he saw faint orange streaks on the thighs of his jeans. "Christ," he said, "what is this?" He brushed at it once, then tossed the jeans onto the bed where Neva was reading. "Can you do something about this crap?"

She and Will slept together less and less. When they had sex, it seemed a little impersonal, over as quickly as they could each manage an orgasm, as if that were the whole point. They slept farther and farther apart in the bed they shared. They didn't see each other often, as the Center asked Neva to tutor more and more hours, as Will's work stretched late into the evenings.

When they came back from the Supermercado, Neva and Kira found Deb at the kitchen table. "Don't get your hopes up," Kira said, when she saw Deb eyeing the shopping bags. "It's not much."

Neva was amazed when Kira pulled a hunk of white cheese and a bag of eggs out. "How did you manage that?" she asked.

Kira shrugged. "I headed straight for Dairy. And then I asked the guy, 'Isn't there anything else in the back?' He had some stuff back there, but this is all he would give me. Five eggs."

"What kind of cheese?" Deb asked.

"I don't know. Maybe Oaxacan." She pulled a knife out of the drawer and cut a sliver. "Here," she said. "Taste it."

"Oh my god," Deb said. "This is fantastic."

"You know what I think," Kira said. They turned to look at her. "I think we should just eat this cheese." She unwrapped it and put it on a wooden board with a knife. "Here," she said, setting it down on the table.

"Maybe we should save it . . ." Deb said.

"Screw that," Kira said, pulling a chair out.

"Wait," Neva said. She sliced an orange and a mango, the last of the fruit. She put a loaf of bread on the table and emptied a package of crackers in a bowl. "Beer?" she asked.

Kira nodded. "Is there any wine?" Deb asked. They looked at her, surprised. Deb never drank. "Well, there *was* an earthquake," she said.

Neva opened the refrigerator but found only a nearly empty bottle of white wine that smelled like vinegar. "Here!" Kira said, holding up a bottle of red wine she found in the cabinet under the sink.

"I think that's Jamie's," Deb said. "He keeps his wine under there because it's cool."

"Nice of him to share," Kira said. She uncorked the wine and Neva put three glasses on the table.

"You've got to get over that," Deb said later. They had eaten everything, drained the wine. Kira and Neva were drinking beer. They had rehashed the story of the shopping trip: from the empty shelves, to Lianna and Susannah fighting over a bag of egg pasta, to Neva's car sickness. "Nobody cares, least of all him."

Kira smiled into her coffee. "What?" Deb looked up.

"It had nothing to do with Peter," Kira said as she put the eggs and the cans of quince juice in the refrigerator.

"What are you saying?" Deb asked.

"Neva," Kira said, "doesn't think she has a right to sit in the front. She'd rather puke her guts on the side of the road—"

"I didn't puke," Neva said.

"Or all over somebody's car." Kira frowned at the label of a can she was putting in the cupboard. "Anything not to call attention to yourself."

"What did you say to her?" Neva asked. "To Lianna?"

"Ask me later. Deb won't like it," she said, smiling at Deb, who raised her eyebrows but said nothing.

Kira was right. That didn't matter. So much had changed when she went up the mountain to La Loma. Neva could barely remember sleeping with Peter, and she did not remember any pleasure. Beer mouth, sweat, the way his dick had curved to the right—something embarrassing but unimportant after the weeks of smelling bodies, after seeing the picture of a woman clawing her sister out of the mud, parents fighting over typhus medicine for their sick children.

She remembered how Lianna had positioned herself to get in the front seat as soon as Peter unlocked the car. How she stood there with her skirt not quite the right length, her fat pocketbook under one arm. Teaching never seemed to make her in the least bit tired. What was it like in her classes that she was never tired? Neva just felt sorry for her.

She never had a body until Tomás, and sometimes she was sorry for the memory of so much pleasure. She didn't think much about the future; daily life was so crammed with post-earthquake life—mud everywhere, standing in lines for bottled water or aspirin, holding your breath when the lights dimmed. The war went underground, briefly, until the rumors rose, like dirty flood water, about graft, medicine sold and shipped back out of the country, and then one day a mudslide uncovered a mass grave.

The Madres stood outside the Red Cross for days trying to get names and identification, but it looked as if it would take months. When the women came to the Madres office, they could only shake their heads. We can't do anything. We can only wait. Neva wondered how often they had heard this. She wondered if she would go on saying it, on and on.

Quiet. It was so quiet. It was so much trouble to live these days, to get to work through the broken streets, to shop for groceries. People finished their chores and went home. The power came and went, and it was easier just to go to bed at eight when it got dark.

Why didn't the government do more? The paper published a scathing editorial asking where all the international aid went. The publisher and his wife were killed the next week when their minivan overturned on a deserted stretch of the highway. There were stories that infant formula was being routed to BoBo, a chain of stores President Ramirez's brother owned, that Ramirez himself had a basement full of blankets and flashlights. Besides, they had a war to fight. Debts owed to the Oligarchs, whose fincas and mansions on the western side of the city were largely untouched by the earthquake. Whose greatest headache these days was how to get workers there to pick the coffee. That the charity art show and its black-tie fiesta would have to be postponed.

It was like that in Alabama. Tornadoes leveled the houses of the poor, the mobile home parks built on floodplains. She and her grandmother sorted clothes at the Red Cross in Butler City after a tornado had ravaged two small towns in northwestern Alabama. Neva had helped unload the trunk of a Jaguar while the owner sat behind the steering wheel and waited for them to finish. She'd taken the box to her corner to sort it and found torn, stained T-shirts, unmated socks, and some dishtowels that looked as if they hadn't been washed. There was a winter coat missing all its buttons.

You are awful people. Neva looked at her students and saw blood. The girls tipped their nails with bright red polish. She'd been seduced by the mere fact they liked her. Been that sad, that lonely when she'd first come here, to this country. That's when things get dangerous—when people have so little. She'd learned by the time she got to high school that it was better to be aloof than left out, to be quiet instead of shy. But she had never been popular. She thought how ashamed her parents would be of the person she had sometimes been here. Of the person I have often been. As if nothing else mattered but what happened to me and my family. What happened to me. She started latching the door during her prep period, sick of them lounging around as if they owned her classroom, the way they owned the whole country. She saw Marta García crying in the hall one day and almost relented. But she walked by, wondering what *she* could have to cry about.

Months before she had gone to a party of the Ladies Hospitality League, one of those women's organizations where bored Coatepequen wives entertained bored American wives, and a few single women, like Neva and Susannah, got to tag along. The Americans entered in a group, passing under a huge jacaranda tree so loaded with purple flowers that Neva felt dizzy. She lagged a little behind, until Virginia Edwards, a missionary wife from Ohio, caught her arm. "Now, come on now!" she said, pulling Neva through the door. "How beautiful!" she exclaimed a moment later, in what seemed an ordinary house, with table arrangements featuring plastic flowers and miniature Coatepequen and American flags.

She was miserable throughout the party. The other women spent a lot of time talking about where to buy things.

They all thought everything was beautiful. "Isn't it just beautiful?" Virginia Edwards said again when they went into the dining room for a lunch of oily chicken and salad with Italian dressing. When the women on either side of her leaned forward to gush about a shop in Santa Clara, "where they have the best cheeses," Neva had asked, "Can you get there on the bus?"

There was silence. "Well, no," one of them said. They settled back in their chairs. "I shouldn't think so," said the other. They started up new conversations, and Neva waited out the meal like an island in a sea where the waves rose and fell, higher and deeper, a tide running away from her shores. She had been so lonely for the company of women those last few months with Will, but she never went again.

She had been patient, waiting for her life to change. Waiting. Life in a holding pattern. Well, she was through with all that.

She dreamed a man held a gun to her face. The next day, a man held a gun to her face. She wanted to hand him her purse, but her arm was frozen to her side. Around the corner, she heard two people arguing. "The Left," she heard someone say, and someone else argued back in Spanish. She was on the sidewalk, stopping to fix the loose buckle on her shoe. When she stood up straight, there it was, the gun. She could smell the metal.

The purse, she thought, the purse. But there it was: her frozen arm, heavy as lead, lead spreading to the rest of her body, which suddenly wanted just to lie down there, it was that heavy. And then a shout, the gun leaving, a slight figure in a white shirt and brown pants disappearing. So slight he might have been a boy. He might have been a girl.

I will remember you forever, Neva thought. For my whole life, even though we never spoke. And then the heaviness was so great, she did sink down onto the dirty sidewalk.

People were hungry, and they stole and robbed, breaking into houses, holding guns or knives to throats. They had lost their houses, their shoes. They lost sofas, photographs, washtubs, bicycles. Huge piles of rubble and junk lined the streets. They never grew smaller or moved, but each week the crowd of people rooting through the dirt, rock, and broken plastic grew smaller.

Seven hundred people died. It was really seven hundred and four, but on the news they said "seven hundred," and when anyone talked about it, they said "seven hundred." Neva wondered about the four. Mother, father, sister, brother. A single mother and three thin children. Four: the sides of a house, the sides of a box. The directions in which you could pray or travel, if you wanted to travel. Unless you counted up and down: a plane, rocket, or the soft hand of God. Fire and brimstone, God shaking you like a fly over a pit of cold fire, a special circle for women who lay down like a rug while their husbands wiped the dust off their shoes, for vain women who didn't mind being adored by murderers.

Or, if you didn't believe, a mouth full of dirt, an eternity of worms. She never had. Seven hundred and *four*: a father, a mother, daughter, son. Not dead, but disappearing. Not dead, but traveling. Not dead. At least not yet.

22

The Talladega Forest

"I have to go back to the States," Neva said, after she hung up the phone. "Some family stuff. I have to go. For a few days anyway."

"Now?" Deb asked.

Neva nodded.

Kira whistled. "Not likely. Pretty long wait for an exit visa right now."

"They always make exceptions," Deb said. "Neva, is it serious? Did someone die?"

"Not recently," she said. She felt a giggle rising in her chest. Oh God, is this hysteria? she wondered. "Excuse me a minute," she said. She went into the living room and sat on the couch. We never sit in here, she thought—only when there's a party. And then everyone stands. The giggle had turned into a fist-sized lump of something, wedged deep behind her solar plexus. I would like to cry, she thought, to feel it dissolve and run out the ducts of my eyes. Enough salt to burn the skin of my face. She slid to the floor and felt the cold tiles pressing against her cheek.

"There's some news," Harker had said. They didn't even know the phone had started working again, were all startled when it rang.

"For you, Neva," Kira had called from the hallway.

Some news, Neva thought. You and Rhonda are getting married. She thought of the brick house in Wisconsin, the snow piling in the yard. The antidote to this life's fever.

"Neva?" Harker asked.

She saw the snow melting. The house a place where she visited, not lived. "I'm still here," she said, trying not to begrudge him his good news, trying not to let it show in her voice.

"They found the car," he said.

"What car?" she asked. Then, before he could answer, she said, "The station wagon. Oh my God, Harker. Oh my God."

The tile had grown warm against her face. She could sense Deb and Kira in the other room waiting. The white station wagon in north Alabama, deep in national forest land, in the Talladega Forest, buried in scrub and kudzu. Spotted by teenagers panning for gold. Panning for gold. Surely they would laugh about that someday, she and Harker.

"I have to tell you the rest," he said. Bones, he said. There has to be an autopsy, but them, Neva. It has to be, he said.

"I don't think I could ask for an exception," Neva said to Deb and Kira, who sat at the kitchen table.

"Does this have anything to do with why you went to La Loma?" Kira asked.

They waited. "Please don't ask me," she said.

"All right," Deb answered for both of them.

"You could go to Guatemala," Kira said.

"I guess we could," Deb said. "They didn't have an earthquake."

"I can't go to Guatemala," Neva said. "I have to go home. I mean I have to go to the States. For a few days."

"No, I mean you could get out of Guatemala, Neva," Kira said. "You can probably get a visa at the airport, but if not, you could always go to the embassy."

"Are you sure?" Neva asked Kira. She heard the teariness in her voice.

"I'm pretty sure," Kira said. "Worst-case scenario: take a puddle jumper across Guatemala, then cross the border into Mexico, at Chetumal."

Deb was nodding. "She's right. It might take a few days, but it could take forever here and you know how it is."

Yes, Neva knew. A visa was supposed to take three days, but something almost always went wrong—a signature missing, a seal in the wrong place.

"I'll go with you," Deb said. "We'll go in the morning."

They must have headed north, Harker had said. After they left you at Grandmother's.

"Or maybe they were coming back?" Neva said.

"Maybe," Harker said. "But Magruder didn't think so."

"It doesn't seem real," Neva said. "I can't make sense of it—why they didn't hike out, why no one found them."

"You know what it's like back there, those old logging roads, not really even roads."

"You just want it over," Neva said.

Harker was quiet. "You're wrong. I want it not to have happened. I want them back, I want that life back. The life before, when we got to be kids—"

"I'm sorry," Neva said. "Harker, I'm sorry." She had never heard him cry.

"And no, I don't know everything. I'm afraid to ask and find out that they suffered, how much they suffered—" His breathing was ragged. "The FBI is doing the autopsy, Neva. You should probably come home."

"The FBI? Where did you tell them I was?"

"They knew, they knew where. Remember? They always know everything."

Not everything, Neva thought. There was one thing they hadn't known. "I'll come," she said. "I'll come as soon as I can."

Everything had happened just as señor García had told her in his RV that day just after the earthquake. The barranca was rumored to be full of Frente guerillas—"Crawling with them!" Rolando's girlfriend Linda had said, one night when Rolando came by to talk to Kira about something. They'd announced shutdowns—paros, they called them— twice a week in the three weeks since the earthquake, warning people not to go out to restaurants or the movies. Especially not to US-owned restaurants like the Pizza Hut. They'd bombed it last week. But it still didn't seem like war exactly, just inconvenience when the power was off for a few days or when they couldn't order a pineapple pizza.

The bus station was crowded the next morning, and the eleven o'clock was the first bus they could get seats on. The city disappeared slowly, the buildings and noise fading little by little until they were between a mountain rising, all moss and granite, to their left, and a rolling field to their right. There was no ash this far out. "I forgot what green looks like," Deb said.

Neva dozed off for a minute until sharp voices behind them woke her. She and Deb turned to see a man and woman arguing. The woman folded her arms, and the two of them stared straight ahead, not speaking.

"You're lucky you never got married," Neva said, leaning toward Deb so that the couple behind them wouldn't hear.

"No, I was married," Deb said. The fields looked like spring, a blurry green through the rain that had just started.

"And he was awful to you?" Neva asked. The driver honked the horn and held it down. Two boys chased a burro from the middle of the highway.

"No, he was nice to me," Deb said.

"Then why did you leave?"

"He was nice, but it wasn't what I wanted. I thought about leaving, and I thought about it and I thought about it. And then I tried. He was so sad. He said, 'I just want you to be happy,' and I would go back to our house to get something I needed and he would be in front of the television. In my chair. When I got there, his face would just light up."

"You went back to him?"

"Once. Then I left and I started going over while he was at work, trying to move out in bits and pieces. I would take some books, then rearrange the shelf so you didn't know anyone had been there.

"And then one day my friend Martha and I went over to get a chair, and there he was, sitting in it. It was a Monday, and he'd been in that chair all weekend, watching TV, drinking coke, and dozing. There was a pile of cans next to the chair. I think when Monday morning came, he just couldn't get out of the chair to go to work."

A family of four lurched down the aisle, and the driver pulled to the side of the road and stopped. Where were they going? The fields ran seamlessly along the highway, unmarked by village or side road or even a path. They disappeared into some trees.

"So Martha left and I got Doug—my husband's name was Doug— out of the chair, and he showered and changed into some clothes I laid out. I started calling around, looking for a psychologist for him. He was so depressed he could hardly speak.

"I didn't love him, you know." Deb turned toward her. She looked over Neva's head out the window. "But he was a good person. He didn't deserve to suffer.

"He wouldn't go, so I went." Deb coughed.

"Did the psychologist help?" Neva held out her water bottle to Deb, but she shook her head.

"The psychologist—" Deb's voice was harsh. She coughed again and reached for the water bottle, gulping once and spilling a few drops onto the front of her blouse. "The psychologist told me we were clearly 'co-dependent'—that was the brand-new cool diagnosis—and that I should go home and tell Doug to 'grow a spine.' She actually said that—'Grow a spine.'"

"And did you?" Neva's stomach knotted up. Everyone had so many stories, so many you could never know them all. Living somewhere, in the cells of their bodies. Touch the soft spot behind someone's left knee and she might remember tenderness. Wound the liver and watch anger flow out of the body. An ankle once twisted that throbbed each time you tried to dance. Three long scars on the inside wrist. She didn't think Will was sitting in a chair watching television, waiting for her to return or come back for a chair she'd missed. But who knew what had hurt him, what wounds he carried.

"I did exactly what she told me. I made my speech. I told Doug I'd be back on Thursday to get the rest of my stuff." Deb's mouth twisted. She looked straight ahead.

"What?" Neva said. "What is it?" But Deb waved her quiet with one hand and they sat in silence. It was quiet on the bus.

"You haven't figured it out?" Deb said. Her voice was low. "The whole story's such a cliché."

"Oh no," Neva said. Don't say it. Don't tell me. I would rather watch these long fields go by, the clumps of green like messy ponytails, a field of messy ponytails. She imagined tying them with ribbons, braiding them, combing them with her grandmother's long-handled garden rake. Don't show me your scars, Neva thought. But she knew she should have seen, should have looked around enough to see something besides her own sorrow.

"He drove out to the reservoir and ran a hose from the exhaust pipe to a window. The car had run out of gas when they found him. I almost called, so many times. Once I went out for a walk because I knew if I stayed home I would call."

"You aren't to blame." Neva put her hand on Deb's forearm. She shook it off.

"Who cares about blame?" Deb said. They sat in silence, listening to the hum of the bus's motor, the clunk as gears shifted, something rattling in the back.

"What does blame have to do with anything," she said to the seat in front of her, to the floor, to the mountains in the distance, to the gravel crunching under the tires of the bus. Neva reached for Deb's hand and held it. She could think of nothing to say.

The driver's radio squawked. The driver listened for a moment, then picked up his microphone and spoke into it. He drove a few miles more until the highway's shoulder widened, then did a U-turn so rapidly the bus tipped a little and bags tumbled from the overhead rack.

Neva and someone's father stowed them back in place, nodding at each other before they sat back down.

"Well, that's new," Neva said. "What is it, you think?"

"I don't know." Deb looked out the window. Everything was quiet, the countryside green and beautiful as the sun came out after the brief afternoon rain.

The bus was about half full. Talk filtered back that the guerillas were active. "Or maybe something's wrong with the bus," a Canadian tourist told them.

"You think we can get another bus?" Neva asked no one in particular. But when they returned to the station there were no buses leaving for Guatemala. "Trouble, lady. On the road" was all the man at the ticket counter would tell them.

It took hours to get a cab.

"The embassy will be closed," Neva said. "Deb, I have to get home." She paced outside the bus station, but the queues were long. It was nearly six when the cab dropped them off at home, promising to return at seven the next morning to take Neva to the embassy.

Deb swept and dusted the whole house while Neva paced, picking up a paperback she'd read in November, then tossing it onto the couch in disgust. "When do you think they'll reopen the library?" she asked as Deb swept through the room, picking up shoes and bottles.

Deb paused. "I don't know. I think that one wall was pretty bad." She held four beer bottles between the fingers of her left hand, the brown glass fanning out like the spokes of a wheel. "It doesn't seem like a high priority, Neva."

"I'm going crazy," Neva said. She wanted anything but to think about it.

"The movies," Deb said. "They reopened the theater yesterday. You want to go?"

They heard Jamie coming in the side door. "Jamie," Deb called, "do you have the paper?"

"God, you are desperate for something to read," he said. He laid the paper on the coffee table.

"The Cinema is back up and running. We're going to the movies. You want to go?"

"What's on?" Jamie asked.

161

Neva shook her head. "It's not in here." She and Deb looked at each other and laughed. "Who cares? We just want to go to the movies."

"What about the paro?" Jamie asked. "The guerillas said that movies and restaurants are off-limits." He looked queasy from last night's drinking.

"I'm sick of paros," Neva said. Deb nodded in agreement. "We're warned and warned and warned. Don't drink the water, don't sit near the window—except the embassy people take all the other seats. Don't walk by parked cars. Don't stay out after curfew. I'm sick to death of it."

"Nothing ever happens," Neva said. "Sometimes I almost wish something would happen—"

"Neva—" Deb cut her off.

"Yes," Jamie said, his head deep in the refrigerator. "Be careful what you wish for."

Wish for the worst thing to go ahead and happen. Then you don't have to be afraid anymore. Waiting for someone to come, to take her father and mother away. Waiting. For the news that they were dead, that their lives had gone on elsewhere, with new, more lovable children. Neva had never before understood why Harker had chosen to think of them as dead. Live the worst thing, and it cannot take you by surprise, leave you hollowed out, on a dirt road in northeast Alabama. But they didn't leave at all, Neva thought, not really. They never made it out of the state.

"If we went now, we could go to Don Tono's first. I wouldn't mind a beer and a pupusa," Deb said.

Neva stood up. "Okay. Jamie?"

Jamie shook his head. "Not me." Jamie had been less of himself since the earthquake. "You girls be careful. People are crazy right now." When Neva looked back from the doorway, he was rummaging in the refrigerator, his bony back bent stiffly like a little old man's.

The city was ashy. They picked their way across piles of rubble, leaping across the sidewalk where it had cracked and buckled. The air smelled clean for the first time in weeks, and beneath a light coating of dust Neva could see the jacaranda blossoming in the trees beyond the plaza.

"You think Don Tono's is open?" Neva asked.

"Don Tono's is always open," Deb said.

But Don Tono's was closed. They bought cold pupusas from two women wheeling their grill home and ate them as they walked to the movie theater. There was hardly anyone there. An American film that neither of them had ever heard of. It had barely started when there was a loud pop, so loud Neva was deafened and couldn't hear what Deb was saying to her. The screen split down the middle, and yellow smoke began pouring into the theater. It was very dark. Deb pushed her down and they crawled out the side exit, coming out into the still bright early evening. "Oh my god!" Neva said, wiping her eyes.

"Shit!" Deb said.

They were both coughing; the coughing turned to laughter. "You never swear!" Neva said.

"I never got bombed before." Deb's eyes and nose were running. "We better get out of here before the guardia arrive. Come on—" She grabbed Neva's arm and they began running. They ran past Gabriela Mistral Park, the library, closed and shuttered, Don Tono's—they saw no one.

"Do you know what the film playing is, was? Do you know what it was?" Deb asked, breathless as they jogged away from the theater back toward their house.

Neva shook her head. "What?"

"*Baby Boom*!" Deb said. They stopped in their tracks briefly, bent over laughing. Behind them, to the east, another bomb went off. "Come on," Deb said, grabbing Neva around the wrist, tugging her on.

They ran faster and faster. Neva could hardly keep up with Deb. She focused on the tight sinews of Deb's calves, watching the muscles tighten and release as Deb ran ahead of her. Deb, the former marathoner. This was nothing to her. Neva felt as if her chest would burst.

Deb circled back around to her, running more slowly now, by Neva's side. "It's okay," she said. "We're nearly there."

They rounded the corner. The street was empty, dead quiet except for the sound of helicopters far to the east, over the Colonia Presidente.

"God, what is going on," Deb said, fumbling for her key, and then they were in the living room, collapsing on the bright red and blue rug Kira had brought back from Guatemala.

"Shit," said Neva. And then they began to laugh.

"Is that the scaredest you've been?"

"Yes," Neva said, "No. Maybe. The night the guards picked us up. Well, I was so drunk."

The night Will took out his knife. The night he broke her records one by one. Twisting her arm behind her back as he dragged her toward the stereo. "Maybe," she said. "Deb—"

"What?"

163

"Where is everyone?"

"I don't know. Kira should've been back long ago. I don't think Jamie is upstairs. His windows were dark."

"Deb," Neva said.

"I don't really want to talk about Doug. I never talk about it. I don't know how it came out."

She patted Deb's hand. She wasn't good at comfort. There had always been sadness there, in that face. What else had she failed to see? The past had kept a tighter grip on her than she realized. It had let her off the hook, or so she allowed herself to believe. There was so much damage—the same words she'd thought a week ago as she walked past the endless piles of rubble on the way to the bus stop. So much. And if you're not careful, the damage will make you unable to see, to see yourself, to recognize the murderer, the accomplice.

"I'm so sorry, Deb," she said. They were quiet together, the room still. "Do you want something to drink?" As she rose, she felt a flicker of something outside, a small current running through the muscles of her stomach. But, she thought, it's always like this. Each emergency, The Emergency. Every paro, the coup. Nothing ever really happened.

Much later Neva remembered the whistling and the way the small panes of glass in the louvered windows rattled like chimes. But when it happened, the crash seemed sudden, instantaneous.

"Okay," she said, trying to laugh. She and Deb huddled on the rug before the loveseat. "That was the scaredest." She realized the crotch of her jeans was wet. She was glad it was Deb, not Kira. "Christ!" she said, determined to make a joke about it. "I've peed my pants!"

Deb didn't answer, but remained curled against the wooden legs of the loveseat. There was dust all over both of them.

"I think I'm too afraid to go change," Neva said. "I wet my pants in the fourth grade. In the library. My friend and I, we were looking for books for the weekly book report. It was Friday, when you did that. She didn't like any of the books I picked out. You know, I don't think Allison was very smart. I wanted *Caddie Woodlawn* or *Island of the Blue Dolphins*, but Allison kept saying no. Finally we got to the last bookcase, which had only two shelves and was over in the corner. When we squatted down in front of it, everything let loose."

Deb didn't say anything. "I knew if I had asked to go to the restroom that I wouldn't have gotten a book. I really wanted a book. I can remember how desperate I felt as that fifteen minutes wore on—we only had fifteen minutes—and Allison kept saying no. We had to walk out in front of the fourth graders—they were lined up to go in. My mom came and got me. I remember how my legs stung when we went outside. Atlanta could be cold in November. It was November. Did you ever wet your pants, Deb?"

Deb didn't answer. She seemed to be sleeping, curled on one side, her hair and eyelashes white with the thick dust. Neva shook her, reached to brush the plaster out of her hair, and saw instantly how the mortar had come in through the window, how it had erased the back of Deb's skull, leaving the rest of her body curiously intact. Blood and brains seeped in a slow circle behind her head. Neva sat back on her heels.

When the darkness outside shifted into the deep midnight blue of late night, Neva knew she had been sitting a long time. She tried to rise, but her legs were so cramped she had to turn over on one side and stretch them out, one by one. Her left pinky trailed in the dampness on the tile floor. Well, that's blood, she thought. She had forgotten about Deb, even as she sat staring at her body.

Now what? It was so still. She couldn't imagine where everyone had got to. Kira. Where was Kira? She listened carefully, but there was nothing but dead silence, not even the usual firecracker sounds of maneuvers on the mountain.

23

Before and After

She had not slept when the knocking started the next morning. By then she knew something was terribly wrong, that she and Deb should not be there. The phone didn't work and there was no one in the adjoining houses. Or if there were, they didn't answer the door.

The pounding was fierce. "Neva!" She heard Tomás's voice. "Neva, are you in there?"

She opened the door cautiously and reached for him. He picked her up and pushed them both back through the door, glancing over his shoulder as he slammed the door behind them. "Jesus," he said. "Why aren't you at the embassy? Don't you know what's going on out there?"

She wet a washcloth and washed the dirt off her face and hands, took off her jeans and panties and washed her crotch. Her skin itched, but even if there'd been time, she couldn't have showered, couldn't have done anything that required taking all her clothes off to shower. She had just finished packing a shoulder bag with her toothbrush, the packet of letters from her brother, socks, underwear, and a bottle of water, when she heard voices below, footsteps on the stairs. Kira stood in the doorway.

"The basement of the Brit Club," she said. "Then people went to the embassy."

"Why didn't you?" Neva asked her. She didn't look at Kira. She looked around the room, her shoes lined up on the floor of the closet like trusting pairs of creatures ready to board the ark. The chukka boots were sad-faced camels. Her yellow slippers tired birds who'd lain down for a rest. She would leave them all. She would leave.

Kira shrugged. "Some stuff to get."

"Tomás says we'd never get to the embassy."

Kira shook her head. "Yeah, I don't know if anybody got there.

There's a lot of shelling in the Sonsonate district. Your boyfriend has a gun."

Neva looked at Kira for a long time. "He's not my boyfriend." The gun thing—was that important? It was too hard to think. All night she had tried to think. That there was help to be had, somewhere, if she could only think. She had never seen Tomás with a gun, but so many people had them down here.

Kira lingered in the doorway. Then she said, "I've gotta pack," and disappeared.

Neva went through her closet one more time, then closed the door. She opened the shutters and sat on the bed, remembering how it felt to wake in this room. Life had no plot, she thought. It was just one long series of comings and goings. A necklace of leavings, the cord broken and the beads scattered everywhere.

Downstairs was empty. She heard a thump in Deb's room and found Kira sitting on the floor in front of Deb's bureau, a drawer open in front of her. Kira looked up. In her lap was Deb's red datebook that she took everywhere, a black-and-white photograph, the empty frame on the floor next to her. She saw a flash of gold, and when she moved closer she saw it was Deb's high school ring. "It's hideous, isn't it?" Deb had said when she showed it to Neva. "My grandmother thought this would be a great graduation present. She was sure my mom wouldn't get me one. I could never bring myself to get rid of it."

"What are you doing?" she said to Kira. "What do you think you are doing?"

"Neva." Kira gestured toward the bed. "Don't you want to sit down?"

"No, I don't want to sit down. I want to know what you're doing in Deb's things."

Kira took a long breath in as if she were about to go under water, deep diving in the chilly ocean. She gathered Deb's things together in the scarf in her lap, brought the corners together and tied it into a tiny bundle.

"Deb's sister lives in Minneapolis. I thought she should have something." Kira shut the drawer in front of her. "Something," she said.

As if Deb were really dead.

Neva sat down on the edge of the bed and began to cry. "I'm sorry," she said. "I am so sorry."

They walked in a circle around Deb's body, which Tomás had covered with the beautiful Guatemalan tablecloth from the dining table. That was the weekend they had all gone—Deb, Kira, Susannah, and her. They had stayed out so late they had to wake up the owner of the pension when they got back, only to realize there was no drinking water, so thirsty from the long night's beer after beer that first Kira, then each of them, stuck their heads under the bathroom tap. "This is living dangerously," Susannah had said, the front of her white shirt splashed. But none of them got sick.

Most of the blood had pooled in the depressions of each red tile and dried black. So much blood, Neva thought. Each of us is like a wineskin, walking around, waiting to break open and spill, empty out, until we're a bundle of cloth huddled next to a dirty loveseat. A winding cloth knotted in someone's lap.

"When we get back," she said.

"Neva, we will never come back here," Kira said.

They could hear mortar fire and helicopters in the distance—nothing too unusual. "It's pretty quiet," Kira said.

"Maybe they're taking a coffee break." Neva's bag slapped against her shoulder with every step. What would happen to Deb? Who would find what was left of her? Tomás seemed worried about getting out of the city, but things didn't seem so different to her. It was quiet—that was all. Deb might've been hit by a car or contracted a deadly flu from one of their students. She might be out of town or at work.

Tomás put his hand on her back, but she shrugged him off. His face seemed thinner, his hair matted. They hadn't really talked. "Deb died," was all she had told him, and he had gone into the living room and come back out a minute later.

"Where is your room?" he asked her. She pointed upstairs, and he half led, half carried her, telling her only to pack a bag. That they had to leave. To pack a bag she could carry.

He came back up once with a cup of tea and a plate of bread and cheese. "Try to eat some of it," he said. "Try."

His face looked thinner, and it looked sadder. Her face felt heavy and foreign, incapable of motion, as if someone had stitched a stranger's to hers the night before, when it was too dark to discover.

Half a mile later they hit a roadblock manned by Frente soldiers, who waved them back the way they'd come. They turned east, skirting the edge of the barranca, until they heard a shout and saw half a dozen government tanks clustered under a ridge. The soldier who shouted was standing in the middle of the tank; he spun like a lighthouse in their direction, shoulders scrunched over his rifle.

"Run!" Tomás shouted, taking her hand and pulling. Neva realized the soldier was aiming at them. She crouched and ran, hearing a whistling sound and the bark exploding off a tree to her right. They headed down a path into the barranca.

It was only when they stopped to rest that it hit Neva, a lurch in her stomach and then the thought: Deb is dead. It was nothing like when her parents left. When, each day, she rose thinking that might be the day they returned. Maybe tomorrow she would wake up not remembering. But Deb was dead. She died yesterday, and that would always be the day she died. And today was the first day she was dead.

Before and after. I thought I had lived through my Before and After.

The day her parents left and the day her parents left for good were two different days. And she would only know, when she was so old they had to be dead, which day it was, that windy November day when she was fourteen.

Kira was retying her boots. She saw Neva watching her. "Are you all right?" she asked.

Neva nodded.

"You should pee before we move on," Kira said. "And drink some water."

She was so dry. She couldn't drink enough. "You better save some," Kira said and took the bottle away from her mouth and looked around. They were in a grove of banana trees, the leaves wide and waxy green. It was cooler than it had been up on the trail, but still hot and humid, the air not moving at all. The huge bee she'd been watching in the heliconia was really a green hummingbird with a rust-colored throat, ignoring them. It wasn't quiet, but the noise—helicopters and mortar fire—was at a distance. "Where is Tomás?" Neva asked.

Tomás came down the trail with binoculars in his hand. "We should go on," he said. He didn't look tired. Neva didn't move. "Where were you?" she asked. Her voice was hoarse. She was sick of men and their secret lives.

"We have to go," he said.

Kira picked up her pack and started down the trail. Tomás pulled Neva to her feet. He squatted down to retie her bootlaces, and when he stood back up their faces were close together, almost touching. She thought for a moment he was going to kiss her, but he said, without touching her, "It wasn't my choice," and pushed her up the trail ahead of him.

She didn't dream, she didn't think. She put one foot in front of another, kept her eyes on the trail, and when she forgot, she always stumbled, going down once on the muddy trail and almost sliding off down the steep hill. Kira turned back to look at her from time to time, but Neva kept her eyes down, pretending not to notice. There was the smell of dirt, there were spider webs sticky in her hair, there was itching, itching everywhere, feet that felt like they belonged to someone else, someone old and tired.

She remembered eating a banana. She remembered the first time she squatted down to urinate, and then it became so automatic, she stopped even thinking about it. They walked until it was so dark they couldn't see at all.

It was Kira who said, "We have to stop."

"I know, I know," Tomás said. "I hoped there might be a clearing, a little light. If someone comes along, we won't even be able to breathe."

"Why don't we just head off the trail for a ways. We can go slow, feel our way."

But Neva could sense Tomás shaking his head, even though she couldn't see him. "I think there may be mines," he said.

She sat down, and the muscles in her legs tightened up as if to punish her. "We can sleep in shifts," she said.

"She's right," Kira said. "We'll hear anything, anyone coming. It's only a few hours."

Neva slept first, and they never woke her. A painful sleep, her legs and back hurting right through the hours until first light.

She woke with a start. Someone had taken her shoes off during the night, and Tomás was pulling her socks off and looking at her feet. "I think they're okay," he told her. He squeezed them one by one, pushing them up and down and pushing his thumb into the arch of each foot. "Neva?" he asked.

"Tomás?" she mocked him, laughing. "Oh my god, this is so romantic!" Then she saw the corners of his mouth turn down and saw that she had hurt him in some way she could not identify. He still held her left foot in his hands.

"Thank you," she said. "Thank you." She tried to sit up, but he held her foot, working the stiffness out of the arch.

"We should get there today," he said. "Maybe by noon or so."

"I don't know where 'there' is." He finished massaging her feet. She sat up and began to put her socks on. He caught her wrist and held it for a moment. Why had she never noticed? They had the same skin.

"The border—we're near it now. There are camps, people there. People who can tell you how to get home." He rose and stood in front of her, tilting a little to the side as if his back hurt.

"Home," she said. She began gathering up her stuff. Home? Where was that? He didn't know the first thing about her.

24

The Border

She thought: It must be Wednesday.

She thought: Wednesday was washing day in Alabama. Sheets and towels flapping on the line or drooping down in the still heat.

The same day as any day in Atlanta. Up, dress, egg on toast, brush your teeth, school, my green satchel, parts of a leaf, the pilgrims, Betsy Ross.

She thought: My mouth is so dry. My body: a list of bruises, aches and pains, my hip half asleep from sleeping on the hard ground.

She could see a line of black ants walking through the grass, carrying provisions. One carried a leaf like a banner. I could kill an army, she thought, with a single blow.

I will just stay here until my body goes drier and drier, thin, pared down to hollow bone and sinew stretched tight. I will stay until a strong wind blows away what's left. No houses spinning or small dogs yapping to confuse the issue. Just me, dry and fragile as a leaf. Nothing anyone would ever notice.

She heard someone urinating close by. The sound a rush of water, a sigh midway. Voices. I will close my eyes and feign sleep or death. I am tired of walking, moving, moving on. I am tired. I am sick of everyone leaving. Of loving everyone who leaves.

Ringing the clearing where she lay were banana trees, a waxy green shrub whose name she'd never learned, and a heliconia, with its spiked red and yellow flowers. A hummingbird large as her fist drank from first one flower then another.

It was enough to lie here and watch.

But the voices grew louder. They would never believe she was dead, would be sad to find her dead, would wake her as if she were sleeping; there was no reason she should be dead. Bombs killed people, not grief, not being left behind. No, there was no escaping the voices. She rolled onto her back and sat up, a little lightheaded, and waited.

When the sun had crept entirely over them in an arc and was yellow through the ferns, Tomás made them stop and rest. "The border?" Kira asked. He nodded.

"What are you thinking?"

"I don't know," he said. "Just try to get close. See what's there."

"Neva?" he asked.

"I'm all right," she said. "I'm not an invalid."

They each took a swallow of water, holding it in their mouths and letting it work its way slowly down their throats.

"There are camps on the other side of the border. We should be able to hear them when we get closer."

Camps. She and Harker had gone to camp. Three summers. Red camp, her parents called it, joking.

At their first rest they ran out of water. "I should go look," Tomás said, picking up the canteen and rising to his feet.

"There's not time," Kira said. "And we're out of iodine."

Tomás rubbed his face with the back of his hand.

"We're close," Kira said. "If we don't hear them in two hours, we'll look for water. It's strange," she said. "There ought to be patrols. I don't understand why we haven't seen anybody."

"Maybe they're behind us." Tomás reached a hand down for Neva. "You're right. We should go on."

And after that, she didn't remember. Didn't remember anything clearly and didn't remember most of what happened before she woke up in a tent, her mouth so dry her lips felt glued to her teeth. Only she knew that she had started dreaming, hallucinating, that her parents were walking just ahead and she kept calling them and calling them. She began calling them by their first names when they didn't respond to "Mom" or "Dad" or "Mother" or "Father." She knew someone had carried her part of the way because she could remember the press of a shoulder against her abdomen. And Kira's voice saying, saying more than once, "It's close, Neva," saying "Can you hear me?" then "Is she all right?" And she was sick, sick, sick. Put me down, she thought. I don't like this at all. I think I would like to sleep a while longer. But turn it out, turn out that bright light before you go.

When she could get up and move around a little, when someone found her slippers because her bandaged feet wouldn't fit in her shoes, she went and stood outside the tent where she'd been sleeping. She looked for Kira's blond hair. She knew she had slept too long. "Why is it so quiet?" she asked one of the nurses, who stopped what she was doing.

"We sent a bunch of people to Costa Rica this morning. It's just a lull. They expect a lot of people coming over the mountain paths. How do you feel?"

"I'm okay," Neva said. She felt a little dazed, disoriented. Her feet hurt. "Yeah, I'm okay."

"Maybe you could help. If you could hold this rope while I stake it down." They tied off the tarp, and the woman began stacking crates under it.

"Are you American?" Neva asked.

"Australian. I'm Hilda." She reached a hand out and shook Neva's. "There are no Americans here—well, except you and your friend.

"Are you looking for your friend?" she said, pointing. "Over there."

Neva sat down on the ground next to Kira, who was eating a mango. "Tomás is gone, isn't he?"

"Do you want a mango?" Kira asked. "I'll cut it for you."

Neva nodded. Kira opened her pocket knife, peeled and sliced the mango so that the yellow flesh hung from the pit in cubes. She stuck her knife into one end and handed it to Neva like a popsicle.

"He's gone." They ate in silence. If you held the fruit at the right angle, you could bite off a cube without covering your face in juice. Neva had never been any good at it. She leaned forward so the juice dripped onto the ground instead of her T-shirt.

"Do you want to know?" Kira asked. "I'll tell you if you want to know."

"I already know." Neva put the half-eaten fruit down in the dirt next to her. Kira handed her a bandanna and she wiped her sticky face. "When those soldiers let us by, I knew who he was. Who he worked for."

"Neva—" Kira said. She picked up the bandanna and wiped each of Neva's fingers with it, one by one.

"You don't know, Kira. You don't know the kind of family I'm from. What it means to sleep with one of them—"

"The Silverhorn case? I know about your family."

"My mother was Indian, for chrissakes. Why did I never understand what it meant here?" She stopped and looked at Kira. "What did you say?"

Kira held Neva's hand in one of her own. "We knew about your parents—Deb and I."

"How?" Neva asked.

"When you got your work visa. It's in some file somewhere. They watch that stuff here. You know how paranoid they are at the embassy."

"But how did you and Deb find out?" All those months of hiding, of feeling free of it, and she had been watched as surely as her parents were watched. She had never disappeared.

"Somebody at the embassy told Henry who told Susannah who told me."

"And you told Deb?"

"She would've wanted to know. We thought we'd tell you eventually—that we knew." Kira detached her knife from the mango, wiped the blade clean, and put it into her pocket. She threw both mango pits down into the woods. They heard a *thump thump*, then something scurrying away. They laughed.

"There's monkeys around. They keep stealing stuff and laughing about it. But that was probably a coati."

They were quiet. The sun was egg yellow, slanting low through the green leaves, the ferns covering the ground.

"That was the phone call, wasn't it?" Kira asked. "Before you and Deb tried to go to Guatemala?"

Neva nodded.

"And why you went up to Lake Chichool?"

"Yes," Neva said.

"What happened?" Kira asked.

Neva took a deep breath. The rustling behind them had stopped. "I thought they might have come here, come to Coatepeque.

"We don't really know. They weren't far from my grandmother's house—where they left us—just a few hours. Coming or going—we don't know. The car was wrecked. There are just these old logging roads there, not real roads. I mean, there aren't even those anymore. We don't know when," she said. "Maybe it was later or maybe it was that day. That same day they left us. We don't know."

"You need to take a rest," Kira said. "Dehydration's bad stuff; it takes a while to recover from it. And this may be the only quiet time for days." She reached over and pinched the skin on the back of Neva's hand, watching as it drifted slowly back into place. "You're still pretty dry. You need to drink a lot more water. There may be some of that electrolyte stuff."

Neva felt it. She was bone weary. She swayed when she stood up, suddenly light-headed. Kira put a hand under her elbow and steadied her. "Okay? I'll walk you to your tent."

Neva nodded.

"Get some rest," Kira said.

"You will be here?" Neva asked. Her throat hurt the way crying made it hurt.

"Oh, I'll be here," Kira said.

She stuck her head back inside the tent and looked at Neva. "You're wrong about Tomás.

"Those soldiers—when we crossed the barranca? They were defectors. People are switching sides like crazy. They had ripped the insignia off their uniforms."

"And of course Tomás knew this?"

"He knew.

"Neva," Kira said. "What a risk he took coming back for you. I think he found out who you are, that they were watching you. Maybe that's why he left."

The secret life. You think you can step out of history and live, but it always catches up with you. "And this time?" she asked. "Where did he go this time?"

"He went to war."

She and Neva sat facing each other across the cot. "Those soldiers—" Kira said. "One of them put on a Frente scarf before we left them."

"What, he had it with him? God, Kira, I don't care."

"I gave it to him." They watched each other across the cot, neither of them blinking. "I gave him mine," Kira said.

Neva sat down on the cot. She saw a line of ants making their way along the canvas where the floor of the tent and the walls met. It was worse than waking up and not knowing where you were. Thirsty, she reached for the water bottle on the ground next to her.

"What?" she said.

Kira sat down on the ground across from her. "Did you never suspect?"

Neva shook her head. They would need this tent. They needed it now. The water was so cold this morning when she washed, so cold she thought she'd never warm back up, and now here she was sweating. She wiped her forehead.

Kira sat down next to her. "Well, that's good I guess." They sat apart from each other, Deb like a shadow between their bodies.

"No, I didn't suspect. But I couldn't put you together. The way people would come by the house and you would go outside to talk with them."

"Yeah, and all my hot lovers."

"Those guys?" Neva asked.

"Well, a couple of them. When I worked the medical tent during the earthquake, I thought you might figure it out. But I had to; they didn't have enough people who spoke English."

"You knew Tomás before?"

Kira shook her head. "No. I think he may have known about me. But not until the morning we left did he know—"

"—that you lived with me."

"Right. And we both knew we had to go—"

"You came back for Deb."

"I came back for both of you." Kira stood up. "Neva, you have to sleep."

She had just woken up, was beginning to remember where she was, what had happened, when Kira came back into the tent. "How are you?" Kira asked.

"I'm okay," Neva said. "I could start helping out."

"Neva, you need to go home. You can't stay here."

"You're staying." Neva sat up on the cot and looked at Kira.

"Maybe," Kira said. She sat down next to Neva, leaving a space between them, as she had all those evenings in the courtyard. As if Deb might wander in and join them. The fountain rocking each time one of them moved.

The fountain. She twisted to look at Kira.

"Why the fountain?" she asked.

"There's an old cistern beneath it, though it's dry now."

A cistern? A place to hide someone or something. The guns. Someone was running guns for the Frente.

"It was you," she said. "The guns."

And then it started. She saw the blood on the tiles. She remembered how Deb's hand had lain, palm up, the fingers curled as if she had just been holding something, a rubber ball or an orange.

"Oh my god," she said, scrambling up. "I can't listen to any more." But she turned. "How *could* you?" she screamed. "Deb is dead."

"She's not dead because of them. The government started gearing up a week ago. The Front came into the city because they were shelling the barrancas. Jesus, Neva. I tried to get you out of town."

"You knew, you knew, you knew." Neva screamed so loud the air rushed across her throat like sandpaper. The talk in the camp stopped.

She didn't care. She wished someone would shoot her, let a stray mortar kill her. She wanted to die rather than know this.

"I didn't know." Kira was on her feet coming toward her. Her face crumpled as she wept. "They came for the guns, and I was worried. I didn't know. There were always warnings. How could I know it was different this time?"

Kira squinted into the sharp light on the horizon. Night fell quickly here. They didn't have long before they would have to pick their way carefully back to the camp. "But I never really thought of myself as a communist. I mean, it wasn't about that.

"I wasn't ever very political," Kira said. "I didn't grow up with radical parents or anything. But once when I was in college this woman came to speak from El Salvador. I was a Spanish major and you got extra credit for going. Her sister had been arrested and kept in a box for two months."

"You were a Spanish major?" Neva said.

"Sí, soy de los Estados Unidos," Kira said, lapsing into the clumsy accent she'd used since Neva had known her. She laughed.

"It isn't funny, Kira."

"It isn't not funny, Neva. But it was useful. I'm sorry I couldn't tell you."

She heard monkeys high in the trees squabbling over something. A distant clatter of metal, probably from the camp. She unclenched her fists.

"It doesn't seem possible to do the right thing here," Kira said. "But you have to do something. It seemed so easy before I came. Who was right and who was wrong."

They were quiet for a moment and then Neva said, "No, you're right about Deb—she would have told. She would have told, and what then? Who would've died? You can't always choose the people you love. I mean, you can't choose them over others. You can't."

Blame. She understood now what Deb meant that day on the bus. Blame was just a way to keep looking at your own face in a mirror. But the dead deserved more. They deserved to be remembered. They deserved to be loved.

The jeep was waiting. The driver motioned furiously out the window. "At least he's not blowing his horn," Neva said.

"He can't," Kira said. "They'd bomb us."

They laughed and laughed. Neva's eyes were full of water. "Oh God," she said. "Why is everything so funny here?" The driver opened his door and put a foot on the ground.

"Because nothing is," Kira said.

"I'm sorry, Kira," Neva said.

Kira kissed her hard on the mouth. "Live a long life. Never look back."

"You have to come back sometime," Neva said. "You have to say you'll look me up."

"But you never even liked me." Kira smiled, but she looked at the ground.

"I like you now," Neva said. Will I ever come back here? she wondered. Ripe mangoes lay scattered all around them, their scent flowery and rotten. She looked around. "Nothing will ever seem so green to me again."

"Deb would forgive me, you know," Kira said. She shifted from one hip to the other, more uncertain than Neva had ever seen her.

"Kira." Neva squeezed her hand one last time. "There is nothing to forgive."

Acknowledgments

A version of chapter 10 appeared as the short story "The Door of the Devil" in the anthology *Sovereign Erotics: A Collection of Two-Spirit Literature*, eds. Driskill, Justice, Miranda, Tatonetti (University of Arizona Press, 2011).

Research for this project was supported by funds from the University of Oklahoma, from a New Directions Initiative Grant from the Great Lakes College Association, and from the Robert P. Hubbard Fund at Kenyon College. The VCCA, the MacDowell Colony, Hedgebrook, and the Hambidge Foundation provided artist residencies that afforded me the time and space to work. For this support, I am immensely grateful.

Personal acknowledgments and a reader's guide appear on the author's website at janetmcadams.org.

About the Author

Janet McAdams is the author of two collections of poetry, *Feral* (Salt, 2007) and *The Island of Lost Luggage* (University of Arizona Press, 2000), which won the Diane Decorah First Book Award from the Native Writers' Circle of the Americas and an American Book Award. With Geary Hobson and Kathryn Walkiewicz, she is coeditor of the anthology *The People Who Stayed: Southeastern Indian Writing after Removal* (University of Oklahoma Press, 2010). She is the founding editor of the Earthworks book series from Salt Publishing, which focuses on Indigenous poetry. Of mixed Scottish, Irish, and Creek ancestry, McAdams grew up in Alabama, taught high school in Central America, and presently lives in Ohio with a troubled border collie named Durga. She teaches at Kenyon College, where she is the Robert P. Hubbard Professor of Poetry. In addition to teaching creative writing, environmental literature, and indigenous literature, she is a practitioner and teacher of Integral Yoga.